THE LAST GOD

JEAN DAVIS

All characters, places and events portrayed in this novel are fictional. No resemblance to any specific person, place or event is intended.

The Last God

www.jeandavisauthor.com

ISBN-13:   (print) 978-1546851226
                  (ebook) B072KCMZZ1

First Edition: June 2017

Also by Jean Davis

Destiny Pills & Space Wizards
Sahmara
A Broken Race
Dreams of Stars and Lies

The Narvan
Trust
Chain of Gray

For my husband, the man with the magic hands.

CHAPTER ONE

A small ship decended through the atmosphere, landing deep in the barren desert that covered most of Kaldara. If the strangers were hoping to remain unnoticed, their hopes were misplaced. The General's staff notified her immediately. While she was surprised by the arrival of a familiar vessel, she wasn't at all pleased by the intrusion during this delicate time of quiet evacuation.

East, one of her four points, entered the vast throne room and approached the steep bank of stairs with unhurried steps. The pale green robes of his uniform rasped over the first step as he came to a halt below her. Though his voice was as calm as usual, a tic at the corner of his wide lips betrayed his distress.

"General, six life forms, minimal weapons. Orders?"

"Bring them in. Quietly. The current process must continue."

It had been many years since she'd had occasion to demonstrate her powers. With this planet nearly at its end, an example to keep any possible dissenters in line was in order.

East bowed his bald head and then retreated. The silence in the open room returned to its usual oppressive weight, making the General's heartbeat seem far too loud. Only the occasional shifting of boots over stone from the four remaining guards by the doorway on the far end of the room broke the monotony.

Ten steps above, her parents, the king and queen, sat on their ornamental thrones. Carved with gilded scenes depicting their favorite things from worlds past, the massive chairs held their god-sized bodies. The blue opalescence of oblivion tinged their open eyes and pale skin. Tubes ran from pumps mounted behind the thrones, penetrating their flesh at multiple points. Oblivion preserved and sustained them so they could maintain their expanded form with no effort.

Their bodies hadn't moved in years, but each day attendants cleaned them and adorned them in finery. Today, they wore violet silken robes that left their arms bare. The pulsing fluid shimmered just under their skin, nearly translucent with age. A golden chest plate adorned her father while gleaming bands of silver encircled the queen's neck and arms. Jeweled crowns sat upon their heads, hair brushed back from their serene faces. Her father may have blinked yesterday, but she'd been staring at him for so long, committing his face to memory, that it may have been her imagination.

The king and queen sat watching, as they always did, seemingly aware of everything going on before them. They weren't, unless she raised her voice or touched them. The General had been testing the limits of the oblivion for the past century. Since Kaldara's impending end, and hers along with it, had become clear. She worked to learn the limits of the actions, sounds, words, and volume that triggered her parents to become aware.

The king who had once commanded her to conquer worlds was now content to sit on a throne, lost in his own mind. Yet, he would not go peacefully into the beyond. He insisted on remaining, towering over her in his throne, silently reminding her of all the atrocities she'd carried out in his name.

The only consolation to the continued presence of her parents was that they'd allowed her to oversee the mundane business of Kaldara for the past four centuries. Since the day the pumps had been created to her mother's specifications and installed behind the thrones. They had kissed, a dispassionate meeting of lips to cheek, and taken their places side by side. Her father's points, his closest and most trusted slaves, had inserted the tubes.

Those men had since dwindled away to dust without his care. She wondered if he even noticed that they were gone. Her own points were so much a part of her, extensions of her awareness and power that she couldn't fathom letting them age like a common citizen.

The General closed her eyes, seeing through her point, West, who had gone out into the dead sands to intercept the strangers. They had left their ship and were making their way toward the city with some sort of equipment in their arms. They halted their approach as West landed his four-man transport. Just as he went out to speak to them, footsteps in the chamber recalled her attention to her own body.

Antoni's long legs covered the distance from the archway to the stairs with the speed and grace of a pure Unlata Kai. Upon reaching the base of the steps, he bowed with reverence even though he was the only other pureblood left. It was rare that all four of them were in the same room. For his own well-being, Antoni avoided the king, whether he was in a state of oblivion or not. There was a reason there were only four pure Unlata Kai left, and he sat on the throne behind her.

Antoni spoke quietly, "General?"

"Yes, Captain?"

She admired the way the crisp blue uniform hugged

his body and the conspiratorial knowing in his aqua eyes. His pale, blemish-free skin, and thick hair combed neatly back from his face, held in place just above his shoulders as if by magic, further set him apart from the people of Kaldara.

"We stand ready to launch."

Using her senses, she reached out to the king and queen behind her. They remained as calm and unaware as usual. "Continue."

Antoni gave her the slightest pleading glance. She stared him down until he backed away. He went to the doorway and spoke to the guards there.

They had both agreed that there would be no new rulers. The Unlata Kai had gone stagnant. Their mission complete. Their numbers dwindling to a handful as the old ones left their physical forms to join with the elders in the beyond. All of them but her parents and their stubborn pledge to rule into eternity.

She would never sit on her father's throne with Antoni at her side. She'd given up that dream long ago, instead focusing on creating order with the citizens and structuring the society to the highest efficiency. But now there was nothing more to distract her from the truth.

She'd come to see that the Unlata Kai should no longer interfere with the lives of others. Her kind had diluted their bloodlines with each planet they'd visited, with each civilization they'd raised.

They'd lost many of their own to greed and the allure of power over their followers. Before they'd settled on Kaldara, her father had sent her to hunt them down and destroy them. Others had gone peacefully, choosing to remain with the families they'd started, accepting the end of their years and slipping into the beyond.

Kaldara was no different. Only her four points

remained as a reminder of what the original occupants looked like. With every succeeding generation, the short, muddy-skinned people with flat-faced features and wide mouths had given way to prolific-breeding Unlata Kai hybrids, polluted with misunderstood and ever weakening remnants of the gifts of their Unlata Kai ancestors.

Their social cycles had been upended as the entitled and unruly first generation hybrids outlived their great-grandchildren. She'd done her best to smooth the transition, but her father had played favorites and sent her to war against the rest. Now only the obedient later generations remained.

History had taught her that no matter how deeply her kind intended to help, to guide, to instruct—the people they touched wanted more. They became violent and more often than not, corrupted the Unlata Kai who led them, driving them all into a tragic end.

The time of the Unlata Kai was over.

The only thing to do now was end it cleanly. Quickly. And this planet was about to oblige her wishes.

All she had to do was keep her parents calm. If they learned their end was near, they would evacuate and begin the cycle of nothingness all over again somewhere else, bringing destruction on a new planet of worshippers.

If the king and queen remained oblivious, the people of Kaldara could evacuate to safety, to begin again without any Unlata Kai interference. She and Antoni had been setting aside supplies for them for the last hundred years.

Deep below the surface, the first of the tremors she'd anticipated came to life. It was followed by another round and then silence. It wouldn't be long now. The unstable core had had enough, just as she had.

She signaled Antoni to begin the last wave of

evacuations. Three of the four ships were filled and waiting the order to launch. The last of her troops were stationed throughout the city, following orders with the utmost need for expediency and discretion. If the king and queen sensed panic, they would take action.

With a resolved look of calm on his fine-featured face, Antoni departed. Alone, with only duty-bound subordinates to keep her company, the General awaited the next order of business.

With everything in place, as she wished it to be, days often passed without anything of interest. Sometimes weeks. Efficiency had its downfalls. There was no longer a need for the skills that had elevated her to General of all. There were days when she almost reached for a tube of oblivion herself.

Another tremor ran through the core. This one stronger. The end would come soon enough. Just a flash of white hot light and then nothing.

"General." North approached the steps. "West has returned with the other ship. They are landing on the palace pad now."

Torn between relief of something to focus on other than the evacuation and annoyance of the untimely interruption, the General touched the amulet that hung from a thick golden chain around her neck. Jeweled and engraved golden armor spread over her body. It never failed to make an impression.

She often wore her armor in standby, covering her torso and legs, but leaving her arms and head bare. She preferred the freedom of movement. Nothing had truely threatened her well-being in a very long time. However, she didn't know these people, and a part of her relished playing the General one last time.

The helmet bearing a formidable androgynous

face clicked up the back of her neck, plate by plate, the flexible sections keeping her agile yet protected. The sleeves clicked down her arms, mimicking muscle and bulk beyond her own, giving her the illusion of a large threatening figure. Not that she needed the armor for that. Scars earned in hundreds of conquests covered her body, illustrating her experience well enough.

"Do they have weapons?"

"West has removed them."

"Their language?"

"Not one we know."

"I'll take care of it when they get here." Even knowing she'd soon be dead, adding another language to her collection held a small thrill.

It would be best to meet them elsewhere, but a deviation from the standard would alert her parents. She needed to keep this meeting short. If her father caught wind of a new people he'd not yet manipulated, it might well entice him to do just that.

She addressed North, "Why don't you go welcome our guests and see that the palace staff is following procedure."

As her lead point, North knew better than to speak of the plan plainly. His boots clicked in a steady rhythm as he made his way across the stone floor inlaid with jeweled representations of all the planets her parents had touched in their long lifetimes. She'd been to most of them herself.

The floating globe lights high above made the facets shimmer. If she hadn't been looking down over the expansive floor for the last several hundred years, she supposed it would be an enchanting sight.

North, along with West and his four men, returned with six unarmed beings built much like descendants of Unlata Kai. Though their skin varied in color and their bodies in shape and size, the main features were there. They wore clothing much more fitted to their bodies than the loose robes the Kaldaran's favored. She sensed no gifts among them. A race long ago touched then, she decided.

Yet they traveled in one of her ships.

The awe-struck faces of the newcomers confirmed her thoughts on the throne room. The thinnest of them even had the audacity to whistle. The rest were silent, standing uncertainly at the bottom of the tall bank of stairs.

With a long unused command, she summoned her staff from the armored palm of her left hand. The narrow, jet black snake that wound around the bottom three quarters of the golden staff shimmered, seeming to slither upward. She dropped the end onto the step with just enough force to send a heavy reverberating ring through the room. Their eyes widened in a suitably gratifying manner.

"What do you want here?"

A man took a step forward, the toes of his black boots butting against the bottom step. Tall, with a few greys peppering his short brown hair, he appeared healthy and lithely-muscled beneath his beige and black uniform. He spoke, his voice deep and pleasant sounding, yet the sounds made no sense.

The General held up her free hand, halting him. Descending the stairs in well-practiced regal manner, she came within one step. Then, retracting the metal that covered her hand to her wrist, she reached out to rest her palm against his cheek. Rough hairs formed a dark shadow that followed his jaw. It had been a long time since she'd felt such a primitive thing. The rush of forgotten tactile sensations gave her a shiver of pleasure.

"Speak," she ordered. Her voice booming through

the helmet with utter authority. Experience told her that even though he might not understand her, the intent would be clear enough.

Her eyelids closed as she dipped into her well of power, speaking the command in whispers that unlocked her mind to acquire new languages. A chill raced up her back and into her brain. Accessing her well drew her closer to Anika, her other half, the ruthless part of her who wanted full control. She much preferred to keep Anika behind the veil. Her other half often had her own agenda and it aligned far more with her father's than her own.

Slowly, the sounds he made began to form words in her mind and then in her ears. His tone was rushed and worried. His body language even more so. Three of the men behind him looked ready to bolt while the other two, a large man and a petite woman watched her with calculated focus. The man, in particular, caught her attention. While the others wore matching uniforms and all carried the same empty holsters at their sides, he wore a black shirt, stretched tight across his wide chest, his arms bare, showing off thick muscles under dark skin. Grey pants drew her gaze down to the same black boots the others wore. Tawny eyes watched her from beneath arched black brows. His full lips were drawn into the slightest of scowls, right hand hovering over an empty holster at his hip of a design different than those worn by the others. He seemed to place himself just in front of the woman beside him.

The words of their leader became clear, distracting her from the soldier. Images associated with those words sped through her mind. One of them, the ship in which he'd arrived, grabbed her attention.

"Your ship, where did you get it?"

Startled by her sudden use of his language, he faltered in his repeated statement, stammering and glancing at the others. Then he returned to what he'd been saying all along, his voice louder and more insistent.

"I'm Colonel Adam Rice. We've come to inform you that your planet is in danger of imploding. The core-"

She wanted to scream. The kind of scream that would burst the ear drums of men like these. Perhaps, she considered, slicing out their tongues would be a better solution. In the interest of not attracting undue attention, she instead covered his mouth with her hand. While his language was new to her, it might not be so for her parents, and even if they didn't understand the words, the alarm in his tone was clear.

"West, escort these people out and send them on their way. When this task is complete, your time has come. Thank you for your service."

West bowed low. "Yes, General."

She reached out along the connection she shared with South and East, confirming that the evacuation was near completion. She gave South, who was aboard the first ship, his order to launch. The ships had been provisioned for the long-term. Her points had been given orders to oversee the journey to a new home.

West and his guards ushered the now distraught group of strangers out of the throne room. Colonel Rice remained in her grasp, watching his men go, confusion plain on his face.

She gave him a stern look of warning and then removed her hand, only then remembering that with her helmet on, he couldn't see her expression. She deactivated it so there could be no misunderstanding.

His gaze locked onto her face, darting from one scar to the next. "We only wished to warn you. You won't harm them?"

"No harm will come to your people. They are merely being escorted back to your ship."

His volume rose again. "Our readings show the destruction..."

"If you wish to rejoin your men, you will talk quietly. The situation is under control."

His not quite handsome but charming face contorted. "Under control? Our readings indicate that there is a large population here. They'll all be killed."

"Was I unclear?"

His voice dropped to a hiss. "You'll kill them all?"

"Hardly. You may be wondering why you are still here?"

His gaze ran over her armor and back up to her face. "That did cross my mind."

"Your ship. It is familiar to me. Where did you come by it?"

"It's from our home, a much larger ship."

Her heart thudded unevenly. "This ship was not built by your people. Who built it for you? Who do you follow?"

Could there be another Unlata Kai out there? She'd been sure they were all gone. If there were others... Uncertainty niggled at her determination. She couldn't allow them to live.

"Follow? No one in particular, which is why I'm out here. I work for Naptcha."

"And who is Naptcha?"

"Not a *who*. A corporation. A government supported business. It's the government who pays my bills, technically. I'm protecting their interests in-"

She waved him to silence. "So not anyone you consider a god? You worship no one?"

The colonel shook his head slowly. "Never been much for church."

Relief washed over her. "Then how did you come by the ship?"

He squared his shoulders and lifted his chin. "I don't believe that's any of your business."

"Your ship belongs to my people."

"We came here to warn you of danger. We haven't harmed anyone. You can't think to commandeer our home."

The General laughed. With her threat of any remaining Unlata Kai put to rest, she let out the remnants of panic with a deep exhale.

"It's you who have done the commandeering. Show me you can build a ship equal to the one you have taken, and you will be free to go."

He took a step back, glancing to either side. Finding no guards in his immediate vicinity, Rice darted from her reach, racing toward the archway where the others had exited.

Again reaching into her well of power, the General uttered the command, "Halt."

Rice froze mid-step, his muscles straining but still unable to continue forward. Even his voice was strained. "How did you do that?"

"Silence."

His jaw strained, but no further words came from his lips.

If she reached much further into her well, Anika would demand full reign of her body. She couldn't let that happen. Not now at the end. Even with what she'd borrowed, Anika stirred, interested in the General's need for energy. She'd be listening. She couldn't allow Anika to fully grasp the situation.

It was too late.

Have you lost your mind? We must get on one of those ships immediately.

The General gave East his silent order to launch.

You can't do this! Anika screamed inside her head.

A headache of epic proportions blossomed in her head. Her legs threatened to buckle as she battled for control. She had to let Rice go or risk losing her body to Anika.

She released the colonel. His footsteps thundered down the hall outside the archway. Not wanting to chance Anika ruining her plan, she signaled West to launch.

It was then that she heard movement behind her, the creaking of ornamental armor, the sole of a golden sandal brushing on stone. The General turned to find her father's eyes focused upon her.

His voice boomed, matching the size of his expanded form. "What is the meaning of this disturbance?"

She gestured at the empty throne room. "Nothing, Father."

"Why are you in your full armor for nothing?"

Caught, the General had no choice but to disengage her armor and resume her usual dress. The amulet again rested on her loose-fitting white shirt, her only ornamentation. "We had visitors. They have been dealt with."

The King's fingers tapped out a steady rhythm on the throne controls. "Why has one of our ships launched?" He scowled. "It is not the first ship today. Explain." His voice, ancient, annoyed, and filled with the same power she'd exerted on the colonel, compelled her to answer.

She fought to control the extent of the truth that flowed from her tongue. "Our people are leaving. This world is tired. We have destroyed it with our wars as we have ruined so many before it. I am tired. You are tired. Let this be over. Our time is done."

"How can you speak such lies? We have done great things for these people. They have lived in centuries of peace. Look at the city before you." He jutted his chin toward the archway. "We have created this place, a city where everyone is cared for. No one is hungry. Every citizen is useful and valued. We have done good here. As we have with every world we touch."

Unlike Rice, she possessed her own power. The General broke his hold and climbed the steps to face him directly. The queen remained in her own oblivion, inactive and uninterested. The crown, resting atop her perfectly sculpted blond curls, sparkled in the soft glow of the lights.

"We ruin every world, just like this one. You pit the citizens against one another."

"The strongest survive."

"And what of the weaker? They die. So many die in your name."

"What of it?" He lifted a hand that hadn't risen farther than his throne controls in a decade. "Look at what we offer."

"Yes, look at it. Look outside the city boundaries. It's a wasteland. Most of a once fertile world, poisoned in your name."

"We don't need it. We have what we need here. No one goes hungry. No one suffers."

"No one is left. These people are all hybrids. We have obliterated their bloodlines, contaminated them with our own. There have been no pure Unlata Kai children after me. We're all that's left. Don't you understand?"

"There are more of us out there. We are not alone."

"They are only words, Father. I have never seen an

Unlata Kai that was not one that I did not already know, and you would allow none beyond Antoni to live. You think there are more, but I hunted them as you ordered. I have not heard whisper of another. Have you?" She shook her head. "You haven't left this room, that chair, in centuries."

"Enough." His giant fist smashed down on the arm of his throne, narrowly missing the controls. Do you wish to relinquish your role as my General? Perhaps it is time for me to stretch my legs and see what new amusements the universe has created for us."

A rush of footsteps signaled an interruption the General sorely did not need or want. "Out," she decreed.

North's voice rang out crisp and clear. "General, the ships are away, but for one. Captain Antoni requests your presence aboard it."

With her father's presence bearing down upon her, the General turned to face her point.

"That is not part of the procedure." How dare Antoni think to escape the fate they had both agreed upon? They had both sworn on the blood of their kind that they would see their plan through.

"He insisted." North gave her an apologetic look. "I agree with his assessment."

It was then, in the midst of a haze of betrayal that she noticed Rice had returned with his soldier. They hung back in the archway, but their holsters were no longer empty.

Though she didn't free Anika, she had no qualms about sharing her rage and redirecting it. Power flowed through her voice. Her body vibrated with energy, muscles bunching and endorphins surging. "North, what is the meaning of this?"

"Antoni told me of your intention, General. We

swore an oath. We cannot let you continue down this path. You must be saved."

"I do not wish to be saved. It is for you, that I do not wish to be saved. Don't you understand?"

"I do." North pointed his gun at the Queen and fired.

A furious scream erupted from the General's mouth. Anika burst out of the veil, sharing her rage and using her moment of weakness to assert herself. Her body expanded, her joints straining and stretching, eyes altering and voice changing to project farther and louder.

The compassion she held for North, who had been with her since they had settled on Kaldara, vanished. His life had been prolonged by her power until this moment when she chose to end it. He dropped to his knees, robes puddling around him, and fell over, lying still on the stone. Blood dripped from his ears and nose.

Shifting noises from behind made the General spin around. Her father struggled to rise, fighting against the tubes that fed his body. His long-unused legs shook under his weight, but he managed to take two steps to his queen.

The queen rested in her throne just as she had for centuries. The only difference was the fluid that maintained her now oozed from the gaping hole in her chest. She did not breathe. Her eyes were empty of the opalescence of oblivion, dull and blank.

"What have you done?" The King held his hand over the wound.

The General could feel the summoning of his power, the healing already beginning. He would bring her mother back. Then where would she be? She'd committed to killing them. Though it had been her plan that the planet they'd ruined so effectively should get the honor. She'd planned to go with them to absolve herself of any guilt, but now she had to hunt down Antoni. None of them could be allowed to live. Doing so would only guarantee that another world, another population, would fall to the whims of an Unlata Kai. Even if it was one she liked...prior to his betrayal of their plan, a fact that only solidified her resolve.

If the queen were allowed to return to life, she would have to face both of her parents and by then, they would have both drawn energy from anyone nearby, filling their wells to obliterate her. Her father had to know their murder had been her plan, her and Antoni. As much as she needed to make sure he went to the beyond with her parents, she had to protect the other innocent passengers on the remaining ship, a quarter of the population of Kaldara. The king would have no qualms about destroying it and everyone on it to kill Antoni for his part in her plan.

The king had to die.

With her father's focus on the queen, the General lunged for the extended tubes of life-sustaining fluid. Her parents had long ago given up eating and drinking, of processing their own wastes. The blue fluid of oblivion did that for them. Now she ripped those tubes from his flesh. Grabbing one after another, yanking them from his body with enough force to pull him away from the queen. He stumbled against his throne, his steps unsure.

He stared down at the fluids flowing from his open wounds. "What have you done?"

"What needed to be done."

His power flared, skin glowing until it was hard to look at him directly. It had been so long since she'd seen her father this way, this powerful. This was the man she had damned herself for, beautiful and radiant. A kind word from him had washed away all the blood on her hands along with terror-filled screams and desperate pleas for mercy.

Even Anika faltered in her race for self-preservation. Together in one mind, they gazed at him in wonder, basking in his presence.

Without her father's efforts to delay the natural process of death, her mother's power well exploded. The searing burst of unhindered energy knocked them both off their feet. It washed the room with heat and light.

It was only reflex that activated her armor a second before the blast overtook her. The king did not react as quickly, his body blackening, skin peeling away. He healed seconds later, resuming his beautifully terrifying form.

She shivered inside. Her mother was nothing more than a black stain on the shattered ruins of her throne. Then she realized that her father had just expended a good deal of his own energy to attempt to bring her back and then to heal himself. If she truly intended to destroy him while he was fully alert, there would never be a better chance than now.

They both scrambled to their feet, circling one another amidst the crumbled remains of the thrones.

His first bolt of energy sizzled against her armor. The energy bolt, even somewhat diffused, emitted an electrifying shock that stunned her body and scrambled her thoughts.

Her own well surged at Anika's command, power gathering. A golden glow surrounded her, just as blinding as her father's white light.

Her voice thundered throughout the room, "You dare strike me?"

She fired a bolt of her own, aiming directly for his head without mercy.

Blue fluid leaked from the King's mouth and nose, his eyes narrowed and gleaming. He fired again and again, even as he staggered, slipping down to the ground beside his throne. The glow of power about him faded. He was too focused on her to heal himself.

"Stop this madness," he said.

"You are the madness." She had no care for the others in the throne room, those that had forced this violent end upon her and her parents.

She hit the king again. The powerful blow shattered the mostly ornamental armor he wore on his chest. His crown toppled to the floor, rolling toward the stairs. The golden circlet hung on the edge of the top step and then tipped just enough to fall, bouncing step by step with a metallic ring that imprinted itself in her mind. A massive explosion of energy erupted from the King as he released the whole of his well.

Time slowed as the glowing ball of white light raced toward her. She braced for its impact and released the ties to her remaining points, allowing them to live on after she was gone.

The ground beneath the throne room shook. Cracks ran up the walls, rending the thick stone that had sheltered them through countless wars.

Debris rained down. Anika formed a shield, but the General directed it over the others in the room rather than herself. Anika shrieked with rage. So did the General.

The connection with Antoni was brutally severed as her father's rage exploded in a massive blast that ripped through the planet and vaporized an entire ship full of a thousand souls. The sheer loss of them all turned her hollow inside.

The ball overtook her, enveloping, crushing her within the confines of her armor. She focused on the shield covering the others. Her plan would still find fruition. Antoni was gone. Her parents were dead. Three ships full of her people had escaped. Today, the Unlata Kai would vanish from the universe.

CHAPTER TWO

Logan watched in horror as the king left the side of the queen and erupted into a towering being of light.

And then that's all there was, heat and light. He shielded his face with his arms. Huddling against the wall, he blinked rapidly and waited for the ringing in his ears to subside while he got his bearings.

Beside him, Colonel Rice swore. "What the hell was that?"

Logan had no answers. He could only attest to witnessing the woman he'd seen when they'd returned to the massive chamber cover herself in the same golden suit of armor they'd spoken with. Then she grew taller, brighter, glorious. His mind reeled with what he'd seen, and he was only half certain this wasn't another one of his nightmares. He hazarded a glance to where the king and queen had been.

The two beings of light exchanged blows of massive proportions. Bombs of energy exploded against their bodies. He couldn't fathom how either remained standing.

"I'm pretty sure the queen exploded," he said, knowing how absurd that sounded but having no other explanation.

Everyone else in the room had gone to their knees when the king had stood. The uniformed men that they had followed back here, now had their arms outstretched and their faces plastered to the floor.

While beings of light danced in his vision and bombs exploded against his eardrums, he achieved a single glimpse of clarity. Everyone who had been near the throne was blackened. Dead. Bile rose in this throat.

A thunderous clamor claimed his attention. He tore his gaze from the bodies to see the being of white light, what had been the king, sprawled among the remains of the thrones. He dimmed and then was nothing more than a battered and bloody man. His crown lay at the bottom of the stairs.

A shimmering sheet flowed from the General to hover over him and Rice. The ground beneath them rocked and the walls shook. The ceiling above began to crumble.

The colonel didn't move. Logan found he couldn't move either. He wasn't easily scared, but he had no idea what was going on here and safety anywhere on this planet was questionable.

Without taking his eyes off the General, he said, "We've overstayed. The planet is going to go with us on it."

"Maybe." The colonel also stared at the giant golden glowing figure.

Debris thundered down on the sheet above them. A shield of some sort.

Logan prayed their ship wasn't being crushed where they'd left it with the rest of their team inside. Then he wondered if he should hope that they'd left. He and Rice might not make it back. The shield didn't look able to stretch that far. In fact, it didn't even go as far as the archway.

A giant explosion struck the General. For a moment he was blinded again. Another blast of scorching air blew past them, though it seemed the shield protected them somewhat as the heat wasn't near as intense as the first time.

"Holy shit," muttered Rice.

The King was gone. Only a large scorch mark on the floor where his body had been. The General lay sprawled on the steps, her feet just below where the thrones had been. Her armor missing the golden glow and blackened. Blood dripped down the steps from the seam at her neck where her head was suspended over the edge of one of the stairs. She lay on her back as if she'd been blown over, unable to catch herself.

She was still moving. Slowly, but twitching enough to indicate she wasn't as bad off as the rest.

"We've got to get out of here."

"Agreed." Yet, Rice crept forward instead of back the way they'd come.

They checked the bodies of the others as they moved closer. All of them had burnt to death. Pain on his own arms registered. He glanced down to find them blistered. Rice's face and neck was red. He guessed his was too by the tightness that hit him now that the shock had worn off. His clothes were singed.

"Good thing we weren't any closer," Rice said, working his way toward the armored woman.

Logan rushed up the stairs. He knelt beside the General, who seemed to have returned to her original size. She weakly pushed him away but said nothing beyond a faint moan.

"Let me help you."

She pushed at him again. He tugged on the helmet to free her head so he could better assess the damage.

The voice that came from the blackened metal face was a ghost of the powerful voice that she'd used earlier, barely a whisper. "Leave me."

He pushed her hand aside and felt up the back of the armor, searching for a lever or latch of any sort. There was nothing there but blood. He wiped his hands on his pants. "How do you get this thing off?"

"You don't." Her voice grew slightly stronger. "Now go, I can't hold the shield much longer."

Rice crouched down beside them. "You're coming with us."

"No."

"Can you get her?" he asked.

Logan took stock of the armor and the size of the woman that would fit inside it that they'd glimpsed momentarily. "I think so."

"Do it."

Rice addressed the General, "I don't know how you're creating this shield, but can you make it follow us if we take you with us out of this room? We need to get back to our ship."

"Only if you promise to leave me on this world."

Rice gave Logan a long look. Logan nodded. As much as her voice was wavering now, she'd be unconscious by the time they got too far. He hoped that she could maintain the shield while she was out of it and that she didn't die. Rice had said the General might know about their ship and how to repair it.

If it was true that she knew the workings of the deserted ship they'd come across a year ago and now inhabited, they needed her. There was so much they didn't understand, but they dearly wanted to. This ship was the answer to all their prayers. Solid, whole, armed, and in theory, self-sustaining. It even had its own short-range shuttles, like the one they'd taken here after Hanson had encountered the abnormal planetary readings. They could help so many more people than they had been able to on the ship they'd been forced to desert after a brutal encounter with Matouk's army.

Logan braced himself and then reached under where the General spanned the stairs, carefully picking her up. She wasn't light by any means. His muscles strained under what he guessed to be as much the weight of her armor as herself.

The metal was still warm from the blast and that only aggravated the burns on his arm, but he held on. He made his way down the steep stairs, his thighs straining with the additional weight.

Once back on level ground, they made better time. Rice led them out the arch and down the long hallway. Not having to duck in and out of doorways to remain unseen made the trip much simpler. The palace was deserted. Not a single body on the ground or fleeing from the crumbling walls. A slab of carved stone plummeted from the high ceiling, landing right in front of them. It hit the shield with enough force to knock him off balance.

He stumbled, twisting awkwardly to keep the General from smashing against the wall before he did. He scraped his shoulder and felt a twinge in the muscle along his left side that he knew was going to catch up with him shortly.

The shield wavered, shrinking until it covered only a few surrounding feet over and around them as they moved.

"Hurry," she whispered.

The courtyard where they'd left the ship was just ahead. The wall to the left toppled inward. Rice jumped over the mess but Logan wasn't as light on his feet. The colonel reached back to help him along. The shield faded with each step until the air around him suddenly felt stagnant, like the very planet itself had stopped breathing. The sounds of the crumbling palace were louder and sharper. The armor was still stiff but the weight in his arms was heavier, unresisting.

"She's out."

"Out or gone?" asked Rice.

"Can't tell with the damned creepy helmet on."

They burst from the palace and into the open air to find the ship unharmed and waiting. The other ships, like the one that had guided them here, sat unattended. Where had everyone gone?

Nana, their pilot waved from the controls, urging them to move faster.

"We'll get her inside and have Hanson take a look. Bet he'll figure out how to get that thing off in no time."

Rice banged on the bay door. It dropped open seconds later.

Logan snorted. "Like Hanson knows how to get a woman out of anything?"

"Give him a break." But Rice grinned. "Lay her down and let him have a go at her."

The door sealed shut. The ship shuddered as it left the surface. Logan tried not to think about the crumbling city below or the fate of anyone left behind.

Hanson, as if summoned by Rice's comment, appeared in the bay. His eyes narrowed.

"She's hurt," said Logan. "We need her armor off."

Logan knelt on the hard floor. Rice helped him ease the General down so Hanson could have a look.

The lanky man ran his hands over the blackened metal of her arm and up her shoulder. "That's quite amazing construction. No open joint of any sort, everything overlapping, metal yet flexible."

He ran a handheld scanner over her prone form.

Logan moved out of the way, standing behind Hanson. His vantage point allowed him a view of the scanner. The readings showed a broken body inside the metal shell. Bones shattered, organs a tangled mess.

"How is it activated?" Hanson mused, running the scanner over her side and then the helmet.

Blood began to pool under her neck. Not near as much as before, Logan noted.

"We need to get that armor off right now."

Hanson nodded. "I'm working on it."

The armor took on a glow like it had before the General had collapsed, however, it wasn't as brilliant as before, nor did she expand in size. Which was just as well. The bay wasn't all that large to begin with.

"Did you do something?" Logan asked.

Hanson shook his head, tapping madly on his scanner and muttering to himself.

A clicking sound reverberated against the floor of the ship. The helmet began to fold in upon itself, each thin panel sliding into the next until it had vanished into the back of the armor, leaving her head and neck open. The plates covering her arms also retracted. The armor at her legs followed suit. Within seconds she wore only a golden amulet encrusted with small jewels on a chain around her neck. It rested against what had been white linen according to the small patches that weren't burnt or soaked with blood.

Her eyes opened to reveal a golden shine that was difficult to look at. Her skin pulsed light.

"Who are you?" The General asked in a weak whisper.

"Travelers," Hanson said, using their standard answer.

Her unfocused eyes blinked slowly. "Can you save her?"

"Her? You?" asked Hanson.

"Yes."

"Who are you?" asked Logan.

"Anika."

The word was strange, like the first words she had spoken to them in the palace. It wrapped around his mind with warmth and comfort. Even his strained muscles relaxed.

"We will try."

Anika's lips drew into a tired smile. Dried blood at the corner of her mouth cracked. "Don't tell her you spoke to me. You'll only anger the General."

"Does the General have a name?" If she did, Logan sorely wanted to hear it or anything else she had to say in her own language.

"No." Anika focused her eerie shining gaze on him. "Her name is not meant for your tongue."

The king had yelled at the General in a flurry of sound. All he'd understood was that it was a tirade full of threats and then pleading. Their exchange had been beautiful and terrifying at the same time, his body not wanting to move, his mind slowing, almost like being on the edge of falling asleep. Their language was so fast and full of strange intonations that he couldn't fit it into the rhythm of individual words.

The light faded from Anika's skin and eyes, leaving the critically wounded shell of a scarred woman in rags on the floor. Rice came in, a question clear on his face before he took in the General.

"I see you got the armor off, but where did it go?"

Hanson lightly tapped the amulet. "In there, I guess. Somehow."

Rice's brows rose. "And she's still alive, I take it?"

"For the moment." Hanson turned to Logan. "You

tell him. He'll just say I'm nuts."

Logan cleared his throat, wondering how to not sound crazy himself. "She glowed again."

"Well she didn't blast either one of you, so that's a good sign."

"It wasn't her exactly," Logan said.

Hanson shrugged. "She said, Anika."

Rice definitely had the look of someone who thought they were both confused. "Maybe that's her name."

"Not unless she makes a habit of speaking of herself in the third person."

Rice chuckled. "From what little contact I had with her, I wouldn't be surprised."

"How long until we're back to the ship?" asked Logan.

"At least an hour."

She wasn't going to make it. "Send Rhodes back and have her bring everything we've got."

Rice nodded and ducked back out of the bay.

Hanson picked up his gear and stood. "Better make space for her to work. I'm going to head up front."

"I'll hang here in case she needs help."

"Rhodes?" Hanson snickered. "I'm not an expert in this sort of thing, but desperate triage on the floor doesn't sound like a great date. Or did your charming wit chase her away already?"

Logan glared at him. "Weren't you going up front?"

"I was, but this might be entertaining enough to make the cramped quarters worthwhile."

"Go." It was bad enough that there were no secrets onboard when it came to relationships, he didn't need Hanson to have a front row seat to the tension between the lead medical assistant and himself. And for the record, they'd only managed to have one date. It wasn't his fault

Rice called him along on nearly every mission or that when he was free, Brin had six crew members vomiting all over the clinic. Sadly this little mission of mercy was the closest thing to a second date they'd had in two weeks.

When Brin strode into the bay with her bag and the case that held the sum of the shuttle medical supplies beyond what she'd brought, thoughts of anything date-related evacuated his mind. Her petite form was all business. She hadn't even spared him a single glance.

She had been all eyes before their first date. It had been her that initiated it after all. Either he must look like total shit, or she was still pissed about the flower he'd picked for her that had turned out to be a host plant for hundreds of slimy micro slugs. Hanson had cleared it. It wasn't intentional.

Logan looked into the doorway that led to the rest of the ship, deep in contemplation. The damned tech lord had sounded awfully in the know about the trouble between him and Brin. Had he cleared the flower, knowing full well the trouble it would cause? His fists clenched. When they got back, and this situation with the General was under control, he would have a word with Hanson and find out the truth.

"Let me know if you need any help," he offered, backing out of Brin's way as she walked around the General, surveying the damage with a scanner and examining closer with her hands.

"Is there any part of her not broken?" Brin sighed and dropped down to her knees. "If I pull this one off, I expect a glowing review worthy of a promotion," she called out. Likely to Rice, who was one of the few people who had influence when it came to the commander and Naptcha, who signed their paychecks.

Brin dabbed a swab into the blood still seeping

from the General's neck and inserted it into a cube she had pulled from her bag. She held it in her hand, waiting.

"Come on." She glanced at Logan. "It doesn't usually take this long."

"What's it doing?"

"She's lost a lot of blood. I need to know more about it so we can find or formulate replacement fluids when we get back."

"If she's still alive by then."

Her eyes narrowed as she turned back to her patient. "Thanks for your vote of confidence."

"That's not what I meant. She's in bad shape. I'm sure you'll do everything you can."

"Maybe you should just keep your mouth shut."

Logan backed away, conceding that any further friendly opportunities with Brin weren't looking likely.

He watched her work, applying gauze, patches and salves. She injected various fluids while muttering to herself, and consulted handheld devices from her bag from time to time. Occasionally she swore and moved quickly to a different area. Through it all, she pulled unpleasant looking tools from the case and applied them to the General's body, working efficiently by herself to the degree that Logan was rather in awe of her skill. He'd never had cause to observe her work before.

Finally, she asked for his assistance. "Help me get her on her side."

Logan did his best to gently turn the substantial General onto her side. She easily weighed twice as much as Brin and was covered in hard muscle. Ashen hair slid over her face, covering features twisted with pain even in sleep. He recalled the sight of her standing on the stairs before her armor had come up. Her wild tousle of hair just brushing her shoulders, longer in the front, and, as he watched her now, exposing the nape of her neck in the back. Brin worked quickly, stitching up the deep cut the impact of the armor on the stair had caused.

With her head resting on his thigh as he held her still for Brin, he tried to recall what her face had looked like. His memory told him hard and implacable. That did fit with someone who went by The General. Yet, he kept seeing the peace in her glowing eyes and hearing her beautiful language. And then the General's demand to be left behind once they'd reached the shuttle. The demand they'd ignored.

He'd seen this woman grow larger than life, glow like a radioactive beacon, shoot bombs of light from her person into another and take those same blasts herself. And she was still alive. She'd survived the heat that had rendered men farther away to charred remains. Twice. And from the sheer number of scars, thin, thick, jagged and otherwise, adorning nearly every visible inch of her body, and he could see quite a lot of it now that Brin had cut away the remains of her shirt and pants, she was no stranger to this level of damage.

Brin rocked back on her haunches, wiping her brow with her forearm "So what does Rice want with her?"

"She might know about the Maxim." Logan carefully returned the woman to the floor. "She didn't want to leave."

"She'd be dead. That whole planet was going into a meltdown that would have cooked them all to well done in a flash, given another couple hours."

"I think she knew that."

"So she's crazy."

"I didn't get that impression." Desperate maybe, but not insane.

Brin went back to work with her scanner. "Well,

you may get the chance to debate that with her in a few days. She's relatively stable. Not good, by any means, but not in a freefall of impending doom."

"That a term they teach at the academy?"

Brin cracked a smile. "No, but that's going in my report to underline the gravity of her status."

Rice returned. "I let the doc know you had the situation under control, Rhodes." He peered around them to see the General. "It is under control?"

Brin lifted her chin and looked him in the eye. "Of course."

"Good. We need to know what she can tell us about the Maxim. Which means, I need her alive and talking. Think you can make that happen?"

"I'll do my best, Colonel."

A shudder passed through the small ship signaling they'd docked. Logan looked to the General.

"Want me to carry her to the clinic?"

"That won't be necessary," said Rice. "Doc said he'd be waiting with a team."

"I better be part of that team," Brin muttered, packing up the last of her equipment.

Rice smiled, "I did mention my preference on that matter."

"Thank you." She flashed him the smile Logan had enjoyed until that slug incident.

The medical assistant gathered up her bag and set the ship's supply box in Rice's hands.

"You'll want to restock that."

She ignored Logan completely as the bay doors opened to reveal Doctor Adams and two assistants with a gurney between them. With practiced efficiency, they shifted the General onto the gurney and headed off to the clinic.

"Well then," said Rice. "Guess I have to go report to the Commander."

"Have fun with that."

Rice grinned. "Thanks for tagging along."

"Anytime."

Blood and tattered scraps of the General's clothes lay among the pile of scattered disposable packaging of all the implements Brin had used to save her. While he was glad of this particular miracle, he'd seen far too many impossible things today. His mind was still trying to process them all.

Logan took his leave of the ship, trailing behind the others, who were part of the Colonel's official team. Hanson followed Rice, likely to relay their final findings on the planet.

He had no interest in the tech talk. Hitting and shooting were more his lines of expertise. Which was why Rice kept inviting him along. His own security force was small, and even more so since the attack that had cost them their previous ship.

Naptcha was far more concerned with trade, research, and humanitarian efforts. Paying the government for the loan of more than a few well-trained men to protect their assets was not the highest priority. Though Rice kept watching for others to recruit, so far, he was the only one to take the offer. If he went along with Rice, that left the rest of the small security team onboard in case of another attack by Matouk's army. The crew still hadn't recovered their nerves after the last one.

The majority of Hanson's team could fire a gun with decent results, but it wasn't something they enjoyed. Logan didn't mind being the muscle.

He went to the lift, glad to find it currently unoccupied. With the General in the clinic, Brin no longer interested, and Rice and his team off fulfilling their duties, he gave up pretending to be remotely socially inclined. He only made the attempt because Rice asked him nicely to do so. Apparently, his usual demeanor set Hanson's team on edge. Which he didn't mind, except he needed the pay.

The faint tremble in the lift flashed him back to the tremors he'd felt on the General's world. Those tremors quickly became the bombs shaking his home, the city, everything on Hijn. Logan found himself trapped in memories of screaming and whimpering and then the eerie silence of bodies in the streets that he'd woken to. The grand buildings had crumbled into ruins like the palace and city they'd escaped today.

He fought for control of the paralyzing sounds and images that took over his mind far more often than he wanted to admit.

Logan took a deep breath as the walls of the lift came back into focus. Damaged goods, that's what he was. Thanks to the army of Matouk.

He rested his head on the cool wall as memories swirled around in his head, sloshing to and fro, disorienting him. Sweat beaded on his forehead as his palms met the wall to steady himself, offering reassurance that the Maxim was whole and safe.

He'd only been with Commander Tate's people for a week when Matouk's army attacked their ship, likely having been following them since they'd left Hijn. Tate had quickly lost that battle, their ship damaged beyond repair. Matouk's blue-striped followers had terrorized them after Tate had refused to join their army, picking off the unfortunate few that had tried the life pods, firing random shots at the already disabled ship until none of them dared to think of escaping. They sent taunting messages, making Tate think they had a chance.

He'd known better. He'd tried to tell them, but Tate had refused to listen. Rice had finally taken his words into account, and agreeing, turned off all but a minimal level of life support until Matouk's men had left them for dead.

They'd done that to him twice now. He hoped there was never the opportunity for a third.

Had the General been beyond hope too? Thinking her planet destroyed, had she done what she had to in order to save her people? Or had she been like Matouk's followers, heartless in her actions? He'd watched her kill her own man with sound and the king with light. Matouk had been rumored to use the same weapons.

Whatever she was, he'd brought her onboard.

He walked the mostly empty halls of the ship to the doorway of his room where he palmed the entry pad. The door slid open, granting him access to his refuge from the wary conversations and forced smiles of the others. Most days he didn't feel like smiling. This had become another one of them.

The rooms were all furnished similarly. He'd chosen this one for the simple fact that the suites on either side of his were unoccupied. Part of his agreement with Rice had been keeping them that way. One furnished room, three meals a day, access to medical and training facilities, and a modest sum of weekly credits in exchange for sharing what he knew of the army of Matouk and acting as guide and guard when needed.

He was free to leave at any time. No contracts, no signatures, not even a handshake. He'd been a soldier once, with a signed contract and a firm handshake by an honest-looking man, much like Rice, but that man was dead. His people were dead.

Biding his time with this crew let him interact with them on his own terms, gave him a reason to leave his room and escape his memories, but they weren't his people. He'd tried to make an effort with Brin, with Rice from time to time, but he'd yet to find any sense of ease here.

Logan passed the small dining nook, suitable for two. The other side of the room contained two comfortable chairs and a low table. A single bed on the far side of the room and a bathroom completed the suite. Whoever had occupied the ship before Rice's people had discovered it, had left long ago.

Layers of dust covered all the unused rooms. Rice had explained that they only had the manpower to clean what they needed. The lower three of the five levels of the ship had been damaged at some point, the sensors dead. One floor was flooded with contaminated water. The others, the ones he'd taken teams of cautious techs to explore, were filled with discarded equipment, most of which had baffled them. Some of the rooms down there had been living quarters or maybe rooms people had used to sleep between whatever work they were doing in the eerie, silent labs. Clothing and random personal belongings littered the floor and furniture, as if the ship had been attacked or suffered a massive collision that had caused them all to leave in a rush.

The only thing he could think of that was powerful enough for that was the army of Matouk. And while part of him wanted to destroy the army for what they'd done to Hijn, the more rational part never wanted to meet them again.

Logan took off his singed shirt and changed into pants not stained with the General's blood. The blisters on his arms convinced him to remain shirtless for the time being. If life followed its usual cycle on the Maxim, Rice would leave him alone for a few days, and then he'd drop by with the offer of something to do. By that point, Logan was usually ready to face people and action of any sort sounded good. Right now, though, he just wanted to rest his body on the long comfortable mattress.

He stretched out, reaching for the blanket he'd shoved aside that morning, but then left it be. He wasn't tired. Not in that way at least. Just tired inside.

Closing his eyes, he took a few deep breaths, letting them out slowly until his mind and body began to relax. As much as he tried to keep his mind empty, to ignore the memories that led to nightmares, his thoughts wandered to the General's city.

The tall spires that jutted from the city fairly glittered in the sun. The rest of the planet was one giant desert. No water other than ice that had built up in some areas more than others. Hanson had remarked about the lack of oceans or plant life. It was as if the planet had been sanitized.

The army did that with unruly worlds, sometimes only taking out a major city, turning the area into vast swaths of useless poisoned soil. This sand was different according to Hanson, lacking the effects of bombs. It was simply empty.

Had the army been to the General's world and used a different weapon? Regardless, how had the one city in all its glory survived?

The buildings and roads had been pristine, like something out of a far-fetched tale, beautiful and fanciful in the design. Trees and flowers filled the open spaces between the hardscape, softening the edges and furthering the notion that the whole thing had been just a dream.

If the General had escaped or fought back against the army, he needed to know how she'd done it. The king and queen had looked grand and awe-inspiring in all their finery and jewels, resting on their giant thrones, but neither of them had the look of ones who had seen battle at any recent time. If anyone on that doomed world had stood against Matouk's forces, it was her.

The more he thought about the city that he'd walked in only hours ago now wracked by quakes and a volcanic explosion that had likely turned it all to ash and rubble, the more he wanted to talk to the strange woman they'd rescued. Or abducted, he supposed was probably a more accurate term.

He got up and gingerly worked his way into a shirt. A walk back to the lift to the only other habitable level, down several corridors, and past the communal dining room brought him to the clinic.

Brin caught sight of him the moment he walked inside. Standing several inches taller than everyone else did make him easy to spot. "About time you have your burns seen to."

"I'm fine." He'd made several steps toward evading her before she cornered him.

"Like hell." Her full lips tightened as did her jaw. "Would you rather someone else take care of that for you?"

"That's not what I meant."

"Sure." She turned away from him. "May, can you see to this patient please?"

Brin walked away, head high and eyes forward. She went to talk to the lead doctor. Both of them stood near a bed that was cordoned off from the rest of the clinic by two portable screens.

May turned out to be a kind-faced woman with grey hair and soft hands. "Don't mind her. It's not you she's mad at. Doc Adams didn't allow her on the team for the Colonel's prize patient."

"Oh, it's probably me, but that would certainly piss her off too. Why'd he do that?"

"Says Brin exaggerated the woman's condition. Accused her of lying on her report." May shrugged, examining his arm. "Didn't see the patient myself, so I wouldn't know the truth of it."

"I did. She was definitely critical. I'm amazed she made it here alive."

May applied a spray that immediately took the pain from his skin. "You're welcome to talk to the doctor if you think it will put you back in her graces."

He hadn't had occasion to talk to Adams before and wasn't excited about doing it now, but the old man must be blind. Brin deserved proper credit. "I can do that."

"Good boy." She patted his shoulder and finished wrapping gauze around his arms. "I'll send him over shortly."

Brin had vanished while he was talking to May. He could only see the shadow of the doctor behind the screen until he emerged from the temporary room. May sent him over with a quick word and a point in Logan's direction.

The head doctor, a stern-looking man with salt and pepper hair and almond-shaped eyes, approached Logan as if he were yet another distraction that he didn't have time for. "You have something to offer regarding the new patient?"

"She was dying, a real mess. Rhodes worked very hard to get her stabilized. It's only because of her that the General made it here alive."

Adams caught him in a dry stare. "And you got your medical training where?"

"Ask Hanson then. He has the scans to prove it. He examined her before Colonel Rice called Rhodes in."

Hanson's name did catch the doctor's interest.

Neurotic and annoying as Hanson could be, he was well respected. Not that he was a medical doctor either.

"I'll take that under advisement."

The doctor's conciliatory tone gave him hope on Brin's behalf. "How is the General doing?"

"Other than not being half as low on blood as noted, many of her supposed damaged organs looking healthy as could be and her third degree burns only being first, I'd say fairly well."

Confused but not wanting to aggravate the doctor, Logan merely nodded.

He didn't get the chance to ask anything further because Commander Tate chose that moment to make her appearance. For once, Rice wasn't at her side. That was unfortunate as he'd come to quickly understand that Commander Tate had little use for a tall bulky man who ate a lot, intimidated her crew, and answered everything in stock single word answers. She much preferred the conversation and company of her techs, which gave her a lot of options since they comprised most of her crew. After all, they were supposed to be exploring and helping others, not antagonizing them. He'd overheard her views on his presence on several occasions. Thankfully, Rice stood up for his actions. The Commander didn't seem to understand that there were others in the universe that didn't share her views on their missions.

Adams left him in a flash to relay the status of their guest.

"She's stable?"

"Yes, quite. We expect a full recovery," Adams said.

"You understand what Colonel Rice said about what she can do?"

"We will keep her sedated but able to talk."

"Let's just hope that's enough."

Adams nodded. "I'll make sure she's safe."

Logan scowled. Safe for them to talk to, maybe. But what about the General's safety?

The two of them went behind the screen. Try as he might, he couldn't hear them.

May came back over. "Did you need something else?"

"No."

"Then you should get something to eat and rest. Your arms will take a few days to fully heal."

"I'll be fine."

She nodded, still watching him as if unsure how to get him to leave.

He didn't care. He was staying until he was sure the General was going to be all right. The way Adams and the Commander were acting as if she were some sort of rare specimen didn't sit well with him.

"I'll wait here for awhile."

"Oh." Her face brightened. "I'll let Brin know you're waiting on her."

"No, don't do that."

May's brows drew together. She bit her lower lip and looked around as if hoping someone else would come take this unpleasant task from her. No one did.

"I'm going to have to ask you to wait outside if you insist on lingering. We have to keep this area available for incoming patients."

Logan looked from the doorway to the otherwise empty area but for him and May. "There are no incoming patients."

She further drew herself up, but he could see her hands shaking where she held them pressed against her hips. "Please."

If he caused a scene, Rice would be called in to

wrangle him. He didn't want to make life more difficult for the colonel. He already had to walk the delicate line between Commander Tate's humanitarian mission and the safety of the crew.

Tate had shown her true selfless colors when their last ship had been attacked by Matouk's army. She'd held off defense in hopes of talking things out. And now they didn't have their ship anymore. It was only a gift of fortune that they'd limped their way along to stumble across the Maxim and that it was deserted. Because, he grumbled to himself, she probably would have tried to talk her way through that too. That may have worked, but in his experience, it usually didn't.

Just when Logan had resolved to leave peacefully, the Commander and Adams emerged from the screen. Tate held the General's amulet, the gold chain dripping from her hand. His resolve went to shit.

He addressed Commander Tate without any prelude. "What are you doing with that?"

Commander Tate's displeasure was just as clear. "That's none of your concern."

"That belongs to the General."

Adams inserted himself between them. "And we'd prefer that she didn't blast the ship with light or whatever it was she did."

Anika's warning to not anger the General flooded back to Logan. "Then don't take that away from her."

"We're certainly not leaving her armed until we have a chance to talk to her. We don't even know what exactly she is," said Adams.

"That's armor, not a weapon. She won't be happy to find it gone." At least he hoped it was. But his gut was telling him to keep the amulet with the General. If she woke up to find it missing, he didn't want to be responsible when she expanded and started blasting.

Commander Tate said, "Colonel Rice shares your sentiments. However, I would like Hanson's opinion. So, Mr. Klevo, if you would like to continue your stay with us, I would suggest returning to your quarters and remaining there until we have need of you."

Having no further recourse other than snatching the amulet from her hands, which would get him summarily deposited on the next habitable planet without so much as a goodbye, he gave her a curt nod and headed out of the clinic.

CHAPTER THREE

Hearing voices, the General drifted up from the darkness. She hadn't expected to join the elders, not after all she'd done. She'd thought her eternity would be filled with silence, maybe blackness, or perhaps perpetual torture if her father had any say in the matter.

Had the elders forgiven her? Was she truly part of the elder collective now? She could watch over her people, those that had fled Kaldara. There had to be a few of the hybrids receptive to the voices within the beyond, as she had been before the elders had shut her out. Even in death, she could guide her people to a better life.

Two voices hovered around her now, a man and a woman. Thankfully, they were not her parents, but she didn't recognize them. The man sounded concerned, the woman, excited.

She drifted upward a little farther and was startled to find that she was in pain. A lot of pain. Much of her body was unresponsive.

Elders never mentioned feeling pain. They never sounded concerned about the physical self at all. She shouldn't even have a body. Unless this was how the elders were going to punish her.

The voices faded. She concentrated on trying to make her arm move. Sharp knives shot through her body.

No moving then.

Anger built up within her. Anika sat just below the surface. Instead of her usual urging to take control, she called for patience. That alone told the General something had gone wrong.

It struck her that the voices weren't speaking her language. They were using the one she'd taken from Colonel Rice. She wasn't dead. And he hadn't kept his word.

Rage surged, forcing healing energy from her nearly depleted well into her body until the pain subsided enough to allow her to move. She reached for her amulet. Wherever she was, she was broken and she wanted protection immediately.

Except the amulet wasn't there.

The bed grew too small to contain her. She spilled over the edge and onto the floor in a tangle of heavy limbs. Her head hit hard. Her eyes opened to see bright lights and gauzy rectangles that seemed to fall in upon her. She tossed them aside.

On the outside of her awareness, as she fumbled with her uncooperative and unprotected body, she was dimly aware of shouting. Men and women raced toward her. Some of them bore what she sensed were weapons. It was hard to focus on the people with the power swirling inside her. Anika pleaded for her to relax, to be calm. That only fed the panic.

She stared up at blurry walls and a ceiling with lights that reminded her of her childhood.

Dimly sensing the ship itself, comfort seeped up from the cool floor through her hands. The walls were familiar, they felt right, but the people around her were not. They weren't Unlata Kai. The Unlata Kai were gone. Except for her.

Her people were on different ships, just like this one. She tried to reach out to them, but then she remembered that she'd cut the connection to her points. There was no way to contact them now.

This ship was in pain. So much pain. Like her. She groaned as she tried to sit up.

Several bodies shoved her to the floor. They fought with her arms and legs and tried to hold her down. She gathered a burst and was about to let it go when a calming voice reached her ears. This one was male. Not Antoni, but another. One she found pleasing. He'd carried her through the palace. She'd shielded him. Him and the colonel who had broken his promise.

"General, you are safe. Lay still. You're injured." He rested a tentative hand on her shoulder.

She dimmed her energy so as not to burn him. "Why am I here?"

"We couldn't leave you there to die."

"You promised."

"Blame it on the colonel." He sounded like it wasn't all the colonel's fault, but he was Logan's superior. If anyone would suffer her wrath, it would be the colonel.

He nodded to the three men who were holding her down. They let go and backed away.

"Can we get her a chair or something?"

A woman came forward, dragging a bench large enough to seat two and then retreated. Logan helped the General off the floor and onto the seat. Standing would have made her feel more secure, but her legs weren't ready for that yet. In fact, the effort of getting to the bench left her lightheaded. Her bare feet maintained contact with the ship, offering her something other than her weak body to focus on.

"Your name?"

"Logan Klevo."

"No rank?"

"Not anymore." He hovered close, keeping one hand on her and warning the rest to stay back with a fierce glare.

An older woman in a tan uniform stood nearby. Disregarding Logan, she came closer. "What is your name?"

"You may address me as General." She was pleased her voice still held power. "Who are you?"

"I am Commander Tate. This is my ship."

Her ship? The General vented her frustration with this new reality with a deep growl that had the desired effect of eliciting a worried look on the commander's stark features. "My ship."

The commander's voice remained firm. "No."

That was the best this commander could do? No wonder she had the colonel to do her job for her. If this woman had come to her world, she would have killed her on the spot.

"Did you build this ship?"

"We discovered it, deserted and damaged."

Anika lent her a little more strength so that she could reach into the ship and feel for what the woman said. She accessed the logs.

Standard reports documented the original crew tracking the aftermath of a trail of ruined worlds, some of which they had overseen. The entries quickly became more scattered. The faces of people she'd known long ago dissolved into despair as their ship suffered from repeated attacks and more worlds fell to a vast army following one who called himself Matouk. An Unlata Kai.

She wasn't the last of her kind.

The General read further, speeding through years of records, finding more mentions of the cruelty and chaos caused by Matouk. She watched worlds covered in fire, shattering, empty, through the eyes of those who also ultimately suffered from his tyrannical stampede through the universe. Matouk was no different than her father, except he showed no signs of slowing down.

She'd missed him in her hunting and he'd taken every advantage while she'd grown bored on Kaldara. Left unchecked, every living thing could eventually suffer his attention. Everything the Unlata Kai had worked for since the beginning would be for nothing, their legacy only blood and ashes.

"This Army of Matouk, who are they to you?"

Her face lit up. "You know of them?"

"Only what I just read in your ship's records."

The light instantly faded and a pinched look took its place. "Those records are secured."

"For you." She breathed out, flowing what energy she had into the ship, taking control of the main engines, the navigation, and the power. She cut them all.

"What's going on?" the commander called out in the darkness. "Report, now."

The General allowed their communications to remain active. Reports bombarded the commander, voices filling the blackness with unwelcome news.

The General couldn't force the wounded ship to ignore their requests for long. It was in enough pain without her demands. Connected as she was, its aches added to her own.

Anika was already cautioning her to sink back into a healing sleep. Her body had a long way to go before full recovery.

"You wish for the light?"

"What?" The commander's voice wavered.

"Ask for it."

Silence stretched out until her very strained voice finally spoke. "Can we have the lights?"

She allowed the ship to fulfill the crew's urgent commands for light. They flickered back to life, bombarding blinking eyes with their harsh glow.

Logan watched her quietly, his gaze intense. She found herself smiling despite her broken body.

"Engines and navigation will remain in my control until I am ready to continue our conversation."

The commander scowled. "You better pray Matouk doesn't find us while you're sleeping."

She turned to Logan. "Since you seem to have some measure of control over this creature. I will hold you responsible for keeping her out of trouble." She turned on her heels and left.

"You should probably get back to bed," he said.

As much as Tate's words grated on her...no one had control over her...the black spots at the edge of her vision agreed with Logan. She let her body go, returning to her natural size so she could fit back onto the bed.

He helped her to her feet, which was mostly him holding her up, and then up onto the bed. Needing help at all put her in an even worse mood. Her father had done his best to take her out with him. It was going to take time for her to recover on her own with no points to feed her energy.

She'd killed North.

She refused to let tears fall. Not for the faithful man who had been with her for centuries, or Antoni whom she'd known her whole life, or even the ship full of Kaldarans who lost their lives to her father's last fit of rage. As much as this loss hurt her, she needed to remain focused. She could grieve later once she was dead. It would give her something to do.

Logan lifted her feet onto the bed and scrambled to return the pillows just as she leaned back, not exactly of her own volition.

"Should I get the doctor?"

She was losing hold of the ship and her body. Not willing to lose what little control of the situation she held, the General put a command lock on the controls and then pulled out, leaving the ship to suffer without her to dull the pain of the crew's attempts to subvert her control.

First she had to heal herself, then she'd ease the ship, returning it to its full glory. The previous crew hadn't followed her father, they had no experience hunting a fellow Unlata Kai. Not like she did. All she needed was time.

Hopefully, Matouk didn't find her before she was ready.

ᚷ

Whether her eyes had slipped closed or she had passed out, she wasn't sure, but she came to hours later. Her body still seemed distant but the room was in focus again, as was Logan who sat on the bench beside her bed. The wall screens were back in place, offering her a measure of privacy from the voices and bustle on the other side.

"You're still here?"

He nodded.

"You do realize you have no control over me, correct?"

Logan snorted. "Wouldn't dream of even considering it."

She was unsure whether his casual air was refreshing or an affront to the respect she deserved. Either way, he served as a distraction while she waited for the pain to hit.

"Did the meds help? If you ask me, I don't think he knew what to give you or how much. They didn't make anything worse, did they?"

That explained the disconnect with her body and the welcome lack of pain. "Yes, they helped."

"Good." He leaned back against the wall.

She hadn't realized how tense he'd been until seeing him visibly relax. He'd rolled his sleeves up and held his arms out straight on his lap. Red patches and blisters peeked above slouching bands of gauze.

"You were wounded? My shield should have kept you safe."

"When the queen...exploded. Your shield protected us the second time. We wouldn't have escaped without it. Thanks for that."

Her skin tingled where he'd held her to get her back into bed. He'd helped her. Calmly, confidently, not as a scrambling servant or follower hoping for favor. An unfamiliar warmth crept out of her cold center where her well resided.

She made her uncooperative arm slowly move outward, reaching for him. "Let me see."

He unwrapped the gauze on one arm.

Her fingers met with hot brown skin. She closed her eyes, summoning a bit of energy from her well to heal him. Gripping his arm, she appreciated the muscles she felt there. He wasn't one of the soft ones, not like the others who had been in the room around her.

Moments later his voice filled with awe. "How did you do that?"

"I can do a lot of things." She let go, her eyelids already feeling heavy.

Anika muttered in her mind. *You shouldn't have done that. We have no energy to spare.*

He's been kind to us.

The mission comes first. Always.

It always had, but right now, whatever the doctor had given her made her light and hazy. She rather liked it, and she decided that she liked Logan, too.

He unwrapped the other arm and tossed the gauze into a bin by the bed. He stood beside her, concern clear on his face. "You should be resting. You're really pale."

He was right, but the thought of being defenseless while she slept kept her from giving in. "Where is my amulet?"

"The commander has it."

"It would benefit her greatly to return it. I should hate to have to destroy you all."

"I would hate to be destroyed."

His dry tone made it hard not to smile, but she had to maintain what little control she had. There was one burst left in her well and hopefully enough to heal her if she worked slowly. Without her points or her army to defend and feed her, she was vulnerable. She hadn't been in that position in a very long time. She had to dig deep into memories to remember how to protect herself.

She needed an ally. Logan had proven himself to be one for now. Until she could learn more about the rest of the crew, he would have to do.

"You will stay." She wasn't sure if she was asking or commanding. The uncertainty of the whole situation left her raw and floundering.

He nodded without argument.

Before her hold on her emotions dissolved, she gave herself over to a deep healing sleep.

☙

When she woke, Logan was still on the bench, but sat slouched against the wall. His eyes were closed and his chin rested on his chest.

Though she had need of a lot more sleep herself, she was curious as to her amulet and her situation. Sensing that his body was also still in need, she let him rest. He must have remained awake for a long time. She reached out to touch the wall so she could access the ship. She'd been asleep most of two cycles.

The silence of the ship's engines left her feeling even emptier than before. The agony of the ship denying the persistent manual commands of the crew filled her with guilt. Yet it was necessary. If she showed these people weakness, they would not hesitate to ensnare her in a promise, and she'd seen far too many of her kind fall victim to that.

Was Matouk truly like her father, or were his worshippers using his promises as their weapon and protection? He needed to be destroyed either way, but the thought of his defeat in the light of delivering him from a life he didn't want was more alluring. Sending her father into the beyond hadn't given her the relief or sense of accomplishment she'd hoped for.

She sat up slowly, using the level of pain and discomfort to ascertain how many of her injuries had healed while she'd been asleep. From the dwindling amount of energy left in her well, she hoped it was most of them.

The haze of medication didn't hit her so heavily this time. Her arms moved without hesitation, no sharp pains in her chest or stomach, and her vision was clear. She tried her legs and found them responsive, but still painful to move, though more in a strained muscle sort of way. At least the bones had healed. Sore muscles she could deal with.

She caught sight of the doctor, the one they called Adams, scanning her from the opening in the screens.

"You wish to come closer?"

He glanced at Logan's sleeping form, and then with a look of resolve, nodded.

"You may enter."

Adams stole inside the room even though he had been given permission. He timidly waved his scanner over her legs and then her torso and arms.

"It's miraculous. You've healed almost completely in a matter of two days."

Another ally would be beneficial, at least until she fully recovered. She recalled the soft light in Logan's eyes when she'd healed him, the way he'd looked at her and the warmth she'd felt inside. Noting the doctor's stiff posture, she said, "You're suffering from pain in your back."

He smiled weakly. "Every day."

"Come closer."

He did. Logan woke, jumping to his feet.

She held the doctor in her gaze, keeping him focused on her rather than Logan. "Lift your shirt and turn around."

He did so, baring a stretch of sallow skin marked with a varied assortment of moles and age spots amongst sparse wiry silver hairs.

What are you doing? Anika demanded. *We have nothing to spare.*

He made us comfortable.

We owe him nothing. He could have just as well killed us with his lack of knowledge.

Ignoring her irate other half, she sent heat and energy into the doctor's body, healing not only his back but a spur on his hip. Once she was done, she pulled back into herself.

Logan stood next to Adams, who stretched experimentally. Though she found she enjoyed the grateful shine to his smile, the tingling warmth she'd felt when she'd healed Logan didn't come. Curious, she sunk into herself to try and figure out why.

Shadows against the screen and hushed voices interrupted her thoughts. A rush of determined footsteps drew closer.

The doctor took a step, then another. "That's amazing. How did you-"

Commander Tate strode in without invitation. "I demand you return control of my ship."

The General sat up farther, pulling close the thin cloth of the wrap in which the doctor's staff had dressed her. She cleared her throat, hoping for some semblance of the power her voice normally held. "You *demand*?"

"The Maxim is under my control."

"It would seem not."

The doctor cleared his throat. "Excuse me, but I think-"

"This ship belongs to us." Commander Tate said.

"Again, it seems not."

Her jaw tightened, making her left ear rise against her short brown hair. "We can't just float here. We're mostly defenseless if we're discovered. We have a mission."

"This ship had a mission before you, and we shall see that through."

"If you could please..." The doctor attempted to place himself between the bed and the commander. "I have work to do here." He fumbled with his scanner, his hands trembling.

The harsh lights of the clinic cast a heavy shadow over Logan's eyes, but the downward turn of his lips revealed enough of his disposition.

The commander gave way to the doctor, her fingers twitching at her sides, as if she wished to curl them into fists. "And what would that mission be?"

"According to the logs, eradicating the one who calls himself Matouk."

"We have no desire to involve ourselves in a war."

"From what Colonel Rice told me, you already are."

Commander Tate shook her head, her voice firm. "We did not provoke any attack, nor will we."

"I wasn't asking your permission."

The woman stared at her, teeth grinding. "My crew already has a mission."

"You may take your mission to another ship. One built by your own people, and you may take your crew with you. I have need of only four men. Leave them and you are free to go."

"We've seen the destruction he and his army have brought upon entire planets first hand. You know nothing of the army if you think you can defeat Matouk with four men."

The General smiled, the kind that made her servants cringe and scatter. "You know nothing of me."

"I've read the colonel's report," she said stiffly.

"I'm sure you have. The few moments we spoke to one another do not define me either. You should leave me before you find yourself cast adrift in a lifepod. I see there are still a nominal amount remaining."

"You wouldn't dare do such a thing."

This woman really didn't know her at all. "I assure you, I would."

Commander Tate's mouth dropped open. "My superiors will hear of this."

"If you would like me to speak to them-"

"I will speak to them." The Commander stormed off.

Colonel Rice arrived in her wake, turning to watch the commander leave. "I see you two are well acquainted."

The General refocused her displeasure on him. "You're just in time to explain yourself."

Logan, who had appeared markedly uncomfortable during her exchange with the commander, glanced between her and the colonel and then addressed the doctor who was prodding at her right foot. "Shouldn't she be resting? Maybe without visitors?"

Adams nodded. "Yes, exactly that." He gave the fleshy part of her heel one last jab with his thumb and then slid the scanner into his coat pocket, nodding toward the opening. "Shall we?"

The colonel stood his ground. "I'm sorry, we couldn't leave you to die." He looked her in the eye. "You're an asset we couldn't afford to lose. If you can take out your king, you might have a chance at making an impact on Matouk's army. We need that."

While she didn't appreciate her original plan going awry, knowing now of Matouk's damage, she agreed with the colonel's logic. More than that, she admired that he spoke plainly.

The doctor gave them all a look of warning, shook his head, and left.

"Your commander does not share your mission."

"There has been some heated debate over that topic. It's not exactly my mission either, but after what his men did to our last ship..." He shook his head. "We can't go through that again."

If the colonel might be able to sway the commander, she would not be opposed to utilizing their crew. She regarded the wrap she wore. "I shall require clothes and a place to reside while I evaluate the best course of elimination for Matouk."

Logan spoke up, "You know him?"

"He is also Unlata Kai, of my people. He is corrupt, or he's being made to act so. He must be eliminated and his worshipers diffused."

Rice lifted a single brow, coming closer to stand beside her, his voice lowered. "And you can do that?"

"I can. I was the General, yes?"

He glanced at Logan, who shrugged. They both nodded.

"You're not anymore?" asked Rice.

"One cannot be a General without an army. Without them, it is just a name."

"The other ships, the ones the Maxim saw departing during our time on the planet, did they contain your army?"

"My army has been disbanded. My people dispersed to begin again elsewhere in peace. The Unlata Kai of my world have been destroyed, that they should not corrupt anyone else."

"You meant to destroy your kind? Why?"

"Did you not see that world?" She shook her head, swishing her hair across her face. She shoved it back with force, annoyed with everything and everyone, even the very air she breathed.

"When we arrived, it was beautiful, lush and green, with plentiful food and an abundant but simple population. The man you saw as King, my father, his hobby, as you would call it, was to play survival of the fittest. He would pit his worshippers against others, converting or killing in their wake to rule all. He's done it to so many worlds.

Raking her hands over her face, she tried to dislodge the visions of populations falling before the armies she led in her father's name.

"He grew bored and became as you saw him. All I could save was that single city after the destruction he had caused. I was sick of his games. The universe is old enough now. It no longer needs our guidance. We haven't been good about giving it for a very long time."

"Gods?" speculated Rice.

"Some would call us so."

"And this ship was created by gods."

"We prefer Unlata Kai, but yes."

"Well then," he cracked a smile, "with a god on our side, how can we lose?"

"Matouk's army also has a god on their side."

Logan exhaled loudly. "There is that."

"So clothes and a room?" asked Rice.

"And my amulet and four men."

"I'll see to the amulet. Hanson will have to wipe his drool off it, but I think I can pry it from his hands. About the four men...may I ask your intentions?"

"My points are gone. I need to replace them."

"May I ask what that entails? We would obviously prefer to have men volunteer."

"Men I can trust to uphold the tasks I assign them."

Rice shifted from foot to foot before asking, "And those tasks, would they involve harming anyone on this ship?"

If Tate was floating in space without a suit, would that count as harming her on the ship? The General sighed and let the pillows take a bit more of her weight. She wasn't ready to promise anything. She barely knew these people.

Promises were binding. Breaking one could mean losing all that made her Unlata Kai. While that might have been welcome a few days before, she now needed to remain whole for a while longer.

If she couldn't give him her word, the odds of him providing men for points who could, in time, recharge her, were slim. As much as she needed that energy, she wasn't ready to make that promise with the consequences it carried. For all she knew, she would end up no better off than Matouk—if he really was conquering against his will.

"We will resume this conversation tomorrow. How about the room and clothes for now. Maybe something to eat?"

Colonel Rice rolled his shoulders and took a step back. "Of course. Though, what we have here, is very likely not what you're used to."

"And just what do you think I'm used to?" she asked, knowing it would make him squirm. She was beginning to not dislike the man, but he didn't need to know that just yet. After all, he had broken his promise, no matter what his reasoning was.

"I would imagine..." he said, looking to Logan for help.

Logan turned to examine the empty wall.

Rice spoke cautiously, "You would typically wear something akin to what the king and queen were wearing?"

"And how would I dispense justice in that?" Her eyelids were growing tired already. All she wanted right now was a quiet and secure room. "What you found me in is about the extent of my taste for finery. Anything whole, serviceable, and comfortable will do for now."

"That, I think we can manage." Rice offered her a smile that made her like him a fraction more. "I'll be right back."

The colonel left them to speak with another man who stood outside the screens. When he returned he said, "I've located a room for you. If you'd follow me, please."

"Can you walk?" asked Logan quietly.

For a moment she considered asking him to carry her. What little she remembered of that experience brought another rush of warmth to her insides. Instead, she broached what little energy remained in her well, borrowing enough to finish healing her legs and feet, but leaving her without enough for a burst. Hopefully, she had them cowed enough for now that they wouldn't require a show of power.

"Yes, I think so." But that didn't stop her from reaching out to take his offered arm until she got her balance. Having no further excuse, she regretfully let go of him.

She tugged the flimsy wrap around her and followed Rice. It wasn't until she'd made it past the stares of the men and women in the clinic and out into the corridor that she realized Logan wasn't with her. Her side felt empty. How quickly she'd allowed herself to get attached to his somber face and impressive frame.

That isn't wise, whispered Anika.

Get back behind the veil. I have no need of you.

You will always need me. You're weak.

She shut out the disparaging voice and picked up her pace to walk beside Rice. "Do you favor Logan?"

"Do you?" he asked without looking at her.

"Not in a way that would take him from your service. He would not make a good point."

"Why do you say that?"

"He is done taking orders, I think."

Rice chuckled. "You don't miss much, do you?"

"I make it my business not to." The corridor was just as she remembered, clean lines, wide enough for four men side by side, glow lights overhead, lending their skin a healthier appearance than in the clinic.

"If you are no longer the General, and Logan tells

me we shouldn't attempt to pronounce your name, what are we to call you?"

"What name do you wish to call me? I've had many. They matter not to me."

"Well, you're not exactly a Jane Doe. Let me think…"

"What is that?"

"What we call an unidentified female."

"Short and simple. Jane. Yes, I like it."

"Really?" He scratched at the short brown hairs on his chin. "You wouldn't prefer something with a little more…I don't know. The General had a ring to it. Something with a little more oomph?"

"We had several generals long ago. The word was nothing other than a rank. When I defeated them and became the only general, it was still the same name."

"Yes, but your people pronounced the with a capital *The*."

"So you were able to understand them."

"Only a little after you touched me. What did you do?"

"I took on your language. Doing so opens a path for whomever I am taking from. However," she regarded him closely. "Comprehending our language isn't something most people can do even then. Somewhere in your distant past, one of your ancestors must have been part Unlata Kai."

"You do that? Breed with the locals?"

"Not me personally, but yes. Many of my people did as we roamed."

"But not you."

She shook her head. "I had Antoni. But my father killed him when he destroyed the last ship before it could leave Kaldara."

"You were going to kill him anyway."

"I think perhaps you understood more than I like."

Rice regarded her cautiously. "I'm not judging you."

No reason to hide the truth. He knew enough already. "We had made a pact, an agreement that we should leave the universe in peace to go its own way without our interference. Meaning all of us who were pure would remain on the planet." She stared ahead, still angry about Antoni's betrayal. "He told me he would stay with me. But instead, he boarded the ship. He'd planned to escape with the others."

Rice grimaced. "I'm sorry I brought that up."

He came to a stop and palmed the door panel. "This suite is vacant. It's one of the larger ones. And clean."

"You know very little about the mechanics of this ship."

He ran a hand through his close-cropped hair. "Well, it was apparently created by gods. Shouldn't be surprising that we common mortals don't understand it all."

"You are frustrated with your position in this new development."

He turned to face her in the doorway. "I don't know if you plan to fry us or laugh us off until we've got no dignity left. I'm not in favor of either one."

His blunt honesty helped her to relax a little. "I am not ready to make any vows regarding the whole of your crew, ship, or future, but I will promise that you, Colonel Rice, will not find death from my hands and your dignity will remain safe from me as well."

"Well, that's something." He stepped out of the doorway, allowing her entrance.

"You seek help with this ship, yes?"

He nodded.

"It would benefit us both to have it in better working order." She took in the room, the simple elegance of a typical living space, yet lacking the personal touches that might declare it a home. "I propose then that we work toward that goal together for the time being, allowing us to evaluate each other further as we do so."

"I would appreciate that."

"Good. Where might I find a meal?" If she didn't have points to siphon energy from, she'd need to refuel the slow, common way.

"We haven't got the equipment working in the rooms, but we have set up a dining hall. You're welcome to eat there, or I can have someone deliver food to you if you'd prefer."

She studied him for a moment before answering. "You would prefer that. My arrival has already caused quite an upheaval in your daily lives, I take it?"

"You could say that."

"I wouldn't be here if it weren't for you."

His shoulders sagged. "That point has been made abundantly clear on all sides."

"Well then, Colonel Rice, we will endeavor together to make the best of your decision."

A smile spread over his otherwise weary face, slow and shy. "Thank you."

"I don't know what you consider edible but it if sustains you, I'll deal with it. And please see that Logan is rested. He is tired."

"He stayed with you the whole time. Said you asked him to."

"I did."

After having talked to Rice alone, and with the prospect of refueling solely from food laying starkly before her, she decided to make some concessions. "I will require those four men we spoke of. They will not harm the ship or the crew."

"You on the other hand..."

She settled into one of the chairs. "I make no promises about myself."

"Duly noted."

"Good skilled men, but I do not wish to disrupt your crew. And, of course, my amulet."

"I'll get on it." He turned to leave.

"One more thing."

He turned slowly. From his stance, he seemed to be waiting for something terrible to finally hit him.

"Rest. You'll need a sharp mind to deal with Commander Tate and your superiors."

He nodded. "I will."

The door closed behind him. The soft surface of the chair molded to her body, embracing her in comfort. It had been a long time since she'd had occasion to sit aboard a ship like this. Not since they'd made the choice to settle on Kaldara.

Had her father destroyed that same ship, the one that had served as her home between worlds all her life? She'd run through its corridors, dreamed in a room just like this one, and learned the language of creation in its walls.

Perhaps it had been one of the three her mother had created during their first years on Kaldara. Ships they'd set aside for trade or travel and then ignored as they'd settled into their perfect palace surrounded by worshipers with no threats or challenges to distract them.

Anika remained silent beneath the surface, leaving Jane to her own thoughts. Just before she'd fully nodded off, the door chimed. Not knowing who it might be, she rose and went to open it manually.

Logan stood in the corridor, a tray in one hand and a stack of clothing tucked under his other arm.

"I thought you were resting," she said accusingly, making a note to speak to Rice about better following her instructions.

"I was on my way to do that, but it seems you scare the living hell out of everyone. The colonel didn't trust anyone else to get these to you."

Logan didn't appear hesitant to be in her company at all. In fact, he seemed even more at ease than Rice had. In that regard he reminded her of Antoni, her perpetual companion throughout the long years. A companion might help fill the void left by the loss of her people. At least a little.

She took the tray from him and set it on the table beside the chair where she had been resting. Logan remained in the doorway. She returned to him and held her hands out for the clothing.

"They weren't sure on the boots so you'll have to get those later. I'm sure Rice will take care of you personally."

"Because no one else will," she added.

He cracked a smile. "After word spread of the whole light shooting from your body thing, I'm afraid you're likely stuck with the two of us."

Being stuck with Logan would be no hardship.

"Until I claim my points," she said.

"About that..."

She shook her head. "I am aware of your interest, but I meant what I said to the colonel. I would not remove you from his service. He needs you."

"But-"

Resting her empty hand on his arm, she enjoyed the hard sculpted heat of his skin. "You do not wish to be a point. I would not waste you in such a service."

"So you might have a need for me then?"

He looked so hopeful. Clearly, he was lost here, not

fully part of Rice's team but needed for his skills. The commander had little regard for him. She'd witnessed that.

She needed time to decide who Jane was, apart from her people, no longer the General, not in charge of an entire race and city of her creation. Maybe he could help her figure that out.

"After we have rested, if you are not required by Rice, I would like you to walk with me." She took her hand from him, clutching the clothing instead. It didn't offer the same tactile enjoyment in the least.

"Walk where?"

"I have made an agreement with Rice to assist with repairs of this ship. You have traveled most of it, yes?"

He nodded. "I've escorted the techs."

"I would like you to escort me."

"You don't need me. You can protect yourself just fine. You're standing here like nothing is happening, yet are in complete control of this ship. You did that in your sleep even, and I have to tell you, it's driving Hanson and his team crazy. The Commander has verbally flayed him repeatedly since you took control."

She frowned. "It is not his fault. There are many better uses of a mind like his. Why is she pitting him against an impossible task?"

"You don't know Tate."

"I don't like Tate."

He grinned. "You're not alone there."

His words, no matter how casually uttered, solidified her intentions. "That," she said, "is why I want you to walk with me."

"Because I'm not a fan of Tate?"

"No." She ran a single finger over his still upturned lower lip.

He looked startled but not entirely disagreeable. And more importantly, not ready to bolt or so full of himself that he took the initiative to try for more.

"It's rare that your kind are at ease enough to smile like that around me. I quite enjoy it."

"I see." His smile took on a new shade that she didn't quite mind either.

She enjoyed the view for as long as possible before the silence stretched to awkwardness. "I should eat."

"And I would like to utilize my bed for a few hours."

She nodded. "Later then."

Logan took his leave, a single backward glance over his shoulder before he turned the corner that led to the lift. She watched him go, enjoying that view as well.

Once he was out of sight, she closed the door and examined the tray he had brought. She sampled the array of offerings ranging from hearty bread with a nutty taste to sweet fruits and a cup full of a creamy but tangy substance that she ate only because she was hungry. Setting the empty tray aside, she examined the clothing.

Underclothes had been tucked safely inside the shirt, away from prying eyes, she supposed. When she shook out the stack, the outfit did not resemble the more form-fitting clothing worn by the women she'd seen so far on the ship. Though, considering her size, she wasn't all that surprised. And she'd asked for comfortable over elegant. The loose-legged pants and flowing shirt that dripped about her hips were warm and moved easily with her. They were far superior to the thin wrap the clinic had provided.

She again sank into the chair, liking the feeling of the furniture conforming to her body rather than the open loneliness of the bed. She didn't need any reminders of how alone she truly was. Somewhere between trying to force herself to sleep and the realization that sleep wasn't going to happen, her door chimed again.

Grateful for an excuse to give up her fruitless quest, she got up to answer it. Rice stood outside with her amulet in his hand.

"Thought you wouldn't mind me waking you for this."

"I thought I told you to get some sleep yourself," she chided.

"You're my last stop. Hanson took some convincing." He shrugged. "Convincing takes time."

"Not if you do it right." Her words came out more harshly than the jest she'd been trying for. She forced a smile to attempt to take the sting out of it. "Sorry, I'm having difficulty sleeping."

"Not surprising, considering the past few days. Have you tried a drink to help you relax?"

She gestured toward the empty tray and the glass upon it. "There was water. It didn't help."

"I was thinking something stronger."

"What did you have in mind?"

He held out his hand, offering her the amulet. "Put this thing on it gives me the shivers."

"Energy field. Yes, you would be sensitive to it, I suppose." Jane took the amulet from his open hand and dropped the chain over her head, resting the metal on her chest. She had to admit, the plain white shirt did allow the amulet to shine. The familiar weight of it helped put her more at ease.

"This room isn't stocked, but if you want, I could bring you something to help you relax."

"That would be appreciated."

He nodded. "I'll be right back."

She watched him leave. While his uniform did have

a flattering cut, his backside didn't have the same smirk-inducing effect that Logan's did. Jane left the door open and returned to her chair, the closest to a throne that she intended to get. Once she'd solved the problem of Matouk, her obligation would be fulfilled and she could be done with this existence once and for all.

Rice called softly into the room, "You still awake?"

"As I can hear you, it would seem so."

He held out a bottle of brown liquid and two glasses. "Mind if I join you? After dealing with Commander Tate and Hanson, I could use a little help winding down myself."

"You talked with her already?"

He opened the bottle and poured a small amount into each glass. Handing her one, he took the other chair across from her. "I couldn't very well have you skulking about the ship doing whatever it is you plan to do, without her knowledge. She had to be made aware of our agreement."

"And?" Jane took a sip of the liquid. She found it smooth and pleasing to her tongue.

"And she's pleased that you will assist with the repairs." He tossed back the contents and set the empty glass on the table between them. "You were right about needing to sleep before broaching the rest."

"Good." Not to be outdone, she emptied her glass as well.

"You like it?"

"Yes." She held out her glass.

Rice filled it halfway this time and did the same for his own. "Whiskey. They make it better back home, but this isn't half bad."

Half bad was making a nice heated spot in her stomach. They sipped their drinks in silence. She to avoid anything snide slipping from her tongue that might spoil her enjoyment of drink and company and Rice looking like he was about to say something several times but thought better of it.

He finally said, "The clothes are suitable?"

"They will do."

"I'll have someone bring some shoes to choose from in the morning."

She considered mentioning that she could simply engage her armor and have golden boots that fit her perfectly, but covering herself in armor was too close to the General. She wasn't sure who she was right now, but she did need a break from who she had been. At least for a little while. She would focus on the repairs and learning what the Unlata Kai of this ship had to offer toward her goal of defeating Matouk.

It had been a very long time since she'd allowed herself the frivolity of inebriation. She considered that she should be questioning Rice about the vital members of his crew while his tongue was loosened, but her mind was weary. Instead, she let him wander in small talk, answering only as necessary to keep him going.

As the contents dwindled, he became melancholy. "We lost thirteen of our crew when we were attacked."

His losses seemed minimal, though, she considered, so was the Maxim's crew. She slowly sipped her drink.

"His army is full of fanatics. They're every bit as cruel as I've heard he is. Our people were picked off one by one as they tried to escape. It was difficult to watch."

Had one of those people lived in this room? She considered the lack of personal items, but those may have been removed. Rice had mentioned the room was clean and that most of the others weren't.

"You were close to these people?"

He studied the contents of his glass, swirling them

around methodically. "Hard not to be with a small crew. Not like we can stop home and pick up more to fill the gaps. Our crewmembers were just gone. Holes in our days, where people had been."

"The place you come from, Matouk has not been there?"

Rice shook his head. "Not yet, at least. Naptcha fears if we head for home, Matouk's army may follow. Besides, we can help people out here."

"Have you tried to recruit more like Logan?"

"Hanson's people are specialized. Most of the colonies we've visited have either been decimated by attacks or are not established enough to have an excess of bright minds. Muscle, we can probably find." He sighed. "It's not like we have much to offer in compensation, especially with the ship in poor repair and Matouk on the loose. His people found us once. They could do it again, and we're not prepared for that. It will be far worse this time."

"Have you met Matouk directly?"

Rice shook his head and emptied his glass. "From what we've heard, he has his men do most of the work, sends them off to find targets. He only shows up personally if there's something worth taking."

"He can control a wider network that way."

"He's got a vast network all right." Rice rubbed a hand over his face.

"We happened upon Hijn in the wake of the attack. Matouk's heavy forces had left long before, leaving only a few that we later learned were gathering slaves and the remaining food. With only one ship, there wasn't much we could do but search for survivors far from where the slavers were. We'd barely picked up Logan when Tate got spooked by a passing ship. Though we got out of there, it wasn't long after that they caught up with us."

"Join or die?"

He nodded.

That sounded like her father all over again. She rubbed her eyes but couldn't remove the image of him bursting into light, his well shattering as he destroyed the last ship, her people. He'd tried to kill her too.

"I will see that you are better prepared when we meet Matouk's men again."

Rice poured the last of the liquor. They drank in silence while she tried to bring to mind the faces of those who had been lost on the ship her father had destroyed. From the forlorn cast to the colonel, he seemed to be doing the same with his own crew.

When the bottle was empty and so were their glasses, he stood, wavering on his feet. "I think I'm well and ready for bed now." His words slurred, but she wasn't positive that wasn't her own imagining.

"I might sleep now as well." She did wish then for one of the blankets from her bed. She could have further adjusted her body temperature, but the effort of doing so almost seemed more than getting up and retrieving a blanket.

Seeing that she was on the way to her bed, Rice went to the door. She heard him pause there and turned around.

"Calling you Jane just feels wrong," he said earnestly. "You're more than that."

"True as that is, I'll remain Jane until it is clear what more I am to be."

He nodded, seeming pleased with her answer. The door closed behind him.

CHAPTER FOUR

Logan wasn't sure what he expected when Jane opened her door, but she wasn't hungover like Rice had warned him she might be and was himself. He still couldn't believe Rice had the nerve to drink into the wee hours with the General, or Jane, or whatever she was now. Looking alert, though her hair and clothes were rumpled, she seemed her usual self–when she wasn't bleeding to death or firing light bombs from her armored chest. She stood watching him, amusement flickering in her gaze.

"You expected to find me heaving over a toilet?"

"Not judging. We've all been there."

"I can heal myself, remember?"

"So never a hangover?"

"Maybe once or twice when I was much younger, before I'd come into my full power, but otherwise, no."

"I'm jealous."

She smiled, her eyes twinkling like the amulet resting on her chest. "Are we off to find shoes then or am I to walk barefoot through the halls?"

"Rice is sending someone. They should be here any minute."

"And you're here to assure them of their safety?"

Was she teasing him? Did gods do that?

He took a chance that he'd read her correctly. "I

don't think there's much I can do to assure that in your case, but yes, in theory."

Jane cocked her head, gaze growing distant. "That is the value you hold for them. Safety?"

"I suppose so."

"And you are good at this?"

What kind of question was that? How was he supposed to answer? He didn't want to sound cocky, especially not to her, given her experience. He knew his mouth was hanging open uselessly. He closed it, trying to compose an answer. "They seem to think so."

"Perception is important," she said, nodding. "Shall we sit while we wait? I've heard I'm less intimidating when seated."

"Do you wish to be less intimidating? I mean..." His tongue stumbled, and he cursed himself for not keeping his mouth shut.

"Will I lose my power and leverage if I attempt to appear more average?" She shook her head, sending her tousled hair into her face. "I haven't decided what to be here yet. You'll have to abide by my whims until I do."

Again he wasn't sure if she was teasing or just so used to speaking her mind that she didn't give it a second thought. He really hoped whomever Rice was sending got here any second to save him from blundering his way out of Jane's good graces. Conversation was not his strong point, especially not with anyone like her.

But there was no chime to save him from her studious gaze and silence. Logan worked himself up to take another leap. "Is that how it normally works? You find a new place and decide on a tactic to take it over in the midst of it all?"

Her friendly demeanor faltered. Just when he was sure she was about to order him to leave her presence and never come back, the door chimed.

He jumped up to answer it.

The youngest member of Rice's team, having clearly drawn the short straw, bumbled his way in with a box half as big as he was. He stood just inside the doorway, dark spots discoloring the uniform under his arms and more sweat beading on his forehead.

With what may have been lingering impatience from his question or only annoyance with the timid delivery boy, Jane snapped, "Well, let's see what you have then."

The young man's throat bobbed up and down, his eyes wide. Logan reached for the box.

"Let him do it," she declared, a clear order in her tone. "Come on then, I don't have all day."

Logan nudged the kid, who found enough spine to heft the box closer to the chair where Jane sat. His hands shook as he pulled pair after pair of assorted footwear from the box, setting each pair on the floor before her.

"These are the...the...th...th ones that looked the... th..."

Jane finally took pity on him. When he saw the moment pass over her face, his resentment of her ordering him around and putting the boy on the spot vanished. Her words whispered in his head. *Perception is important.*

"You do this often?" Her voice softened, losing the edge of imperiousness.

The boy's face burned bright red. "On...on...only..."

"When you're forced to face a god?" she finished for him. A hint of mischief tugged at the corners of her mouth. "Come here." She held out her hand as she had when she'd healed Adams.

His steps were more than hesitant, but over a long painful minute, made his way to where she could just touch him.

She quirked an eyebrow. "Would you make me get to my feet?"

He shuffled a step closer, face even brighter red and sweat dripping down his temples.

"Now then, relax." Jane took hold of his hand and closed her eyes. Her voice was distant as though distracted by whatever she was doing but clear enough to both of them as she talked.

"I once had an older brother. He had a stutter quite like your own. My father hated it, hated him for being weak. And so when I was old enough to take my brother's place, my father ordered me to kill him."

Her brows pinched and she frowned. Then her face became serene again. "He could have fixed him at any time, like I'm fixing you, but my father was cruel and intolerant."

Jane opened her eyes and regarded the young man. "I am not my father."

"Thank you," he said, marveling at his own smooth voice. His skin returned to its normal color by the time she let go of his hand.

She reached into the pile of footwear and examined a pair of low, soft sided light-brown shoes that slipped onto her feet with ease. "These will do."

"You don't want any of the others?" he asked.

"I have no need to diminish your stores."

The boy quickly went about gathering up the shoes and boots, returning them to the box. When he'd finished, he stood looking from Logan to Jane. "Is that all then?"

Jane nodded.

"Thank you again." He grinned as he offered her a quick bow. Grabbing the large box, he hurried to the door and was gone a moment later.

Logan found he couldn't move, not until he asked the question hanging between them. "Did you?"

"Yes." She stared past him to the empty wall. "No matter how weak he was in my father's eyes, my brother had never been kind to me. They were very much alike, in fact. There was no love between us, and so when given the chance to take his place, I did."

"Do you regret it?"

"Yes and no." She got up and wandered toward the door, not looking to see if he was following.

They walked out into the hall where she lingered. "Where to?"

He let the silence stretch between them as they went down the hall. But when they were alone in the lift he turned to her. "What did you mean by yes and no?"

She gazed past him again, hand reaching to her amulet. "He had one of these long before I did. He would tease me, armored as he was and I not, taunt me, kick me around. He thought I was weak and stupid like my mother. But I wasn't."

"You didn't care for your mother?" He remembered his own mother fondly and couldn't imagine someone not having similar memories of the woman who had nurtured them.

"She was cold and distant from the day I was born. She would bear children, but caring for them was beneath her. She had worlds to run alongside my father, after all." Jane scowled. "Our kind is different. I've seen how families are supposed to live. Yours was one of them?"

He nodded, shrugging lightly, not wanting to rub his tame childhood in after hearing of hers.

"To tell the truth, there were five of us at one time. Five children, I mean. I was the youngest. My father killed two and I killed the others. The one I told you about and the one closest to me. That one, I do regret. He had a kind soul."

He found it hard to look at her the more she divulged. What kind of person murdered their own family?

She was quiet when they got out of the lift on the first of the three damaged floors. An hour passed of her going in and out of rooms, examining the contents, picking up this or that and setting it back in place, touching walls and panels, consoles and screens.

"Anything?" he finally asked.

"They were scared. It's painful being here. You can't feel it?"

"No, sorry."

Jane sighed. "You're upset with me after what I said."

Caught, he proceeded with caution. He should have known she could read him far better than he could her. "Not my place to judge."

"It isn't, but being alone with someone who as admitted killing their brothers, who you saw firsthand murder her father, it could be hard to understand."

"I suppose so."

"You don't have to hedge with me, you know. Go ahead and ask."

"Why did you do it?"

"My older brother was cruel. I did the universe a service. My father asked me to, and I took the opportunity." Her fingers wandered over a discarded cup, turning it slowly in her hands. "My younger brother was too kind. He really was weak, though my father didn't see it that way. He loved his youngest son."

"But you still did it."

"Oh yes. He was going to go off on his own, take some of our people, start a new haven of followers, establish a world where he could work his miracles."

"How is healing bad? You've done that here three times."

"But I'm not healing people for gain. I'm not trying to gather followers, raise an army. That's what he did and he brought his children, ones he'd bred upon the natives, the ones with the strongest traits of Unlata Kai. The first generation is always the strongest." She set the cup down and ran her finger through the dust on the table, swirling it back and forth. "He would take them and use them to perform even more miracles. He'd captured the attention of entire worlds of my father's worshippers."

"Doing good."

"Yes." She rubbed her hands together slowly. "But undermining my father's work. I was the General by then. It was my duty to keep his worlds in line. My brother took worlds away. He needed to go. His children also needed to go or they would avenge him.

"You killed them all?"

She nodded, her eyes downcast. "I used to speak to him sometimes, in the beyond."

What kind of madness was this? "You can speak to him?"

"The pure Unlata Kai, when we die, we join the elders in the beyond. Those of us among the living, we can speak to them, access their knowledge. You may think of it as praying."

"But when you pray, you're actually talking with someone, holding a conversation?"

"Yes. It's not faith, not like a religion that an Unlata Kai would set up on a typical world."

"And they answer you?" How many times had he prayed, begging for a cure for his mother, for Matouk's men to leave them alone, and later for someone to help avenge what Matouk had done to his people? No one had answered.

"Yes, that's why they're there. Not to say some wouldn't hold a grudge, but mostly, they are quite helpful."

"And your kind brother?"

"He forgave me."

Even though it must have been long ago, the relief in her voice was clear. "And his children?"

"Weren't pure. They died."

"And he still forgave you?"

She walked into the next room before answering. "It took about fifteen hundred years, but yes."

He froze. "Just how old are you?"

She reached out to take his hand. He was too stunned to pull away. Her calloused fingers entwined with his.

"Very."

He found his confusion and everything else brought up by the utter strangeness of her, rise to the surface. "And you do this often?"

"Touch men?" her tone clearly jesting this time.

"I suppose."

"No." She let his hand go and returned to caressing her amulet. "It's difficult to get close to anyone when you're standing twenty steps above them inside a suit of armor."

"You had to come down sometime."

"I was the General." She flashed him a smile that struck him as sad. "Do you want to spend your free time with the General?"

"Probably not."

"Exactly. Perils of perception. When a man like your colonel is off duty, you can approach him, perhaps have a drink with him and talk of trivial things. But would you do that with Commander Tate?"

"Hell no."

She smirked.

"And not just because of her position. She's not the kind of person I'd want to spend time with."

"Neither was I."

"What about the one you said your father killed with the ship full of others, you spent time with him?"

She spoke a word in her language that was an unintelligible mix of clicks and slur of sound. "He was pure Unlata Kai, like me. We understood one another, our positions and the necessity of them. If it had come to creating children, he would have been my choice, but we were not in a position to do that, with the world around us falling apart and the end of our kind as our chosen future."

She ran her hand along the rough damaged surface of the wall. "Our children were meant to be raised on ships like this one. Like I was. We traveled from world to world, spending a century here and there, sometimes more as the whims of my father dictated."

"You didn't travel with the others of your kind?"

"Too many gods on one world creates war of a degree I hope you never witness. So many died." She shook her head. "We were supposed to guide, to establish morals and set the natives on a forward path, uniting people for the betterment of their survival. But it is so easy to twist that, to fall into the trap of collecting worshippers, to bask in their adulation. The purity of the mission had been corrupted in so many. And in the end, worshippers became their downfall, one god defeating another, servants rising up vast numbers to tear their weak and distracted gods apart when they were pushed too far."

"I never thought of it like that."

"You never had cause to. And you shouldn't have

now. I shouldn't be telling you this."

"Why not?"

Jane took a deep breath and let it out. "Once I have removed Matouk from his army, they should be diffused easily enough. Then my time will be over."

"That's why you wanted to stay behind."

"Yes."

Seeing her alone, surrounded by the destruction one of her own had brought upon those of her kind, and in spite of the harshness of what she had shared of her past, he wrapped his fingers around hers.

Jane's gaze met his, grateful and hopeful. She squeezed his fingers gently. "I suppose I should stop looking at all we have lost here and get to fulfilling my end of this bargain, hmm?"

"Maybe." The realization that he was voluntarily holding the hand of a god, a very old god at that, and that she was smiling at him in a way that made him think a whole lot of things that were entirely inappropriate given who she was, hit him all at once. He loosened his hold on her.

"Thank you," she said, far closer to his ear than he realized she had been a second before. Her hair brushed against his cheek. Her warm breath tickled his ear.

"For what?" He held very still, fearing he would screw something up and send her into a fury that would get him killed.

"Bringing me here. I thought my time was over, but you've shown me that I have one more thing to do."

He wasn't sure if he should ask her to clarify because his gut told him the obvious answer was to defeat Matouk. However, the rest of him wanted the answer to be far more focused on the intimate workings of men and female gods, one in particular of each. He turned toward her. Her lips found his.

She wasn't the General now. In his arms, the two of them far from the watchful eyes of the rest of the ship's occupants seemed to be following the path of any other time he'd found himself alone with a willing woman. And as that had been well over a year ago, he wasn't about to second-guess anything.

With one hand in his hair and the other seeking a way under his shirt, he figured it was fair game to let his own hands wander. Distracted as he was by her eager mouth and the faint sensation of energy buzzing around and through him while they explored each other against the wall in the deserted lab, it took him a minute to realize Rice was near shouting in his ear.

"What?" he growled, adjusting his ear piece and giving serious consideration to flinging it across the room.

"What the hell are you doing down there?"

Jane, slowing her amorous attack, gave his com device a similarly disgusted look to what he knew to be on his own face. But she kept quiet and busied herself with nibbling on his neck.

"Exploring the lower levels with Jane like you asked. Must be we hit a patch of interference."

He only managed to get the last word out levelly by some miracle as she'd chosen that moment to run her hand down the front of his pants and cup him firmly. She pulled back, her gaze dancing with challenge and amusement as she licked her lips.

"I've had enough interference," she whispered in his other ear.

He wouldn't have put it past her to disrupt communications completely. "Did you need something?" he asked Rice.

Jane nodded, torturing him through his pants with

her hand.

"Commander Tate is demanding to see Jane. She's managed to set up a conference call with management."

"Out here?" The strangled sound he made as she released him from his fabric bindings lent the words a somewhat fitting response.

"Yeah. Sparing no expense in this emergency situation, I guess."

Jane's brows rose. She kept a firm hand on him as she finally revealed her presence. "I'm an emergency?"

She didn't sound pleased, and the fact that she was currently in control over a very important part of his anatomy wasn't lost on him. He silently cursed Rice, the commander, the ship, and everything else outside the room.

"It seems so," said Rice. His tone promised a host of questions about how Jane had managed to hijack their communication when she wasn't wearing a device herself.

"Inform Commander Tate that we will be up shortly to attend her meeting."

"Could you please define shortly? Not trying to be a pain in the ass. She's going to ask."

Jane gave him a piercing once over that set his entire body on fire, thankfully not literally. "Roughly twenty minutes." She gestured impatiently at his ear and slipped her shirt over her head.

Logan yanked the device out, turned it off and crammed it in the pocket of the pants he quickly discarded.

Naked seconds later, Logan lost himself in sensations his body had sorely missed as they collapsed into an eager and hungry tangle on the floor. He was glad they were two levels away from anyone else as moans and grunts tore from both of them. Cries of satisfaction echoed in the air before Jane rolled off him to collapse on her back beside him.

The sheen of sweat covering his body quickly dissipated in the chilled air of the lower levels. Jane sighed, reaching for her clothes.

She sat up, running a finger along his jawline and down his neck. "I propose we reenact this later when we are without time constraints."

Logan sought out his pants and tugged them back on. "And perhaps on a bed."

"Agreed." Jane dressed and ran her hands through her more disorganized than usual hair.

Once he had dressed and worked his way back into his boots, they left the room he had no intention of ever forgetting. How often did an average man get to roll around in a naked frenzy on the floor with a god like a couple of incredibly horny teenagers?

And she wanted to do it again. His heart raced. He wanted to touch her, freely like he had just then, to assure himself it had been real.

As if she could hear his pulse race or read his mind, Jane turned to him. "After the meeting."

"You probably won't be in the mood after dealing with Tate."

"Don't be so sure." She backed him against the wall where they lost several more minutes before Jane reclaimed possession of her lips and again straightened her clothes.

"You're going to be there?" she asked as they approached the lift.

"At the meeting?"

Jane nodded.

He chuckled and shook his head. "Not unless hell has frozen over. Beyond the fact we're talking about Tate, management isn't excited about having what they've so civilly termed an *unstable mercenary*, watching over their precious techs."

"But Colonel Rice favors you."

"He's the only sane one around here."

"I could demand they let you in."

The thought of being stuck in a room with Tate and management together made his muscles tense. "I don't really need to be there."

"You don't want to be, you mean."

"I like to do my job and keep to myself, you know?"

She nodded slowly. "Will this cause problems for you?"

"*This* meaning you and me later?"

Jane avoided his gaze. "Yes."

The plain answer was yes. Most of the crew already avoided him or was openly uncomfortable when he was around. Hanging on the arm of the god that had hijacked their ship was definitely not going to gain him any further favor. With anyone, including Rice.

"Would you prefer not to have a later? I won't hold it against you if that is so."

"*That* I don't mind at all, but if we could keep it quiet, that would probably be best for both of us."

"I see." Jane walked into the lift. She turned away from him, her head tipped down so that her hair hid her face.

He reached out to activate the lift.

"Wait." She stepped back outside to place both hands on the wall beside it. Jane rested her forehead on the wall, muttering to herself in her own language. She remained that way for at least fifteen minutes.

As he leaned against the opposite wall, his muscles fully relaxed while listening to Jane speak her language. Only the nagging thought that Rice would be hearing it from the commander by now roused him enough to pull the com device from his pocket. Turning it back on and slipping it into his ear, he didn't wait to get yelled at, contacting Rice first.

"She's doing something. I have no idea what or how much longer we'll be."

Aggravation clear in his voice, Rice asked, "What kind of something?"

He looked closer and stood up straight, body going on alert. "She's glowing."

"That can't be good."

"Probably not."

He stared, waiting for Jane to expand and start shooting light out of her body or for something to explode. As he held his breath, waiting to duck for cover or leap into action, he noticed the light begin to fade. Jane slowly turned around and rested her back against the wall.

Maybe not all glowing was a bad thing.

"Jane?"

She remained silent. He approached slowly, hand outstretched.

Jane grabbed it and held on tightly. "No one will suspect anything now."

"What do you mean?" As she stepped away from the wall, he realized she hadn't just taken his hand like before, she was leaning on him. Heavily. "Are you all right?"

"I will be in a day or two."

He stopped her, grasping her by the shoulders. "What did you do?"

"I initiated the draining of the contaminated water on the fifth level and started healing the outer hull to seal up all the fractures."

"Why?"

"There are near dangerous levels of contaminates in

the air the lower we go and in trace amounts where all of you live. Not that I care particularly about the rest of the crew, but I wished your air to be safe. And for the hull not to give way and vent you into space."

"Thank you." He gathered her trembling body to him, wrapping his arms around her.

She whispered, "They will also not suspect we were doing anything but the repairs I agreed to."

"You didn't just strain yourself to cover that up did you?"

Jane pulled away and made her way into the lift, waiting for him. He got in and brought them up to the first-level room where Tate had set up the meeting. She didn't say a word or look at him as he led her to the room where the colonel and the commander were waiting.

In the brighter light of the active floor, he could see how deeply her efforts had cost her. Her face was gaunt and her eyes drooping, lines he'd not noticed before edged her lips and eyes. She didn't look like the powerful General now, just an exhausted woman in need of a long night's rest.

"I'll see you tomorrow then," she said with an unemotional finality that cut deeply.

She walked into the room as if he were nothing more than a discarded escort. Rice cast him a questioning glance. If he was going to keep up the charade he'd pushed Jane into, though it obviously upset her, he wasn't going to waste her efforts by blowing it now. He shrugged and left them.

Logan wandered back to his room, wondering what exactly had pushed Jane away. She was certainly interested, and he wasn't at all opposed to that. But he liked his freedom here. The halo of unknown threats surrounding her was a host of entanglements and problems that he really didn't need. Between his flashbacks and nightmares and the crew's general aversion, he had enough to deal with.

Though he didn't like the idea at all, not one bit, actually, her best bet would be to spend her free time with Rice. If the two of them were seen publicly together, it would gain her acceptance. But really, if she went that route, he didn't want to remain aboard to see it.

CHAPTER FIVE

Jane took the offered seat at the table across from Commander Tate and Colonel Rice. Four other faces met her as projections that hovered over the other side of the table. Her annoyance with Logan and the subsequent pouring of energy into the ship left her empty. No more healing for her or anyone else and no more progress with the ship until she'd rested. For as silent as she'd been, Anika had to be truly disgusted with her.

She shouldn't have let her emotions get the better of her, but she'd so hoped that things would be different here. That she could be different. But even Logan knew that couldn't be true.

She met the commander's expectant look with a deadpan one of her own. She was too tired for this. If she needed to draw on the General and stand on the verge of Anika to get herself into bed in short order, she would.

"We are to call you Jane?" asked Commander Tate.

"That is the name I have chosen here."

"May we ask why you have chosen this name?" asked the floating head of a woman with blonde hair pulled back into a bun.

"That is irrelevant."

"You have made threats to the crew of our ship," stated a man with white hair and an intolerant expression.

"My ship. You have no ownership of this vessel. It was not created by your people. It was not fought for by your people. They simply found it and moved in."

"And how do you come to own the vessel?" asked the white-haired man.

"It was created by my people, and I control it."

"Our people can control it too," said the third head.

Commander Tate cleared her throat. "What Jane means is-"

Having had enough of being civil, Jane embraced the General. "You do not speak for me." She felt her body pulse, the light around her growing brighter as the room seemed to dim. The chair fell away as she stood. Anika demanded armor, but Jane knew there was no need and it was only more energy to expend. She clutched her amulet with one hand and made a definitive sweeping motion with the other.

"There will be no arguing. There will be no threats. I will simply tell you how this will be. Your crew will be allowed to remain, and your work can continue. I am not opposed to your mission. However, our primary concern is eliminating Matouk and disbanding his army. He is Unlata Kai, like me. You cannot defeat him. He will continue to overrun your colonies and the worlds you are so set on assisting and exploring. Your mission cannot take place until mine is completed. Do you understand?"

"But this ship is in ruins. It is not fit for a battle," said the white-haired man.

"I have begun repairs."

"Colonel Rice did an assessment when this ship was taken. We have his report. Repairs would take months or years depending on the size of the crew and funds to purchase supplies."

Jane cut transmission to his projector.

"You know nothing of this ship," she said to the other three heads and Tate. Rice, she ignored. He seemed amused and was doing his best to cover it.

"My people created self-sustaining ships. You only need a few people capable of initiating the proper commands and expending the energy to speed those repairs along if necessary. I have already begun."

She addressed the woman, gathering she was the most senior of the group after her disposal of the male. "You will have an operational ship at no cost. Not that your people have a right to be using this vessel, but as I said, once my mission is complete, I will allow it."

The woman glanced to either side. The images faded and then vanished. Commander Tate began to visibly sweat.

With the Naptcha heads gone, Rice spoke, "You don't plan on blasting any holes in here, do you?"

"That depends on their response. And yours," she directed at Tate.

"The more holes you make, the longer your repairs will take," Tate pointed out.

Jane had had enough. She shoved the table aside and grabbed the commander around the neck. "You will keep your mouth shut unless I address you in a fashion that requires an answer. Is that clear?"

She was dimly aware that Rice had drawn a weapon and had it aimed at her. "You should put that away. I may hold my promises in higher regard than you do, but I will disarm you by whatever means necessary."

The truth was, if she was going to draw more energy to harm anyone beyond direct physical violence, she would have to release Anika, and in her already weakened state, she didn't want to chance releasing her other half.

"I'm going to have to ask you to put Commander

Tate down."

She appreciated how he made it sound like a reasonable request rather than pleading or a demand.

"And I will have to ask that she no longer speaks to me, as every time she opens her mouth, I am compelled to commit violence upon her person."

"I'm sure we can work something out," he said, coming around to stand beside the commander, his hands free of weapons. "Jane, please put her down. She can't breathe."

Jane set the commander on her feet and turned to face the projectors. "Bring them back if you wish to resolve this peacefully. My patience is gone."

Tate slumped into her chair, rubbing her neck with one hand and madly typing on her terminal with the other. The four heads returned in short order.

"Do we have an agreement?" Jane asked, her body and mind exhausted. Logan was right. She had no desire for anything but her bed. Thinking of him didn't improve her mood.

"If you can guarantee a fully operational ship by the end of your mission, we have an agreement," stated the white-haired man.

"You understand that completing my mission may result in my death and the destruction of this ship?"

The woman's brow furrowed. "You would bring our crew into battle with Matouk's army?"

Unable to pound sense into the woman physically, Jane disrupted her projection. "You expect me to single-handedly defeat a fellow Unlata Kai and his entire army?"

The man's lips pinched together. "So you're conscripting our crew."

"Yes. And if we all survive, they get use of a fully operational ship as payment."

"And if you all don't?" the woman asked.

"Then we don't and Matouk has free reign. I promise you won't like that any better."

The last head nodded. "We have heard of his swath of destruction. We certainly don't want him here."

"Then this matter is settled?"

The white-haired man said, "Yes, it seems we have reached an agreement. Commander Tate, we expect your full cooperation and updated reports. Colonel Rice, your position as head of security for this crew has not changed."

"My men and I will continue to do the jobs we were contracted for."

"Very good. We look forward to the use of a fully operational ship."

The heads dissipated, leaving her with a seething Tate, and Rice, who looked ready to empty another bottle. Having the situation confirmed, Jane took her leave of the room, not waiting for anyone to escort her. She simply touched the wall and accessed the ship to find her own way.

On the way back to her room, she let the power around her dissolve, shrinking back into her common form. With the power gone, waves of dizziness washed over her. She stumbled into a wall and stood for a moment to get her bearings.

It would not have been a surprise to find Logan shadowing her, offering to help her back to her room, but the hall was empty. He'd been unexpectedly kind since they'd met and she wasn't sure how to repay him other than to attempt to be kind in return. It wasn't something she'd had much practice with.

Her tired brain reminded her that she's snapped at him.

He was probably off cursing her somewhere. And

he'd have no way of knowing she needed help unless Rice would have contacted him. Rice had exhaled an audible sigh of relief as she left the room. Help wouldn't be coming from him either. She rested her back on the wall, holding her palms against the lukewarm metal to keep her balance.

She had to let something go or she was going to collapse right there in the damned hallway. Considering her agreement with Tate's people, she released the command on the engines and navigation. The energy she freed barely gave her enough to propel one foot in front of the other long enough to get to her door.

Once inside, she didn't bother eating or drinking, though both sounded important. All she craved was sleep. Dropping into the bed, Jane had to admit she'd overdone herself. She'd be lucky to not wake up with a splitting headache in the morning and not enough energy to heal it. She hadn't overdone it like this since her last campaign for her father, leading their faction of the population in a war that had ultimately destroyed Kaldara.

Jane pulled the blankets up to her chin and rolled onto her side. Sleep came instantly.

CŽ

She woke to the sound of her door chiming and had the distinct impression that it had been doing so for quite awhile. With one hand on the wall, she accessed the controls to her door and opened it. She hadn't been sure who she would face, Rice, or one of his men to escort her below, or maybe even Tate. But it was Logan. He entered hesitantly.

Rejuvenating sleep was not done with her. Getting

up to even a sitting position was more of a challenge than she wanted Logan to see, but she wasn't vain enough to draw on her power to cover the obvious effort.

"I don't think I'm up for a walk today."

A few brisk strides brought him to her side, concern plain on his face. "Stay down. Do you want me to get the doctor?"

Jane shook her head. "I just need to sleep."

His hand rested on her shoulder. "Are you sure?"

"My energy is not infinite, though gods would have you believe it is so. If I release Anika I would have more, but I do not wish to see your people subjugated or for my mission go astray."

He edged himself onto the bed, sitting next to her. He held her hand in his lap. "Who is Anika?"

"I am." She let her eyes slipped closed, the effort of holding them open becoming too much.

"You're cold." He rubbed her arm, creating warmth both from friction and his touch. "Are you sure you're all right? I can have the doctor come here. You wouldn't have to go to the clinic."

Her annoyance with him resurfaced. "Would you want to explain to the doctor why you came into my room and how you touched me to know I was cold?"

"I could tell him Rice sent me to check on you."

"But not the truth?"

"Jane, the truth won't help either of us."

"I've had thousands of years of hiding truths. I'm done." She rolled onto her other side, taking her hand with her. "Stay or go, the choice is yours."

CHAPTER SIX

The chiming in Logan's ear worked its way through his thoughts. He opened his channel. "Yes?"

Rice said, "I'm trying to put together men for Jane to choose from. She requested four. She seems somewhat fond of you."

"If you say so." He gazed down at the sleeping woman beside him.

"You know I prefer that you remain on my team, but being on hers might be more what you're looking for. Less whining techs looking for strong arms to carry their equipment, you know?"

"I'm not sure what I'm looking for yet." And that was the total truth.

"Would you consider helping me out with this? You'd remain on the ship at least. Though, I'm not sure what she intends to use these men for exactly."

"I'll be there. When?"

"After lunch. Would you mind stopping by to escort Jane? The crew seems less panicked when you're with her."

"It's just that you can't get anyone else to volunteer to guide her around." Not that she seemed to need any guiding. Jane knew her way around the ship as well as he did. It was the people she didn't know.

Rice chuckled. "That too. But I did mean it about you sticking with Jane. With her agreement accepted, our explorations have been put on hold. I won't be needing you for guard duty in that capacity."

"They already don't like me. I highly doubt my throwing in with Jane is going to help."

"Logan, if you were hoping for a congeniality award, you joined the wrong crew."

"That's not what I meant. Forget it. I'll be there."

"With Jane."

"Yes, all right."

He ripped the device out of his ear. Was it too much to ask to have a place to fit in that felt right? He didn't mind working for Rice. The deal they'd struck worked in both of their favors, giving him time to figure out what he really wanted to do now that Hijn was devastated.

His body didn't mind Jane at all, but the rest of her was an enigma and her motives ranged from terrifying to a total mystery. Not to mention she had thousands of years of history he didn't know much about. What little he did know, wasn't all that endearing. But she'd completely drained herself to cover for their few minutes of frivolity because of one comment from him and she'd healed two other people for no reason he could see but being kind.

Logan gave her another hour and then shook her gently. Her eyes, slightly more alert this time, fixated on him.

"You stayed."

Even after all his consideration in regard to her, he still hadn't reached a solid conclusion. Ignoring her implied question, he stuck with business. "Rice has the men together for you to choose from."

"Give me a few minutes." She stretched and rose from the bed, disappearing into the bathroom.

Jane returned looking more awake, her hair wet at the tips and face tinged with pink from scrubbing. "Let's go see what he scrounged up, shall we? Or..." She took a deep breath. "Would you prefer I went alone?"

"Rice asked me to escort you."

"Well there's that then." She seemed somewhat satisfied.

He followed her out the door and brought her to the room Rice had specified.

Inside stood seven men, all in uniform. Rice's men, half of his team. Unfortunately, with Jane now taking four of his men, they'd be even shorter staffed than before.

Jane surveyed her choices in silence. She stopped in front of each, pressing three fingers to their temple and then pausing for a minute or two before moving on.

Logan took his place at the end of the line at Rice's silent urging.

When Jane came to him, she smiled and shook her head. "Not you."

Relief washed through him. He knew she was unlikely to have picked him. She'd said she wouldn't, but with things uncertain between them, he wasn't sure.

She was still smiling at him. That was something, at least. But what did he want to do about it?

Logan stepped out of the line and headed for the door.

"Don't leave," she called out.

He turned back to find she had returned to the first man and hadn't seemed to turn around to even know he'd been leaving. He took his place next to Rice.

While Jane spoke to each man, her voice pitched so low that he couldn't hear what she said, Rice leaned toward him, talking at the same volume. "What was that all about? I was sure she'd pick you."

"She had told me she wouldn't," he admitted.

"She said the same to me, but I thought..." He sighed. "Did she say why not? No offense, but explaining the reappropriation of four of my men isn't something I look forward to. Three wouldn't be much better, but at least a little less painful."

"It's complicated." To say the least, he mumbled to himself.

"She likes you," Rice said, regarding Logan with a single-raised brow that said he knew exactly what had transpired between them. "But not enough to become one of her points, whatever that means."

Logan did his best not to confirm Rice's assumption, keeping his gaze steady. "I don't think that's it, exactly." She'd made it sound like it wasn't anyway.

"I guess we'll see." Rice nudged his attention back to Jane and the four men who remained in the line. The others dispersed.

"Are you prepared to give these four men over to my keeping?" Jane asked.

"Not that I have much choice about it."

"Do you or not?"

"Yes."

"Very well. I will require use of this room for a short while. After which, these men will need something other than your uniform as they will be yours no longer. Neither of you should be in the room, though I would have you stand guard outside. If anyone should enter, it would be unfortunate."

"Are you all agreed?" Rice asked the four men.

They all nodded distractedly, their attention glued to Jane.

"What are you going to do to them?" asked Rice

"Make them extensions of myself."

"But they're people. You can't just take them over," said Logan.

"Of course they are. They have agreed to this. Don't worry, they will not be harmed by this conversion."

"Conversion?" Logan managed before Rice dragged him out.

Outside the sealed door, he spun to face Rice. "You can't let her do this to your men."

"We don't even know what she's doing. Why are you so concerned about it?"

"*Conversion* doesn't sound like a bad thing to you?"

"Maybe they're just joining her religion."

"She is a god. She is her own religion. No, that's not it. If she was going to go all god on them, she'd have released Anika."

Rice's brows rose. "You know quite a lot about her."

"We've talked."

"The looks she gives you imply more than talking."

He gritted his teeth, his fists forming against the door at his back. "We've also talked."

"I see."

"I would appreciate your keeping this between us."

"Agreed," said Rice. "Tate would not be pleased."

"No kidding."

Rice nodded to a pair of techs as they passed. Once they were out of earshot he asked, "So what is Anika?"

"I don't know yet. That's who we spoke to when we took her from the city. It wasn't Jane. Anika feels different, her voice I mean."

Rice nodded. "Bigger, more powerful."

"Yes."

He strained to hear what was going on behind the door but picked up nothing. At least nothing exploded.

When the door finally did open. Jane sat cross-legged on the floor with the four men arrayed around her on their backs, staring empty-eyed at the ceiling. They formed the cardinal points.

"The conversion will take time. They need to rest, either here or in their own rooms. I will leave that to you."

She reached out to Logan, "Would you help me back to my room? Our explorations will have to wait until tomorrow."

Logan wondered about the fact that she'd asked rather than ordered. Either she was exhausted again or she was distracted by the conversion. He took her hand and helped her to her feet. Like the day before, she leaned heavily on him.

"You need to stop draining yourself."

"I do." She rested her head on his shoulder, even as they walked.

He felt her drifting away, the strength running out of her body. Strong as he believed the General to be, the energy she was expending couldn't keep up. Her steps faltered. Logan swept her up in his arms. It deeply concerned him that she didn't protest that he carried her the rest of the way.

She was unconscious by the time they reached her room. He debated calling Brin to check on her, but Jane had been adamant that she only needed sleep. She would know what she needed, wouldn't she? He gently set her on her bed and pulled the blanket over her.

With one last look to make sure she was well enough under the circumstances, he went to help Rice remove the prone men from the meeting room and to find out just what Jane had done to them that she wouldn't do to him.

CHAPTER SEVEN

Jane woke to find herself alone. She missed Logan, but given the drain of the conversion on top of the drain of the initial repairs, she wasn't exactly in the mood to be around people anyway, even him. She got up and went to the dining hall to get something to eat. There were only a handful of people there when she arrived. By the time she'd selected a plate full of various items from the buffet, they'd all left.

Alone, Jane ate her meal, watching with a fraction of amusement as other crew members ventured in only to spot her and leave. If they were too timid to share the room with her, they deserved to go hungry.

Stomach satiated, she reached out along the initial pathways she'd created with her new points. Jane summoned them to the dining hall.

Ten minutes later, they arrived and sat with her.

"Eat. You need to regain your strength." She watched them all fill their plates. It was comforting to not be completely alone, even if that was only because these men were under her power now, themselves, but heavily influenced by her needs.

Not the kind of needs she had for Logan.

Others of her kind had partaken of their points, but she had never found it tasteful. After all, points didn't have full free will. It would be like pleasuring herself and she'd done that enough. She much preferred a willing partner.

Rice had come through with alternate clothing for her men. Or perhaps, by the sheer casual fashion of it, this clothing had been their own when they were off duty. Seemingly unaware that their lives had dramatically changed, they chatted amongst themselves as if she weren't there.

The part of her mind that had been empty since leaving Kaldara and seeing North's corpse, was again full. She almost felt normal, not so detached.

"Jane, what would you have us do?" asked East.

She'd already forgotten what his given name was. It was no longer important. They could use those names with the rest of the crew. To her, they had her standard point names.

"You will stay near the commander. If she has need of me, you will let me know. I will expect a report of her interactions with her management and any situations that should arise in the command center."

"West," she said, turning to a middle-aged blonde-haired man. "You will mirror East. Sleep in alternating shifts overlapping the commander's."

"South, you will be my eyes and ears with the rest of the crew."

"North, you are with me to be dispatched as needed for additional tasks."

"You are dismissed. North, we will be going below to begin repairs."

With North beside her, a young man with blue eyes and thin lips, she went down to the level she'd examined with Logan. She rested her hands on the walls and instructed him to do the same.

"You will feel me shunting energy through you. Don't be alarmed. Working together, we will move faster than I can alone."

North kept his hands at his sides. "I don't have power like you."

"You will. Relax." She took his hands and pressed them onto the wall. "You can touch anywhere on the ship, and I will feel you. It is a living thing, passing messages throughout millions of tiny parts that make the whole. Only Unlata Kai can access them, but now, through my blood, you can too. To a degree."

"But I don't know what I'm doing."

"I will not allow you to harm the ship or yourself. I promised to take care of you, didn't I?"

He nodded.

"Good. Now close your eyes and look inward. Feel the ship through your hands."

"I don't..." He gasped. "That's amazing."

"It is. These ships are special. This one is hurt badly and it has suffered for a long time.

"I can feel it."

Jane tried to remember the sheer joy of sensing a ship for the first time. She'd been eight, standing beside her mother. So long ago, her mother had been in love with the ships, maintaining and repairing them, altering them as whims hit her. In those years, she often left the running of civilizations to her father and the handful of others they traveled with, preferring the quiet of space. Jane had been too young to travel to surfaces yet and so she spent her time learning the ship, learning all her mother could teach her of healing and communicating with them.

That woman was so different in her memory from the one who had died on her throne only days ago. She had never been the soft and gentle type with her children,

Jane had shared her love of the ships. It gave them occasions to interact and speak to one another. Even that little contact was far more than her siblings had received.

They had all traveled together, though her older brothers sometimes went with their father, empowering armies in the name of creating overall peace and prosperity. She hadn't led his armies until she was a hundred. And even then, once the rush of battle had worn off, she missed working with the ship. But her father had sensed her gift for strategy, inspiring fear, and instilling loyalty. Having seen her in action, he turned her against her brothers and never left her on the ship again. She'd always stood by his side or on the front lines, leading his armies.

Now she was back where she'd begun, with points who had never experienced Anika in the throes of battle. They were uncertain but eager, and she hoped they remained that way for a while. She needed time to find her way outside of being the General, especially now that she had her points back and possibly Logan by her side. She smiled to herself.

She hoped to find uses for her points that didn't involve battles or intrigue on her behalf. If they could only remain her eyes and ears and extra connections with the ship, she would call her transformation complete.

Working through North, Jane directed small doses of repairs on panels and the inner workings behind them, regrowing connections and parts, sealing cracks and holes. When she felt him lagging, she sent him off to bed and resumed the work on her own. He would grow stronger, allowing her to work longer and accomplish more per session. In return, the four of them would help sustain her far more than sleep and food could. She didn't need a host of worshipers, only four devoted men to provide a suitable level of energy. She didn't require more, not if she used her power wisely. Points were the most harmless way to feed, a replenishing source that also benefited from her working through them. A harmless closed loop.

Once North was sure of himself, she could work in tandem with him rather than use him and then work alone. It would take months for her blood cells to multiply and fully bond with his own.

Some of the Unlata Kai had created entire forces of points, but she considered them weak. She preferred four that she could fully control if needed, rather than spreading her attention through a horde. She'd seen gods go down in battle because they were so distracted with trying to order all their points, flitting from one to the next as chaos overwhelmed them all.

She had just finished repairs on one of the air scrubbers when she became aware she wasn't alone.

"Hello, Logan."

"Jane."

"Come to keep an eye on me for Colonel Rice?"

"No."

She examined her hands, which were blackened with soot and the heavy layer of dust that permeated all the unoccupied areas of the ship. She made a note to herself to work with North on the sanitation system tomorrow.

"Not draining yourself again are you?"

"No need to carry me today. I'm behaving myself."

Logan smirked. "I highly doubt that."

"Well, I have so far anyway."

He offered a conciliatory nod. "Did you really choke Tate?"

"I was tired, and she angered me."

"I wished that excuse worked for me. I would have

done it months ago." He looked her over. "I think it's safe to say that you need a shower and maybe some clean clothes."

"I don't have any other clothes."

"I'm sure I can find something. Come on." He held out his hand.

"Oh like I'm going to contaminate you?" She kept her filthy hand to herself. "Besides, I thought we weren't doing that?"

He dropped his hand to his side. "I would think that keeping your private life quiet would become a habit for someone in your position."

"It was, but I'm no longer in that position, am I?"

She started down the hall to the lift. He walked beside her.

"It would seem to me, that it's pretty close."

"It's not, and I don't want it to be." She noticed he was walking slower, postponing their arrival at the lift. "The drawback to being the General was that every man and woman, though they were not my focus in this matter, was my subordinate. Even Antoni. To prevent issues with favoritism, perceived or assumed, I would never invite the same man to share my bed more than a couple times. They called me fickle and heartless, not to my face of course, but East and West would hear them. I could never form attachments to any one person."

The lift in sight, he'd come to a stop and so did she. Regardless of the dirt she'd not intended to get on him, she took his hand in hers. "I'm not fickle or heartless and I'm tired of being the General. I do enjoy your company, but if you don't wish to be associated with me, just say so."

"Jane, it's not that I don't... I don't know you."

"That we can work on, if you are willing?"

"Answer one question for me, honestly."

She nodded.

"Why didn't you want me for one of your points?"

"Points, in the conversion process, become an extension of myself. I find the idea of sex with my points distasteful. Not to mention, you're not the kind of man who makes a good point. They need to be, not exactly vacant, but open, relaxed in the mind, able to take orders without thought. This is why I always pull my points from the ranks of soldiers. Does that make sense?"

"I was a soldier."

Jane squeezed his hands. "But you're not anymore."

"And you aren't the General."

"And you aren't my subordinate."

"You *are* filthy," he said, pulling her closer.

Jane brushed her lips against his cheek. "And now so are you."

"I happen to know a fix for that." Keeping her in his grasp and his lips pressed against hers, he edged them into the lift.

They straightened themselves just before the lift doors opened and then quickly made their way to her room.

"How hot do you like your water?" Jane asked, pulling the dirty shirt over her head.

"Not painful."

"So short of scalding then." She laughed and removed the rest of her clothes, leaving them on the floor. She was happy to see him doing the same.

By the time they reached the bathroom, the water was already running. Steam filled the air.

"How did you do that?" he asked, regarding the shower with suspicion.

"Magic." Jane grinned. "Not really. I just accessed the controls through the ship. Any bare skin contact works. In this case, my feet with the floor."

"And all your people could do that?"

"Only the pure Unlata Kai. Perception. The first rule of being a god."

"But it's not magic, only that your ships are attuned to you."

"Yes." She ran her finger over his lips. "You're not going to give away my secrets are you?"

"I have a feeling you could convince me not to." His eyes twinkled and the grin on his face made her stomach do a little flip.

"I think we could work something out." She pulled him into the hot shower.

CHAPTER EIGHT

Thoroughly cleaned and sated, Logan lay on Jane's bed listening to her breathe softly in her sleep. He'd even managed a few hours of sleep without nightmares of the destruction of Hijn.

Jane was still sound asleep and that was just as well. The repairs she was doing took a lot out of her. The first round in the steam and the second later in bed had done the rest.

He caught sight of her dirty clothes on the floor. She was going to need more than one change of clothing. One thing he knew about women was that they liked to shop. Gods couldn't be that much different, could they?

Logan inched his way out of bed so as not to wake her and gathered up his clothes. He dressed by the doorway. Glancing back at her hair splayed across the pillow and her face peaceful in sleep, he began to wonder for the hundredth time what he was doing.

She was a god. No, he talked his way through the rationalizations again. She was merely a being that portrayed herself as a god. But what then made a god? She had the powers typically associated with one. She carried herself as one, spoke as one, and she glowed. Holy crap, she glowed. And expanded. And gave off energy that made his very cells hum. What the hell was he doing?

Keeping her happy. Yes, a happy god didn't choke people, blast them with light bombs, or threaten to kick them all off her ship. He was merely doing his part to keep her satisfied. And that was quite mutual and not a bad part to play at all.

It wasn't like she really cared about him. Gods didn't fall in love with humans, not like humans did with one another. She'd had entire armies full of men at her disposal. She'd said so. He was merely a novelty, someone she didn't have to cast aside after a romp or two. Until she grew tired of him. And she would. Thousands of years and she'd never formed a relationship with anyone? That was a big habit that she had no chance of breaking. Not after all this time.

If she did defeat Matouk, would she follow through with her plan to remove all the Unlata Kai from existence, including herself? She'd been rather sold on that intention before, and he had little doubt she had changed her mind now. He'd just be setting himself up for a terrible loss if he let himself begin to care about her. There were far better things to do with his life, time, and energy.

He just couldn't think of any at the moment.

Logan slipped out the door and sealed it behind him. He went in search of Rice.

Finding the colonel with one of Jane's points, he said, "Can I speak with you a moment?"

Rice nodded and excused himself. The man, who appeared unfazed by what Jane had called a conversion, gave him a friendly nod and went about his business.

"He all right?"

"I think so?" Rice watched the man leave, making sure he was out of earshot. "He calls himself East now."

"She called the one who had died in the palace, North. Must be she renamed them to match?"

Rice shrugged. "Other than that, nothing seemed off. His head wasn't spinning around and he wasn't floating, so I'm going to call it a win so far. Jane's been making good progress with the repairs. How's she doing that?"

"Magic." Logan chuckled. "She talks to the ship and gives it her energy. That's all I know about it."

"Weird."

"Very."

"I have a favor to ask of you."

"What?" A bad feeling crept up in his gut. Favors had to do with Jane.

"Rhodes and Hanson, in equally annoying rants, have been begging to observe Jane's healing of the ship. Can you work out a deal to get them off my back?"

"Has she mentioned that no one could be down there when she's working?" Logan asked.

"Not that I know of."

Logan shrugged. "So why don't they just go look?"

"Well, she's already choked Tate and word of that has spread everywhere, despite our best efforts. Hanson gets all jittery when she's around, like he expects to be turned into a newt or something. Rhodes suggested that it would be better to ask than assume. All logic, that one."

Logan snickered. "I don't know if Jane can do that, but I'll ask."

"Logan."

"About the visit, not the newt. Though..."

"Logan."

"Yeah, all right. I'll ask."

Rice consulted his datapad and seemed to suddenly realize Logan was still there. "Did you need something?"

"If Jane is going to be with us awhile, and it seems she is, she's going to need some things."

Rice nodded. "And our supplies are somewhat lacking in the setting up a household department."

"Exactly."

"So what are you thinking? Or should I say, is she thinking?"

"Me. She hasn't asked. But one set of clothing isn't going to get her far and the lower decks are a mess."

"True."

"What if we were able to appease Tate by making a goodwill landing, let her people do their thing, and I can take Jane to get some supplies of her own while we're there?"

"Has she been teaching you diplomacy? Last I heard, you had near the same mind about Tate as Jane does, minus the actual choking."

He was certainly no diplomat, and Rice's disbelieving face made him uncomfortable. "Nevermind, it was just a thought."

"It was a good thought." Rice clapped him on the shoulder. "I'll talk to Tate. You talk to Jane. See what we can work out, yeah?"

"Yeah."

Logan stopped by his room to rifle through his own limited array of clothing. When Rice had found him on Hijn, he'd joined the crew with nothing more than the tattered clothes on his back.

If Jane were petite like Brin, he'd simply ask to borrow a few things, but she was far closer to his own size than the other women on board.

With a pair of loose grey pants he wore to work out and a blue pull-over shirt, he returned to Jane's room. She was awake.

"I brought you something to wear while those get cleaned." He nodded to the clothes she'd worn for the past two days.

"Thank you." She took the items from him. Jane paused and brought them to her face, sniffing. "Yours?"

"We're working on getting you more clothes of your own."

She shook out the shirt and smiled at him as she pulled it on. She wasn't wearing anything underneath.

Standing up, she stepped into the pants and fastened them around her waist with the drawstring. She grinned, noticing him watching her every move. He couldn't help it.

Her hands ran over her breasts, pulling the already taut fabric even tighter. "Do you find this distracting?"

He cleared his throat before he could answer. "Yes. Very." His hands joined hers, massaging the soft mounds beneath the fabric.

Logan wasn't sure if it was something she did to him, like talking to the ship through her skin, that drove him mad or if he just had a suicidal streak of his own.

"Take them back off." He tugged at the strings of the pants.

She slowly pulled one string, then the other. "I just put them on."

"And you can put them on again later." He pulled her toward the bed and pushed her onto it.

She left the shirt on, but removed the pants and gave him a smile that dared him to follow through. Already in way over his head, he went for it.

႞

By the time the sweat was drying on their naked bodies and Logan was beginning to regret the blanket being shoved somewhere off the other end of the bed. His awareness returned to remind him that they hadn't been far below on a deserted deck this time. There were occupied rooms nearby, and unlike the night before, they were far from quiet.

He started to sweat anew. News traveled fast. Rice knowing was one thing, but everyone?

Jane rolled toward him, one finger swirling around on his chest. "What's troubling you?"

"Nothing."

"Don't lie to me."

He cringed as her finger struck a raw spot on his shoulder. He tried to remember how he'd injured it. Then it came back to him. "Did you bite me?"

"You didn't mind at the time." She touched the spot once more. Warmth flowed through his skin like when she'd healed his burns, but this time there was a jolt, like electricity passing through his shoulder.

He grimaced.

"Sorry, rejoining skin was never something I could do with great finesse. I've always been more of the skin sundering sort." When she moved her hand, all trace of the bite mark had vanished.

"Can you do that to anyone? Heal them?"

"Generally, yes. As long as I understand their physiology, and I have enough energy at my disposal."

"Will you still be able to work on the ship today?"

She sat up and stretched. The light glistened on the intricate latticework of scars that covered her body. "Yes, a small wound like that doesn't take much."

While she was in a good mood, he figured he might as well take his chances with Rice's request. "Would you mind a couple observers today? Hanson is eager to see how you work."

Her nostrils flared. "There's not much to see unless you too, can sense the ship. I'm initiating processes. It's not as though repairs happen instantly."

"He's curious. I think it's more that he wants to try to understand what you do rather than that he's expecting to see miracles happen before his eyes."

He traced the scars on her side. "Did you heal yourself or did someone do it for you?"

She reached for the shirt he had loaned her and yanked it over her head. "When an Unlata Kai heals, it leaves no scars."

"But there are so many."

"I'm well aware," she snapped. "My father said I was a slow learner."

"Surely there was someone who could have healed you until you got the hang of healing yourself. Your mother?"

"I could heal myself since I could walk." She tugged on the pants and rammed her feet into her shoes. "I was not allowed to heal myself when I was injured in battle. My father had a powder made that he would sprinkle in our wounds while he berated our performance. It burned and it was impossible to remove the fine particles in order to heal the wound neatly. We all had them, my brothers and I. It wasn't until I'd risen to be his General that he gifted me with the armor I wear now."

He considered his own mother's reaction to such a barbaric treatment. There was no way she would have allowed anyone to mistreat her children in such a manner. "Your mother stood for this?"

"She had little care for any of us. The ship and my father were her sole focus."

"But you were her children."

Jane smiled sadly. "We are not like you. Though, in

some ways, I wish we were."

"Did you treat your own children like that?"

Her brow scrunched. "My children? I've never had any."

"In thousands of years?"

"Never. I held one of the last pure bloodlines. Any offspring I would make with another Unlata Kai would be in line for my father's throne. He permitted me to live because I gave him everything I was, ran everything for him, allowing him to simply bask in the worship he so adored. But a pureblood child would be a further threat. He wouldn't allow it to live."

"But you said your people bred with the original population creating the race we met in your city. It would take a lot of Unlata Kai to overrun that large of a breeding pool."

"I was not one of them."

He recalled his hands on her smooth stomach, not feeling any sign of stretch marks or sagging skin. Then again, she could have healed herself, hiding all trace.

"You do not believe me."

"It's a very long time to be having sex without ever getting pregnant."

"I never wanted children."

"Is that something you can control? I mean," he waved a hand at her stomach trying to put his thoughts into words. "With what you do?"

"Yes. As I said, we are not like you." Jane ran her hands through her hair, ordering her ashen curls. "But to answer your question, no, I would never raise a child in the way I was. However, that was how Unlata Kai did treat their children. It was expected. Hence, my choice."

He nodded, at a loss for words.

"If you promise to keep your people out of my way,

I suppose it will do no harm to have them observe me working with North today."

"Thank you."

Shadows lay behind her eyes after his questions, but she didn't seem angry. He'd have to make sure to threaten Hanson to behave. He wouldn't put it past Jane to snap into angry glow mode at any moment. Her moods were just as mercurial as Brin's but far more dangerous.

She kissed him briefly and left. Though he didn't want Jane to join her elders, he couldn't find it within himself to argue about her desire to end the Unlata Kai.

CHAPTER NINE

Jane funneled her energy through North, initiating the repairs on the sanitation controls for the fourth level of the ship. Meanwhile, she pushed the last of the contaminated water from the level below.

Hanson and a woman she didn't recognize leaned against the wall beside Logan. He overshadowed both of them with his height and bulk. They'd been there for most of an hour, but she'd been too busy to give them much notice.

"North, go up to the first level and locate the same system there. Touch it when you are ready."

He nodded curtly and headed for the lift.

Jane approached the threesome, her patience already on edge by having an audience. "Who is this then?"

"Brin Rhodes," the woman said, holding out her hand. "You were rather unconscious last time we met."

Logan gave her an expectant look. Jane sighed inwardly. She'd never had to concern herself with social niceties before, but if she meant to be different here, it would require the effort. She shook the woman's hand. "When was this?"

"Brin was the crew medic on the shuttle when we rescued you," Logan explained. "She stabilized you."

"Saved you," said Brin, pride shining on her pretty

little face. Her high, round cheeks blossomed a rosy pink.

"Kidnapped me," said Jane. "You were with them when I first met your crew on Kaldara."

Brin nodded.

What Jane remembered more than her face that day was the way Logan had stood defensively just in front of her. Her gaze slipped to him now. He didn't appear to be paying her any undue attention. Perhaps he'd only been doing his job by protecting her in an uncertain situation.

"I removed your armor so she could work," said Hanson.

"And you stole my amulet," accused Jane.

"I gave it back," he said meekly.

Logan watched them all. Jane exhaled long and slow. Her annoyance with his crewmembers was putting him in an awkward position. Her father had done that to her far too many times. Logan had mentioned his strained relations with the crew. He didn't need her making it more difficult for him.

Trying to move to more neutral territory, Jane examined the petite woman. "You didn't take any samples of my blood did you?"

Brin's eyes lit up. "Well yes, we needed to analyze your blood type. I've never seen anything like it."

"Destroy your samples. All of them. Don't let anyone ingest the blood."

"Why would anyone do that?"

"Because sometimes people do strange things." They were skittish enough without learning that her new points had been converted by absorbing her blood. She didn't need accidental points.

She caught the question in Logan's cocked head. "As you might imagine, I've seen a lot of strange things."

He nodded, the recent tension on his face easing.

Brin looked uncertain but she said, "I'll see to it."

Jane addressed Hanson. "Did you see what you wanted to see?"

He looked confused. "We haven't seen anything yet."

"It's more of a feel," she took his hand and splayed it out onto the wall of the room. Pressing her own hand over it, she extended her awareness into the webwork of cables behind the surface, urging them to regain pressure and seal any leaks along the way. It was difficult to work through a filter of non-conductive flesh, but she took him through line after line, riding through the fluid, deep into the sloshing and pulsing thump that was the flow of the ship. Outside the wall, she was dimly aware of his occasional profane expression of awe.

Then she felt North. Dividing her attention between the two tasks, Jane worked to restore the sanitation functions on the third level while still working through the flow of fluids on the fourth where she stood. Working through Hanson, she had to push her energy more forcefully, but she had told Logan she would allow this observation. The faster Hanson and the medic got their fill, the sooner they'd leave her in peace.

"Jane," Logan said in her ear. His touch registered on her shoulder. "Let him go."

She pulled her energy back until the walls stopped speaking inside her head. Hanson's hand slipped from hers. He cradled it against his chest.

"Look at it," he said, shoving his hand toward the medic. "It's burnt. Got to be third degree by now. I could smell it burning."

Brin examined his hand. "It's fine. Not a scratch."

"What?" He held his hand in front of his face, twisting it back and forth. "I could smell it. It hurt like hell."

"What you smelled and felt was the ship itself. Not your hand," explained Jane.

He stared at the walls around him. "The ship can feel?"

"What do you think?"

"That you were messing with my head."

"If I was going to toy with your mind, I'd do a lot more than make you believe your hand was burning."

Hanson took a step closer to Logan.

"And what miracle did you want to witness down here?" she asked the medic.

Brin glanced at Logan before answering. "Could I scan you while you work? I want to see how you do it."

"As long as you don't touch me. He's the only one allowed to do that." She nodded to Logan.

Brin gave him a glare that set Jane's teeth on edge. "Don't give her any flowers. She'll kill us all."

Logan suddenly found his boots very interesting.

"You brought whatever it is you plan to scan with, I take it?" Because if she hadn't, she wasn't getting another chance. Not after the way she was treating Logan.

Part of her told her she should be jealous, but whatever had been between them was plainly over. Not to mention, she'd been quite clear about her own past relationships, if they could even be called that.

"Yes, of course." Brin opened the small bag she'd set by her feet and pulled out a tablet. She held it up vertically, running it up and down Jane's body from where she stood.

From the way the medic was frowning, it was plain that she wasn't happy with the results. "You need to be closer."

Brin sucked on her lower lip and glanced back at Logan and Hanson. Her gaze lingered on Hanson's hand.

"He's fine," Jane assured.

"I can see that," Brin snapped, then caught herself, giving Jane a tight smile.

Jane again placed her hand on the wall, opening her mind to the ship. North returned and stood aside, waiting for instruction. She directed him to the ventilation system on the wall behind her. Closing her eyes to block out distraction, Jane worked through North, who was becoming a familiar signature in her mind, making the process easier. With her attention focused on the two points of repair, she had no time to concern herself with the other occupants of the room.

The ship was slowly sinking into the soothing rhythms she remembered from her childhood. At least in this area, the pain was easing, which allowed the ship to be more receptive to her instructions.

North was flagging. She sent him off to rest. While Hanson had experienced the power flow, he was a bystander. When she worked through North, some of his energy was leeched during the process because of their connection. Energy that could have replenished her own if she hadn't needed him here. If she were at full strength, she might be able to use all four points, but it would take time to fill the well that she'd been drawing heavily from since she'd opened fire on her father.

She could allow Anika out, gather the crew close as worshippers and feed from them.

The thought enticed her. That would accomplish her goal of healing the ship much faster. No doubt, she'd require Anika to fight Matouk when it came to that. Would it be so bad to set her free now?

Jane slowly brought her awareness back to the room while she considered the faces of the crew members she'd met, of Logan and Rice, Adams, Brin, Hanson, Tate and the rest. Did she want to see them every day, drunk on her presence, scurrying to follow her commands?

Learning this new incarnation of herself was exciting, fresh, something she hadn't experienced since finding her place as the General. The crew might not be entirely on her side, but their actions and opposition made her days interesting. She hadn't resorted to oblivion like her parents, but the mundane life of the past few centuries wasn't far from it. Keeping herself under control might make her task harder, but it would be more enjoyable. After all she'd done, she deserved a little joy before her end.

Discovering the others had gone while she'd been working and ruminating, Jane made her way up to the large room these people used as a dining hall. The largest of the rooms on the ship, her kind had used it for recreation or practicing their powers while in full form. She recalled the space as she knew it, filled with plants from various worlds. Sometimes a pet or two lurked in the corners. A colorful array of birds, gathered in their travels, flitted about overhead while the children of the ship worked to learn their powers.

Now a row of tables stacked with bowls and platters sat in the middle of the room. At the rear, two people stood at a counter that looked to be cobbled together from pieces out of some of the suites. They were kneading dough and talking quietly. The tables near the entrance were all empty. She picked through the food offerings and then sat, calling her points to her along the blood connection they shared.

The four men arrived within ten minutes and joined her. She picked through the various food items she'd chosen to try while she listened, slowly leeching energy from the three who weren't as drained as she was.

East and West reported that the crew was settling down in regards to her presence now that an agreement had been reached with their employer. Though, they were still extremely cautious around her. News of her healings, versions of what she'd said here and there, and of choking Tate had made their rounds.

South reported that Tate was excited about a proposal by Colonel Rice, but he was unable to ascertain what that proposal was. Whatever the subject, she was happy about it, and that sent off warnings for Jane.

"If you hear anything else, I want to know immediately. Wake me if you must."

South nodded. She dismissed the four men and returned to her room. Anxious by the uncertainty of Tate's happiness, Jane found she couldn't sleep. Instead, she moved her favorite chair next to a wall and connected with the ship, monitoring and healing.

She awoke seven hours later, still connected and cramped from curling up in the chair, to the sound of the door chime. With a simple command through the ship, she opened the door and then discovered her energy hadn't rejuvenated while she'd slept. She shouldn't have nodded off with an open connection. It had siphoned off her power, continuing her work while she wasn't in control of her body. Concern over what Tate might have in store had left her out of sorts.

"What did you learn?" she called out, expecting South with a report.

"About what?" answered Logan.

"Nothing." She winced as she unfolded her legs and blood returned to her feet. "Did you need something?"

He came in but stopped a few feet away. "Just checking in to see if *you* needed anything."

"Only sleep." Discovering that her legs were not

cooperating with her wish to get across the room to her bed, she held out her hand to him. "And maybe your arm for a moment."

"Please tell me you weren't still working?"

"It wasn't intentional, and I'm not in any mood-"

"Don't fry me on the spot, but you look exhausted. Again." He half-carried her to her bed and covered her up. "You need to take better care of yourself. I don't know how your powers work, but it sure seems that you're going to burn yourself out if you continue like this."

He gave her a stern look that made her smile despite her terrible mood. With a whisper of the energy she had left, she touched his mind out of curiosity. Whatever he might have actually been coming to visit her about was gone from his thoughts, leaving only genuine concern.

He was worried about her.

Not like when the locals worried that their god was angry or worried that they were going to suffer because of something they'd done, but worried for her. It touched her deeply.

"I would never fry you. On the spot or otherwise."

He sat beside her, brushing her hair from her forehead. "That's good to know."

She shifted closer, enjoying the gentle brushing of his fingers on her skin. Not since she'd been a young child had anyone touched her in such a way, not expecting anything, just soothing.

"I wanted to thank you for your patience with Hanson and Brin earlier."

"Did they get the answers they sought?"

"I think it's more that they gained a hundred more questions, but yes, for now, I think so."

"Good." She patted his thigh, wishing she wasn't so damned tired, but he was right, she was exhausted, yet again. "I'm glad you're here, but I need to sleep."

"You do that and when you wake up, we're going to get you everything you need to make your stay here more comfortable."

She drifted off, thinking the only thing that would make her more comfortable was his body nestled alongside her own.

CHAPTER TEN

He knew Jane needed to sleep, but the shuttle crew was getting anxious to be on their way and Tate was accompanying them, which only added more pressure. He ran down the list of food he'd packed so she'd have something to help her recharge. The man she'd appointed as North had been happy to relay which foods Jane liked best from the selection in the dining hall.

"Jane." He gently shook her bare shoulder. He hoped she wouldn't be angry that he'd let himself in. The chime hadn't woken her, and he'd been too excited to wait.

"What?" She rolled onto her back to regard him with half-opened eyes.

He sat on the end of the bed and prodded her feet over the edge. "I have a surprise for you."

"I should warn you, that in my experience, surprises usually don't end well." She sat up and stretched.

"Come on, you're just jaded by all that experience." He handed her the freshly laundered clothing he'd picked up on his way over. "I packed you something to eat."

After shoving her hair out of her face, she got dressed, settling the amulet over her shirt. She got up and went into the bathroom.

"Where are we going?"

"A supply run. Nothing dangerous. Not work. Not

for you or me anyway. Come on."

He stood the moment she walked out of the bathroom. "The shuttle is waiting."

"What shuttle? To where?"

"A colony we've visited before, on a planet they've named Ivium. They're friendly, don't worry."

"I wasn't worried. I just don't like surprises."

She looked so normal, wiping her still half-asleep eyes and yawning. It was hard to imagine this same person could shoot light from her chest, talk to the ship through her skin, and command an army. But for all her soft touches, the healing of himself and others, and the moments of passion they shared, she'd also told him things about her past that chilled him through. She was not normal. He had to remember that.

"Then I should warn you that Commander Tate is traveling with us."

"I'll need my men."

"They're already waiting for you."

She slipped on her shoes. "Prepared, aren't you?"

"I conferred with North and suddenly the rest were there."

"Good. So what is this little excursion about then?"

"Supplies for you while Tate does her diplomacy thing and Hanson and his crew do some further explorations."

"So everyone is happy."

"That's the plan."

Jane gave him a peck on the cheek. "I wouldn't mind a couple hours of fresh air."

Logan walked with Jane to the bay where the shuttle and crew were waiting. Her points silently surrounded her, leaving him little room in her vicinity. Conceding his position to them, he took a seat next to Rice.

Hanson and his crew, equipment, and three of

Rice's men along with a selection of trade items filled the rear of the shuttle. Tate and East sat back with them. He suspected Jane had her points spying on the commander and he didn't blame her.

They left the Maxim and headed down to the blue and green world below. Hanson's briefing of his team drifted up from the rear.

"Who does the trading?" asked Jane.

"Mostly me," said Rice. He tapped his chest proudly. "Son of a successful merchant. It comes in handy."

"You did not also wish to be a merchant?"

Rice gazed out at the blackness surrounding the planet. "Seemed awfully boring at the time. A young man has dreams."

"Dreams usually lead to trouble," Jane said.

Rice shrugged. "I prefer to call it adventure, but I suppose that's a matter of perspective."

Jane fell into a hushed conversation with her points.

Rice leaned in close to Logan. "Hanson wouldn't shut up about yesterday. He's not going to drive Jane nuts today, I hope?"

"She was quite tolerant. I rather doubt she'll entertain him like that again."

She'd been edgy to be sure, but he was still surprised by her acquiescence to his request and her level of cooperation. If she had more days like that the crew might settle in around her, making life on the Maxim less tense. He could even see the two of them enjoying their time off together out in the open without caring so much about the looks from the crew. They were far more bearable when he had someone to share them with.

Ivium slowly grew larger. Soon, he could make out clouds and then water and land below them. As many times as he'd traveled from ship to world and back again since joining the Maxim's crew, Logan was still in awe of each flight. Matouk's army had kept his own homeworld so downtrodden that they didn't have many ships left, and as with most colonies the army had crossed, the few ships they had left were for emergencies or in poor repair. He'd never thought to travel in one himself until Rice's men happened to be there when he'd needed a way out.

"Just so you are aware, Commander Tate considers you Jane's wrangler. So if you could attempt to keep her glowing and light shooting to nil, it would be good for both of us."

"And so you are aware, I'm not a god wrangler."

"Yes, I know. Work with me here."

The ship came to a gentle landing in a meadow not far from the colony. The bay doors opened, allowing warm sunlight inside along with the scent of crushed grass and the distant chirping of birds. Rice and his team departed first, unloading the majority of the goods they hoped to trade. Logan took an armload while he waited for Jane and her points. Tate, Hanson and three of his men, followed along behind, carrying their equipment and ignoring the rest of the baskets and crates. Jane scowled at Tate, though the commander didn't seem to notice. With an almost imperceptible jut of her chin, her points moved quickly to gather up the rest of the load.

"Do you always bring trade goods when you visit colonies?" she asked as they walked.

"Usually. Sometimes we just bring a medic or two. That often gains us just as much goodwill."

Jane nodded. She seemed deep in thought, and he rather wished he were closer to her, but East and West kept him at bay by holding their positions. Standing outside her immediate orbit put him at a distance he wasn't comfortable with. It certainly hadn't been what he'd had in mind when he'd proposed this plan. Now that she had her points, would they ever have time alone together outside of her room?

They walked across the thick grass that brushed against his knees and then a sun-dappled tree line that opened to a field of grain. Taking care, they walked single file along a well-worn dirt path beside the field. Workers in the field of trailing vegetables they came to next took notice of them. A couple hurried off toward the buildings clustered beyond the patch of green.

It wasn't until they'd entered the little colony itself that he managed to get near Jane again. She took in the buildings and the sun-browned people with mild interest. Rice staked out an open place in the town center to stack their goods. When those were all deposited, Jane spoke to her points. He couldn't hear what she said, but East and West stayed with Rice. South walked slowly away into a cluster of children and began to speak with them. North hung back, staying nearby, keeping Jane in sight as she looked into the windows of one of the shops.

Logan made his way over to her. "See anything you like?"

She cast him a sideways glance and smirked. "You mean in the shop?"

Her flirtatious nature made him laugh. "Yes. There are several others we can stop by as well."

"Not a bad selection, but yes, let's look around first."

Behind them, he heard Rice already starting to barter with the colonists who, seeing that the intruders weren't armed, had begun to flock to the center of town. The bare dirt around a large round well was soon full of feet. Children climbed up onto the wide ring of white stone that lined the well to try to see over the adults.

He noted their clothes were clean and well-mended

and everyone appeared in good health. Though he couldn't say they had flourished since the Maxim's last visit, they'd at least not suffered any major downfalls. He smiled to himself, recalling the simple joy of waking up and doing his work, knowing he had a comfortable bed and a meal waiting at the end of the day. It hadn't seemed like a joy at the time, but it sure did now. He sighed and focused on the clear blue sky above, doing his best to clear his mind of melancholy thoughts.

Tate sat in the shade with a silver-haired woman. They were busy talking politics and paid he and Jane little attention. Hanson and his team had separated before they'd reached the town, having gone off to examine a promising mineral deposit they'd found on their previous visit.

They entered the second shop they came across, a building much like all the others, but displaying clothing, round white baskets, and wooden boxes in the front window. North stood in the doorway, watching the goings on in the center of town and keeping an eye on the merchant behind his counter.

"Is there something in particular you're looking for?" he asked.

"Clothing," offered Logan. "For her."

The man stepped out from behind his counter, revealing him to be much shorter than he'd appeared. He rolled up his sleeves and pulled back his outer robe to reveal a wide belt with assorted items fastened to it. North's gaze locked onto the merchant. Logan watched him closely as well.

"Tailor?" asked Jane.

The merchant grinned widely. "Bit of everything by necessity. I learned the trade from my father, and he from his father."

"Wonderful. We can't stay for anything custom, but alterations may be possible if you're speedy."

He grasped a measuring tape in his hands but made no move to use it. "May I inquire as to with what currency do you intend to pay before we begin?"

"Wise merchant." Jane nodded and looked to Logan.

He had an assortment of trade coins from various worlds they'd visited in the pouch at his side. But before he could ask which sort the merchant wanted, Jane cocked her head and seemed to look into the man. Logan wasn't sure what she was up to, but the intensity in her gaze couldn't be mistaken.

"Your family, they are doing well here?" she asked as if it were a simple casual question.

Logan was quickly learning that with Jane, very little was casual or simple.

"Yes, we've been quite fortunate. We built this shop shortly after we arrived. Business is good." His upbeat demeanor faded. "But my youngest, Caroline, she has not done so well here. She keeps getting sick. Medicine is not cheap or plentiful, and I don't believe our doctor knows how to cure her because it keeps coming back. The cost of her medicine is taking everything we make."

He clamped a hand over his mouth, which he seemed to realize looked odd, so he tried to turn it into wiping his face. "I'm sorry, I don't even know you. I shouldn't be burdening you with my problems."

"Don't worry, Isaac. I asked. You answered," Jane said as if that explained everything.

His eyes went wide when she used his name and his mouth dropped open.

"May I see your daughter?" she asked. "I may be able to help her."

"Are you a doctor?" He glanced at Logan. "You

brought one last time. He couldn't help."

"Jane is new. No harm in giving her a look?"

"I suppose not." Isaac took a deep breath and let it out. He then waved them behind the counter and up the stairs to the second story where his family lived.

A young girl, maybe eight years old, she was so emaciated it was hard to tell, lay on a pallet on the floor beside a bed. She opened her big blue eyes as they came closer.

"Everything she eats and drinks goes right through. Nothing seems to stick with her. It hasn't since we came here."

"Are there others like her?" asked Jane.

"Two more. Both young. We don't know what caused it. They were all healthy children when we landed. We fear they will not last much longer."

Jane sat on the wooden floor beside the girl. She rested one hand on the girl's wrist and closed her eyes.

"Have you tried removing the children from this world? It may be something here making them sick," asked Logan.

"We have no ships. We were dropped here with our initial supplies seven years ago. Everything you see here either came with us or was built here. They never came back to check on us or resupply."

"You've done well then." The town was clean and well built and the people, other than the three children he hadn't known about, appeared healthy and relatively happy.

"We've done what we can. It helps tremendously when people like your crew come to trade."

Logan nodded, making note to bring the situation to Rice's attention.

"Logan, could you please bring Isaac downstairs? I

think I can help Caroline, but I prefer to work alone."

"I thank you for anything you can do, but I don't know you. I won't leave you alone with my daughter." He crossed his arms and stood solidly in place.

If Jane didn't want anyone to see her healing magic, he was going to have his work cut out for him, because Isaac really didn't want to leave.

Considering his options, Logan dug into his pouch. Holding out a handful of coins that Rice had loaned him, he asked, "Which of these do you take?"

Isaac glanced from the coins to his daughter and Jane. Unarmed, wearing his unassuming clothing, and sitting on the floor, she might appear unintimidating to anyone who hadn't seen her in armor, eight feet tall, glowing like the sun, and shooting light from her body. Had he not known her, her scars alone would have been enough to make him reconsider leaving her alone with the girl, but he knew where she'd gotten them. Isaac might assume she'd been sorely abused. Which, the more Logan thought about it, was also true.

"Maybe we could get started on her clothes while she works?"

Issac said, "You'll take good care of her?"

Jane nodded. "I'll be down in a bit. I prefer white if you have it."

"For working?" asked Logan. "You'll be filthy in no time."

"The sanitation systems will all be online soon. White."

Arguing logic with her in front of an audience didn't seem wise. He went downstairs with Isaac.

The merchant showed him various designs, from form-fitting to loose and flowing, long and short and three grades of fabric. While he would prefer to see Jane in the tighter clothing, he had a feeling they wouldn't leave her room, or he'd be utterly frustrated while she worked.

In the end, he considered what she had been wearing under her armor when they'd taken her. Loose and utilitarian won. Though, he did pick the ones accented with fine threads of silver, a wide black belt to mark her trim waist and two long overcoats so she wouldn't be cold down below until the climate systems were all back online.

He was busy sorting through his coins to find enough of the type Isaac wanted when Jane came down the stairs.

"She's resting now. You should see an improvement within the first few meals. Make them light at first. Plenty of water."

Isaac nodded, smiling, but his doubt cast a heavy shadow. "You have no tools, no medicines. How could you have done anything for her?"

"Perhaps you should have a little faith." Jane gave the purchases arrayed on the counter a cursory glance, nodded, and strode out with North.

Logan quickly paid while Isaac stacked it all into a neat bundle.

"Thank you." Isaac handed him the clothes. "I didn't mean to be ungrateful for whatever she did," he added quietly.

"Don't mind her." Logan gathered up the bundle, which was quite substantial, and went outside.

Jane was already across the street, making a beeline for the silver-haired woman who was talking with Tate. Logan handed the bundle off to an empty-handed member of Rice's team with instructions to see it loaded on the shuttle. He ran after Jane and North. This wasn't at all the relaxing day with her that he had pictured.

He reached the four-some in time to hear Jane

demanding to see the other sick children. Tate wore a deep-set scowl and the other woman didn't look all that excited about the idea either.

"But you don't look like a doctor. Where are your supplies?"

"She doesn't have any," said Logan. "But she can still help. Would it hurt for her to see them?"

The look on Jane's face said quite clearly that she didn't appreciate his stepping in. North must have picked up her annoyance because he was giving Logan a stink-eyed glare, too.

"Is this woman part of your crew?"

Tate rubbed her brow like she could maybe straighten out the deep lines there. "It would seem so, yes."

"You don't look like a doctor. You look rather... unkempt."

"You would prefer that those children die because you find my current wardrobe lacking?"

"They're not dying. They're just sick. They've been that way for years now."

"They have a wasting condition brought on by the minerals in the water and soil. You are fortunate that only these three were susceptible."

The woman looked uncertain. "They were the youngest of us when we settled here. Children born here seem to be fine."

"Let me see them."

Rather than a carefree afternoon in a meadow, alone with the food he'd packed, maybe a nice breeze and the background noise of birds and a thriving town behind them, Logan spent the day with two sets of distraught parents while Jane worked on their children. Not that he begrudged her saving the children, but he'd really wanted to spend the time here with her alone. Instead, he had North tailing along behind, with East and West popping in twice to confer. South came to take North's place so that he could eat lunch. His own stomach rumbled, wishing it had its turn, but he didn't dare leave Jane unattended. Even if he wasn't in the same room.

When she'd finished with the last child, she came down to take his arm. From the first steps they took together, he realized it wasn't that she was being familiar, she needed the support.

"That bad off?"

She nodded. South tailed them.

"Are you hungry?"

"Famished."

"I did bring lunch, though it's rather past that now."

Around them, people showed off their new acquisitions to one another. A few stragglers still crowded around Rice and his crates. Some had been refilled with food, baskets, clothing and a large carved wooden bowl. One of his men stacked the empty crates while another, arms full, was headed back to the ship.

"North mentioned the others were provided with a meal by the colonists," said Jane.

"I thought we could have a private meal."

"I would like that." Her fingers stroked his arm.

"We could look around more after we eat."

"I appreciate the thought, really, but I'm tired and I'd rather be on our way before those children wake up."

"Why?"

"Because I healed them, and I don't want it to be anything more than that."

Logan grabbed the basket he'd brought from the dwindling pile of goods near Rice's impromptu shop. He led the way to the quiet field beyond the town that he'd had in mind all day.

"What do you mean?"

"People see what I do as a miracle. People who work miracles are revered and worshiped. I don't want to be a god here. Or anywhere." She sat down in the lush tufts of grass next to where he'd set the basket. "This is a lovely spot to enjoy lunch."

"I thought you might like it."

"It reminds me of the gardens on Kaldara."

"Yes, I can see that." Though, the gardens he'd glimpsed on their escorted march into the palace had been meticulously clean and sculpted, everything trim and in its place. Here, the plants grew wild, the flowers amidst the grass, trees clumped together and bushes wherever they happened to find root. There was no hint of a gardener's caring touch here, but it was just as beautiful.

Rather like the woman in front of him, and he wanted to fully enjoy her. Unfortunately, with South looming nearby, he still didn't have Jane to himself, but at least they were away from town and the crew.

"Kaldara was much like this when we came to it. Calm, a little primitive. The inhabitants were happy but struggling. These people are doing much better."

"So this kind of world, in this situation, would your kind stay here, and what would they do?"

She picked at her food despite her admission of being famished. "They would have stayed. My father was incapable of passing up an opportunity. They would be subjugated, their resources managed, their world molded in a way my father found pleasing. If there were any other life forms worth mention here, they would be exploited in the way that best suited my father's desires."

"I'm not sure that sounds all that helpful to the guidance and development that you had mentioned before."

"I told you we were corrupt? It is far too easy, after so many worlds, to see the patterns and just plow through to what is familiar rather than what might be right for that particular people or planet."

"So it was more of a habit?"

She nodded. "You could say that."

They finished their meal in silence, enjoying the sunshine and the sounds around them. The scent of freshly harvested grain carried on the soft breeze that teased her tangle of curls.

"You are unhappy," she said quietly.

"Why do you say that?"

Jane smiled. "You are not that difficult to read."

"I've been told otherwise."

She pulled herself closer, resting her shoulder against his. "They were not me."

"That's true. I can't say that I've had lunch with a god before."

"That's not what I am. Not a god. Unlata Kai. Only those that wish for something to rule over them, who do not seek to understand, call us gods."

"Sorry. It's just..."

"I know." She patted his arm. "Tell me why you are unhappy."

"This day is not going how I imagined."

"Most of mine don't. But really, why does that make you unhappy? Is life not made up of unexpected events? If everything went as we imagined, we would have very boring lives."

"I suppose that's true."

"I did not imagine surviving the natural destruction of Kaldara, yet here I am."

"As I recall you weren't all that happy about your

survival."

Jane chuckled. "That is so. However, I find I am less unhappy about it than I was. We are changed by the events that happen around us, especially the unexpected ones."

He savored her hand on his arm, her side pressed against his, and the ease with which she spoke to him. He especially liked the kindness that lurked just below her turbulent surface. "Those children, will they live?"

"I can say that they will survive and fully recover from the illness from which they suffered, after that, it is out of my control."

"You're all about the fine print, aren't you?"

"I've learned to watch what promises I make. They have a habit of coming back to haunt me."

"Have you ever acted as a god rather than an agent of your father?"

"Many times. All Unlata Kai have their roles. There is always a god who rules them all. But under him are other gods that form a foundation for his control. It should come as no surprise that I am the god of war."

"At least you didn't throw fertility in there."

She smirked. "No one would buy that. My mother took that role, as well as anything else my father required."

"So you rather got pigeonholed then."

She stared at him, looking inward. "Yes. Strange word for such a meaning, but yes."

"How do you do that? I don't feel anything when you're in my head."

"You shouldn't." She stroked the back of his hand. "It would be very sloppy of me if you did. Besides, gods are supposed to know all, right? If we had to ask what you meant every time you threw around words like that, we wouldn't seem very omnipotent, would we?"

He nodded. A dark speck in the sky caught his attention. "What is that?"

Jane peered upward. "An incoming ship. Are you expecting anyone?"

"No. We should get back to Rice."

She helped to quickly gather up their supplies. They rushed back to town, keeping an eye on the sky as they traveled.

"The colonel is alarmed," South announced.

When they came back into the square, many of the colonists had scattered back into their homes. Their doors were closed, and he wouldn't have been surprised to find them barred if he had tried to open one.

"Do we know who it is?" he asked Rice.

"No. I've sent half the crew back to the ship for our weapons."

Fire rained down from the sky, beams slicing through trees and homes. Screams filled the air.

"Not friendly then," Logan muttered under his breath as they sought cover alongside one of the homes near the square.

"How far away are your men?" asked Jane.

Rice scowled, eyeing the sky above. "I lost contact with them."

"I can protect us, but you will need to get me out of here as soon as possible. Do not allow me to stay here." She drove her gaze into Logan. "Do you understand?"

"Anika?"

"Yes."

The beams came at them again. Two more ships raced toward them. The beams sliced through one of the homes. Smoke billowed into the air. A woman wailed.

"Do it."

Jane nodded and closed her eyes. Instantly she

expanded, light burst from her skin. Her clothes expanded with her. A golden glow filled her eyes. She raised her arms, throwing a transparent shield over the entire town.

The ship that had fired first, hit the shield and burst into flames. Shards of the ship flew in all directions, coloring the shield with black and red. The other two pulled up in time.

Anika opened her mouth to emit a high pitched sound he could not so much as hear as he could feel.

The two ships fell from the sky, crashing into the meadow where they'd had lunch. Towering over them, Anika strode to the meadow. She turned briefly.

"See to the colonists. I will deal with them."

"Find out who they are before you smite them, please?" shouted Rice.

Anika's face darkened. "Do not think to order me. Do as I say."

Her vast strides made quick work of the distance between them and the edge of the shield. When she got there, she reached into her shirt and drew out her amulet. In seconds, golden armor covered her entire body, the heavy-featured scowling face helmet flowed over her head.

She walked through the shield as if it were nothing. Logan moved to follow her.

"Go ahead. I'll take this," said Rice.

Logan nodded and ran after Anika. He smacked into the shield. The solid surface hurt like hell.

Anika didn't look back.

He couldn't see her this close to the surface of the shield. Whereas at a distance, it appeared transparent, up close it was swirling opaque gold.

He called after her but his voice sounded hollow, the sound gathered up by the shield and hoarded.

Logan spun around and ran back to Rice where he

was attending to one of the damaged houses with the crew that had remained in town.

"What should we do?" asked the terrified family who had evacuated the ruined home.

"Stay close. Can you stay with another family?"

They nodded and ran to the building closest to their home, pounding on the door.

"You need to remain inside until we get a handle on this situation."

"What was that?" they asked, pointing to where Anika had been.

Rice sighed. "You're fortunate that we had a god with us. No doubt, she'll make quick work of this threat."

"A god?"

"Inside please," Logan urged them through the door that had opened. The pale faces of the anxious occupants inside peered at the shield.

The more he thought about it, he didn't fully understand who or what Anika was and how she differed from Jane. When he'd spoken to her before, she seemed kind, like Jane, as much as he'd seen Jane be anyway. He knew that she could also be cruel, or perhaps just devoted to her cause. Anika may have been the same way, devoted to remaining alive.

If Anika were truly great and kind, why wouldn't Jane remain in her god form all the time? From the way she spoke of Anika, being a god wasn't a good thing. But she could shield an entire town and take down ships with a few words. That didn't seem bad at all. It sounded really damn useful.

Her four points erupted from the square where they had scattered in the attack. They ran to the shield and through it with no issue.

Logan swore.

"What?" asked Rice.

"It would seem that only those keyed to Jane can pass through her shield."

"So?"

"We're trapped here."

"I'm sure she'll be back shortly," said Rice.

"We can't go check on the men who went to the shuttle, and they can't get to us. Assuming they're alive."

"Good point. But she'll be back."

He hoped so. Jane's plea to be removed from the planet as soon as possible left him chilled. If Anika wasn't a threat, then why would she need to be removed. And for that matter, how did Jane expect him to remove her once she was in god mode? He couldn't even get to her.

When Anika did return, it was with her points and blood spattered armor. There was no sign of prisoners.

He tried for the most neutral tone he could manage in light of the obvious carnage. "Who were they?"

"Followers of Matouk. It was fortunate that I was here or this colony would be in ruins and its people slaves."

"And what are your plans for Ivium?" asked Logan, curious if her answer would align with Jane's.

Anika's helmet clicked in rapid-fire succession as the plates slipped into one another to bare her head. He rather wished it had stayed in place. Anika bore none of Jane's scars. The glow emanating from her skin gave the impression of beauty, her eyes were hard and not comforting by any means. It was like peering into a sun.

"You wish to serve me?" she asked.

"I have a feeling it would be preferable to the alternative," offered Rice.

"I was not speaking to you." A thin bolt of light sprang from her hand to knock Rice to the dirt.

Anika motioned to her points, two of which came

forward to remove the colonel. Where they took him, Logan couldn't see. He was too focused on not falling victim to the same fate.

"You asked me to save you, remember? I did. We did." He waved his hand to indicate the remainder of the trembling crew.

Anika came closer, looking into him as Jane had before. "Logan."

"Yes?"

"You will be useful." She gazed upward, retracting the shield into herself with a funnel of shimmering light that spiraled into her chest.

"The three ships launched from a larger vessel orbiting this planet."

"Have they harmed the Maxim?"

Anika cocked her head, closing her eyes, offering a brief respite from her piercing stare. Did she ever blink?

"The Maxim remains operational in orbit. We will secure these people and then return to the ship to destroy this threat."

"But what of our shuttle?"

"Damaged, but repairable."

"You can tell that from here?"

He found himself the focus of her molten gaze once again. "Do not question me, or you can join your friend."

Logan backed away. If they were able to get Anika back on the Maxim, Jane would take over. He hoped. She'd made it sound like she would.

He found the colonel groaning on the ground behind the damaged house. "You all right?"

"Been better." He sat up slowly, rubbing his chest.

"And I thought Jane had a short fuse."

Rice grunted. "Not exactly jealous of you right now. Though, I notice she didn't blast you."

"Wouldn't put it past her." But as he considered their talks of promises, he wondered if that carried over to Anika. It was worth a shot. "I'll be right back."

"Don't do anything stupid."

"Stupid is debatable."

"Logan."

He waved off the colonel's concern. Either he'd get a more cooperative Anika, or he'd find himself rolling around in the dirt beside Rice.

She'd shrunk somewhat, not as towering as before, but still larger than life. Her armor had changed to bare her shoulders and arms, giving her a more feminine appearance, though it was no less breathtaking or terrifying.

He approached her, safe within her points, with caution. "May I speak with you a moment?"

Her gaze snapped away from North, whom she had been speaking with, to penetrate him. "What is it?"

Logan cleared his throat, bracing himself for a bolt of light to the chest. "You made me a promise."

She actually grimaced. "Did we now?"

He nodded.

"I thought we'd learned from our mistakes," she muttered. "And what is this promise that you feel compelled to interrupt me with?"

"That you wouldn't harm me."

Anika pursed her lips and shrugged. "I can deal with that."

"And you also made a pact with the Maxim's crew."

She sighed. "Fortunate that you covered the other one first."

"You promised to repair our ship so that we could aid you in defeating Matouk and his army."

"My ship."

"The ship."

She bared her teeth in what was very much not a smile. "I fail to see why my other half finds you charming."

He wasn't quite sure why either, but didn't push his luck by saying so. "Jane urged us to return to the Maxim with you as soon as possible."

"That is not her name," she all but spat.

"I'm well aware of that, but it's the one she chose for us to use."

"Because you are not worthy to speak her true name."

Curiosity slipped in. "Is she with you now?"

"Yes and no."

"Can you bring her back now?"

Anika came closer, her points milling around the two of them. He'd never been comfortable around anyone taller than him on the rare occasions that occurred. Now, he not only felt short, but he disdained the fact that he had to crane his neck to look up at her. He swore she grew again just to spite him.

"Jane was exhausted from healing, that's why she opened herself to me. I am here to protect all of you, and I will do that until the threat has passed."

"But you already destroyed the three ships. The Maxim can take out the one in orbit with your help."

"Matouk is the threat. I will see him defeated before my other half returns."

He couldn't have Jane gone that long. She'd told him to get her back to the ship. She didn't want to be here, not even to take credit for the healing of the three children. She certainly wouldn't want Anika set free on this colony, not after what she'd said about subjugating and worshippers. Was Anika corrupt like all the others Jane had destroyed?

As if she sensed his thoughts, and she very well

could have, she calmly said, "Who is to say they won't launch more ships to investigate the loss of contact? Or that, discovering the Maxim and in light of our resistance, they will not call upon Matouk himself?"

"You think he would come here?" Logan asked.

Dread filled him. The Maxim's operational weapons were minimal. Defense against a single ship was one thing, but if more were to arrive, the Maxim's crew would lose everything. He might not be fully one of them, but he'd worked alongside them, eaten with them. He knew each of their faces. And then there was this whole colony huddled behind their doors. With Hijn's losses already haunting his nights, he didn't think he could take more.

"We will not leave Ivium defenseless," Anika assured him, taking a step closer.

Far more powerful than the faint hum that often emanated from Jane, Anika's pulsing beat swept him up. This voice, the quiet, rational one was the same as she'd used when she'd asked him to rescue Jane from the city as it fell apart around them. Her very presence made his blood sing. He wondered if her points felt the same way, if that's why they stayed by her side and didn't let others through so they didn't have to share.

He wanted to help. He needed to do anything to remain close to her. "What can I do?"

Anika smiled down on him, her face softening. "Send the crew back to the Maxim. I will remain here to protect these people against any further attacks while the Maxim takes out their ship."

"May I stay here with you?"

She caressed his cheek, trailing a finger down his neck. The most wonderful shivers followed her touch. He could barely breathe in anticipation of more.

"Yes, Logan, you may stay."

"Thank you," he whispered, finding that was all the voice he had. His heart was so full, his entire body humming. He wanted nothing more than to crawl inside her light and stay there forever.

CHAPTER ELEVEN

When Anika had charged Logan with seeing her body to safety while Kaldara collapsed, it had been a simple matter of self-preservation. There hadn't been many options at that time. He'd completed his task and remained by her side even without her field of influence. Even more intriguing, her other half had chosen to keep him close.

He stood before her now, swaying gently, eyes heavily-lidded, drunk on the residue emitted by the use of her full power. She could do anything to him in this state and he would thank her for it. It was unfortunate that her other half had seen fit to entangle her in promises.

She would need to take a different path toward collecting the adulation of these people. Even a small following would help feed her until she could gather a new army, an army that would drive Matouk into the dirt where he belonged. The loss of the people of Kaldara, who had revered and fed her, soured her joy of finally holding control over her body again.

Rather than send Logan to do as she had bid him, she sent East. While she told herself it was to keep the crew from seeing how her influence worked before she was ready to fully employ it, part of her was curious as to why her other half found Logan so alluring.

When she searched their shared memories, it came as a surprise that her other half not only took pleasure in his company but had enjoyed sex with him on several occasions. That was not their usual method of operation. Twice perhaps, but never more than that. Never allow another to become attached, to feel that he should expect more from her than she could give. She had a position to uphold and it had nothing to do with reproduction or servicing another's needs. An hour or evening of enjoyment was one thing, but what was her other half up to with him?

Anika took up a spot near the well in the center of the town. She watched the closed up buildings and verified that her remaining points were on guard. If only Matouk had been aboard one of the small ships she'd destroyed, she might have truly enjoyed herself here. As it was, her other half whispered of missions and obligations, urging her to return to the Maxim.

Her other half had always been too entangled in the desires of their followers, of pleasing others. With her father gone, she was finally free to do as she wished. This world was the perfect place to experiment, to start anew on her own. If only she could appease her other half enough to shut her up. All the nagging was making it hard to think clearly.

"West, I need you to go to the damaged shuttle. Notify me when you have arrived. We will repair it and get these people back to the Maxim."

The point nodded and set off in eager strides to do her bidding. North and South hung close by. Logan stood at her side, his arm just touching hers. Energy leeched from his body through the point of contact. Her other half held herself in such tight control when it came to feeding. She kept her field dampened to a degree that she might as well not even have it. So many foolish self-imposed rules. Anika snorted. That's what these beings where here for. She protected them. They fed her. That was simply the way of things, as it always had been.

Though the adulation and energy he offered were like nectar that was pure temptation, he was a distraction she didn't have time for until the others were gone. She reluctantly pointed to a bench near the marketplace. "Logan, why don't you go sit over there until I need you?"

The heartbroken look he gave her made her other half cry out even louder. *Leave him alone.*

We will not harm him. Rest now.

She tightened her hold on the veil that separated them in the hopes of smothering the irate voice.

Logan's shoulders slumped and his head bowed as he departed. There was a reason she kept a perimeter with her points. Those not of Unlata Kai blood were far too susceptible to the residue of power. While that could be handy when needed to sway unruly citizens or create instant followers, it did tend to take away free will and cloud all reason. If he acted strangely, others might question why, and she wasn't embedded well enough here yet for that.

He slowly made his way to the bench. North and South remained on the perimeter of her field, within her influence, but not overly affected by it. Her blood had begun to settle in their bodies.

A woman approached from one of the homes. From her tan and black uniform, Anika gathered she was of the Maxim's crew. She appeared in her middle years, silver streaking her auburn hair.

"What are you?" the woman asked in a trembling voice.

Anika again consulted her shared memories. "My

other half didn't like you. You know what I am." She dismissed the woman with the flick of her wrist.

"But what you did..." Tate gazed up at the sky where the shield had been. "They just exploded."

"Keep that in mind next time you bother me."

West contacted her through their blood connection. With the distance and the amount of damage to the shuttle, she needed to concentrate.

"Logan, if you value your commander in any way, remove her from my presence."

He appeared more clear-headed, but the hesitation on his face made her wonder if he had sensed the level of her annoyance. The lack of speed he used in getting up and coming over to Tate to escort her away revealed his true feelings on the matter.

With Tate and Logan gone, her other half quieted. Anika funneled her energy through West, repairing the shuttle the same way she had worked on the Maxim. The distance made the process more draining, but she didn't want to leave the colony without making her presence known to the people here, and she couldn't do that until the crew had left.

However, at this rate of energy expenditure, she would need to rest. Her other half had repeatedly drained their power well since they'd left Kaldara and had made little effort to refill it.

It took nearly an hour to get the shuttle back in working order. Meanwhile, Rice and the others helped some of the colonists put out the fire in the ruined home and remove two victims.

West reported that the crew that had returned to the shuttle had survived. They were waiting there, not realizing that the shield was now down. West did not enlighten them.

Feeling the strain of her efforts, Anika sent East to retrieve Rice rather than seeking him out herself. When he arrived, she noted that he had fully recovered from her lesson in respect. He eyed her warily, a look she was well used to and preferred.

"You will take your men and return to the Maxim. Logan will remain here with my points so that he can summon a shuttle when we are ready to return."

He raised a hand and backed up a step. "If I may... It might be wise to keep a few others here as well so that Tate doesn't get it in her head to take the Maxim and abandon you here."

She gave him credit for loyalty. He had a point. She hadn't considered how precarious her standing was with Tate. That was new. Usually lesser beings were eager to please her and wouldn't consider leaving her behind. Perhaps it would be wise to bring Tate into her immediate presence. That would sway her in an instant. But that could also make the rest of the crew, Rice included, think twice about getting near her, and expose her field of influence for what it was. Tate suddenly becoming a sycophant would be highly suspicious.

Anika sighed. These power struggles and building of foundations had never been her concern before. Other Unlata Kai or their followers had taken care of this. But there weren't any others. All she had was Logan and her four points. Taking down Matouk alone wasn't going to be easy, but she was the General. She'd figure it out.

The General had never shirked from confrontation. Matouk was a worthy opponent, not some barely civilized beings her father wished to rule over until he tired of them. She would do this of her own accord, but her well needed to be full before any of that. Her other half wasn't taking care of herself. Anika would have to do that for both of them.

As much as needing help to lay the groundwork for her rise to power annoyed her to the core, it was necessary. She forced the aggravation from her voice and addressed Rice. "Very well, you will remain."

"May I keep two men with me? The colonists could use some help with a few projects while we're here."

"That will be acceptable. I do not wish for your hard-earned trade goods to be at risk if we encounter another attack. They will be safer aboard the ship."

Rice nodded. He sent a man off to continue loading the shuttle. Anika also considered the fact that if they were to suffer another attack, with her energy as low as it was, she would only need to protect the handful of men rather than the entire colony. Another field of that size wouldn't be possible without instantly depleting her and that was something she avoided at all costs.

"You will stay close to the town with your projects?"

"I don't think any of us will be wandering far from you for awhile."

"That would be wise. I will need a place to rest so that I can be prepared to build another shield if necessary."

"That shouldn't be a problem. Between the healing and the exploding ships, you're likely welcome anywhere."

Anika dismissed him with a wave. Logan returned to the bench but didn't sit down. He glanced her way.

"Why don't you assist with the loading of the shuttle? Find me when you are finished."

He nodded, going to join the exodus of laden men. It grated on both her halves to send him away even for a short period of time. Other than her points, Logan was the only one filling her well.

Rice distracted her with an offer from a family eager to host her during their stay. With North and South at her side, she followed the colonel to one of the larger homes near the center of the colony. The woman she'd seen talking with Tate looked up at her, smiling widely.

"Thank you for all you've done to protect us. Truly a miracle that you were here. You're welcome in my home." She opened the door with a graceful swooping gesture.

"I'll let Logan know where you are when I see him," said Rice, taking his leave.

"Are you hungry? Tired?" asked the woman. "I'm Governor Schmidt. You may call me Carol." She bowed.

"Anika."

Confusion clouded her face, but she shook it off. Likely Tate had used her other name. The utterly common one she refused to acknowledge. Why did her other half had to make life difficult? Control and consume, *her* goals were simple.

"You have a family?" If she could feed from a group, the effects would be less obvious.

"Just me and my husband here. My children are grown and elected not to join us in this venture."

The large room where they stood held a long table with benches on either side and chairs at the ends. A cluster of more comfortable chairs sat at the other side of the room near a fireplace. Stairs led upward. The layout was similar to the store where Logan had purchased clothing for her, except in place of counters and racks of wares, were a spacious kitchen, dining, and sitting area. Which would leave a lot of room for sleeping areas upstairs.

The thought of the clothing Logan had picked out for her, prompted her to glance at what she was currently wearing. She'd not given thought to it before now. Men's clothes. Logan's, her other half informed her. Anika smiled, running her hand over the sleeve of the soft shirt. Comfortable, but, she quelled the smile, not how an Unlata Kai dressed. Her other half had always favored ease of movement and comfort over upholding their image. They'd compromised with the armor, her other half getting her way under their glorious metal casing. But armor wasn't always appropriate, and with Kaldara and the chest of Anika-approved attire destroyed, she was going to have to fall back on what Logan considered appropriate for her. It had to be better than this.

Anika realized Carol had been nervously rambling on about housing other colonists who didn't yet have families or homes of their own. Her well of power fluttered.

"Are there others here now?"

"Yes, would you like to meet them?"

"I would." She sent South off to retrieve the clothing bundle. "But do you have a room where I might rest?"

"Of course." Carol led her up the stairs to a hallway filled with doors on either side. "It's like an inn, I suppose you could say. Not that we have visitors often." She gestured to the nine closed doors. "The rooms are on the small side, but everyone is welcome downstairs. Meals are taken there together. With all the excitement, I should go make sure the cook has dinner started or we'll all be going hungry tonight."

North stood between her and Carol, maintaining a distance between them all. Anika breathed deep through her nose, fighting to control her urge to drain the woman dry.

Carol opened the second door on the right. "How many of your crew will also need rooms? I have three open here, but I can find space for more if needed."

The room was indeed compact, a bed, a stool, and a small table with enough room to walk between them all. Thankfully the bed looked like it could hold three average-sized people.

"These rooms should be adequate." Her points would need to remain on rotation. Sharing the bed with two of them wasn't an issue. Logan and Rice and his men could share the other two rooms.

"Very good. Is there anything else I can do for you right now?"

Anika met North's gaze, warning him of what she was about to do. He stepped into the room, leaving the two of them in the hallway.

Just a light touch to take the edge off. She couldn't afford to cause another scene, one for all the wrong reasons. Not just yet anyway. Anika reached out and rested her hand on Carol's arm, drawing her close.

"You've been very helpful."

The woman's eyes slipped closed and a peaceful smile lit her lined face. "Anything I can do for you?"

Energy flowed from Carol, leeching through her skin, up through Anika's hand, her arm, and into the well at the center of her being. A well, like her father's that when ruptured, would cause a terrific explosion, obliterating her body in a ball of light. At least her people died with a show of power that awed their followers. These lesser beings, they met such messy ends, leaving behind remnants for others to deal with.

She saw Carol's memories of the ceremonies her kind held for their dead. So many dead. So much time wasted on ceremony and holding memories of those gone before. If only they had elders like the Unlata Kai, they could continue on without looking back.

Before Carol became someone for others to remember fondly or otherwise, Anika let her go and stepped away. The older woman staggered back, still smiling, but dazed.

"Perhaps you should go see to the meal and then get some sleep," Anika suggested.

"Yes, the day has been quite eventful."

"North, please see our host safely down the stairs."

Alone for a moment, Anika sat on the stool. She took stock of the people around her, some in the rooms nearby, others outside working, of Rice and his men, of Logan making his way back from the now departed shuttle with her points. They would make a good beginning for her return to power.

South returned with the bundle of clothing in hand, placing it on the bed. He left, closing the door behind him. Anika allowed her body to return to its natural size so that she could change into the clothing. Once on, she could alter its fibers to fit her expanded form. She chose a long white tunic with a square neckline, trimmed with silver thread. A pair of white leggings fit nicely underneath. She shed the simple shoes her other half had chosen and activated her armor to provide her with engraved boots that rose up her shins to the tasseled hem of the tunic. On the whole, rather plain, but far better than what she'd arrived in. Anika pulled her hair back from her face, using a tiny bit of energy to bring order to the annoying frayed mop her other half had little care for. With her hair smoothed and shining, her skin cleansed and a fresh scent surrounding her, Anika was ready to face the crowd she sensed below.

She resumed a minimalized measure of her preferred size so she could comfortably fit within the confines of the inn, and descended the stairs. East followed close behind. North and West awaited her at the bottom. Anika was pleased to see the room was full, every chair occupied and no few standing around the edges with bowls in their hands. None of them were paying attention to the food in front of them. All conversation stopped.

Two unfamiliar men at the table jumped to their feet, offering her their chairs. She chose the larger chair of the two, one capable of holding her current form. Carol was nowhere to be seen, but another woman of a similar age hurried over with a bowl and a steaming piece of brown bread. Her hands trembled as she placed the food before Anika.

While she found food enjoyable at times, she favored the sustenance that came from followers. The room was ripe with it.

Anika made an effort to bring the soup-laden spoon to her mouth a few times and nibbled at the bread. Slowly, the room returned to a quiet hum of activity as the occupants resumed their meals and conversations. With the main focus off her, Anika took the opportunity to converse with those closest, reaching out to touch an arm, shoulder, or hand, leeching energy as she did so. It would take a long time to replenish herself at this rate, but it was a start.

When the meal concluded, the room remained full. Those that had sat nearby retired, claiming to be worn out by the day, making room for others to approach her. Anika didn't bother listening to them, their words were the usual mix of gushing compliments and offers to assist her in any way possible. She made sure to bring each one close and to touch them to siphon off the assistance she needed most. Her field, while no longer as overwhelming as it had been when Logan had come into it right after taking down the ships, still exuded enough residue naturally to hold anyone in her immediate presence in thrall for a short while.

By the time the room had emptied to only the older couple who had served the meal and were now cleaning up the last of the mess, and those that had come from the Maxim, Anika felt more herself. She'd made good progress toward replacing what her other half had recklessly squandered.

Both Rice and Logan watched her closely, but she kept her distance, staying within her points. They would be needed for work around the colony tomorrow. Siphoning from them would only delay the additional progress she hoped to make.

Anika reached out, straining, but able to sense the Maxim orbiting in the distance. The other ship was gone. Sensing no debris near the Maxim, she gathered they had fled to report to Matouk or had fallen back to await further orders.

Tate hadn't left them behind just yet, but Anika would have to work as quickly as possible here to keep the ship and Tate under control if she didn't want to resort to anything that would prompt her other half to fight for her body. She looked from one crewmember to the next, weaving a command to interfere with their communication devices. They didn't need to know the threat was gone just yet and Tate didn't need to know what she was doing here until she was ready to add the rest of the crew to her followers.

Taking her leave of the Maxim's men, Anika went to her room with North and West. She sank onto the bed, basking in the energy flowing through her from those she'd touched.

With her points beside her, Anika drifted off, dreaming of how she'd shape Ivium. Her father had relied on his tried and true plan, but she had so many ideas. She'd seen so much in her lifetime and these colonists were eager to please her.

Matouk would come to her in his own time. Until

then, this world and these people would be hers.

CHAPTER TWELVE

L ogan wiped away the sweat intent on dripping into his eyes with his discarded shirt. The sun hung directly overhead as it had seemed to do for the past several hours without mercy. Dirt and sweat covered Rice and the two men he'd kept with him, along with the ones now calling themselves South and East, and a handful of the colonists. He rested his weight on the shovel he'd been using to dig irrigation trenches and caught a glimpse of Anika as she talked with a couple at the edge of the field.

The three of them bent down to examine the plants there. Anika gestured to the soil and the leaves and another field. It appeared the god of war was trying out for the god of agriculture. She'd said she'd had a hand in shaping Kaldara's city and he supposed that population had needed to eat too. He just hoped her advice was good here on Ivium.

"These trenches aren't going to dig themselves," Rice called out.

Logan returned to his task, trying not to dwell on the fact that Jane had explicitly asked him to get her back to the Maxim. Anika appeared in no hurry to leave this world.

A young woman made her way through the field, bringing water and food to the laborers. He gratefully took what she offered and joined the others sitting on the ground in the shade of the tree line. She sat nearby, picking daintily at her meat stuffed pastry while glancing at him through her long lashes. Logan ignored her, watching for any sign of Anika between the buildings or near the fields. She remained out of sight. That fact agitated him to no end.

When she'd come down the stairs the night before, glowing softly, emanating a scent that begged to be inhaled directly from her bare skin, and looking so serene, he wanted nothing more than to be alone with her. But she avoided him, as she'd done all day now. He didn't understand it, but he needed to be near her, to do whatever she asked of him. Instead, Rice had asked him to work out here, and Anika had sent two of her points to help. That wasn't near close enough to her to satiate the itch that was rubbing his insides raw.

What was worse, Rice and the others who had been at dinner with her the night before, all seemed to be watching for her too, and not with the wary looks they'd given Jane. If he appeared half as desperate for her as they did, it would be pathetic.

He'd had her attention, but that had been Jane. Jane had apparently found him *charming*, which was not a word he recalled a woman ever using to describe him. Someone fun to get drunk with, who had their backs, who enjoyed sharing a bed now and then, sure, but charming had never come up.

If Anika was part of Jane, she might be swayed to enjoy his company too. It was the same body after all, just with a slightly different personality. Maybe a little more than slight, but by all that was holy, he needed to be near her again. He shivered, recalling the sensations that had run through him after she'd taken down Matouk's ships.

But Anika stayed away, spending her day with the colonists. Even when they returned to their rooms, filthy and exhausted from their day's labor, she was nowhere to be seen. It wasn't until they'd nearly finished their meal that she came into the dining room from wherever she'd been.

Her white clothes were still pristine, her hair neatly in place, and that smell, like spiced incense, intoxicated him. She moved through the room, touching each person as she passed, lingering only a moment to speak or nod in response to what was said. North and West stayed close but weren't glued to her side as they'd been when they'd first arrived.

When she got to him, she cocked her head, giving him a thoughtful look. He waited anxiously for her to say something, to indicate in some way that she acknowledged they were together on some level, but she remained silent. Disappointment flooded through him. Then she brushed her fingers over his arm, leaving a trail of gooseflesh in her wake. A part of him realized her touch was no different than what she'd given everyone else, but elation from that momentary contact washed the disappointment away. He breathed deeply, filling his lungs with the smell of her before she moved on.

By the time she made her way to the stairs with her points behind her, the weariness of the day caught up with him. He wanted nothing more than his bed, not caring that he shared it with two men instead of one woman.

When he woke the next morning, Rice announced that they would spend the day helping to roof the nearly finished home the colonists had built.

"Not that I don't mind the useful exercise, but shouldn't we be getting back to the Maxim?" he asked Rice as they walked to the construction site.

The Colonel raised his brows. "The commander would let us know if we were needed. Between you and me, I think we are needed more here right now." He shrugged. "Talk to your girlfriend."

"That's not funny."

"Never said I was a comedian." Rice handed Logan the hammer the colonist in charge of the site had passed to him. "Hanson had asked me to get a few samples before we returned. I'll join you here in a bit."

"How am I supposed to talk to her if I'm stuck up there all day?" Logan pointed to the half-finished trusses two stories above him.

"Anika doesn't seem big on talking. I'm keeping you from getting zapped. Think of it as a favor." He headed off toward the plain where Hanson's crew had been two days before. South detached himself from the roofing crew and followed Rice.

So that was how it was. Anika wasn't offering her men to be helpful. They were keeping an eye on everyone. He glanced at West, who was now scaling the ladder to join the others in placing the next truss. If he left would he be followed too, or would West remain with the workers, watching them?

Logan dodged away to avoid getting rammed with a long board that two others were wrangling into place alongside the next truss where it was being built on the field. West appeared occupied with the work above.

"I'll be back," he said to the nearest worker.

He moved quickly, hoping to stay out of sight behind the other buildings until he could locate Anika. It didn't take long. She had a crowd of children and parents surrounding her. As he crept closer, he could hear their pleas for Anika to examine their children and themselves. Word of her healing of the three afflicted children had spread fast.

North stood by her side, peering through the crowd as more of the colonists gathered. East was nowhere to be seen. Anika appeared as she had the night before, softly glowing, only a bit larger than Jane, just enough to set her apart. She wore one of the long cowled overcoats, the extra cloth elegantly draped over her shoulders. By her narrowed lips and eyes, Logan estimated she'd be pitching a god fit suitable to scatter the encroaching colonists in short order.

Using his formidable size to his advantage, Logan plowed through the swarm, jostling people out of his way with little regard in favor of saving them from Anika's temper. North met him before he made it to his goal.

"Why are you not with Rice and the others?"

"We need to get her out of here before she goes nuclear."

"We have the situation under control. Why are you-"

Two men began to shout, demanding the first place in line. Fists flew seconds later. A woman with a small child in her arms shoved a teen-aged girl aside, knocking her into another woman. Children began to cry. The fight between the two men cleared a space as they rolled on the ground, grappling with one another.

"Enough," roared Anika.

To his surprise, she didn't shoot up to tower over them or flash to a being of light. But she looked utterly pissed.

The crowd slowed but didn't cease their brawling.

"Still have this under control?" he asked North.

North shot him a look that mirrored Anika's. "Get her back to the inn. I'll disperse the crowd."

"Where's East?"

"Sleeping. Now go." North nodded toward Anika

before charging into the mass of angry bodies.

Logan approached Anika, grabbing her arm as he came to her side. "You need to get out of here until they calm down."

She turned her irate gaze toward his hand on her arm. "What are you doing?"

"Getting you out of here. Whatever you'd planned to do out here today, it isn't happening." He tugged at her until she put one foot in front of the other and allowed him to drag her along.

Behind them, North yelled at the colonists to go home. Logan tried to hurry her onward before the mob gathered the wherewithal to follow them.

"Can you wake East from here?"

"I already did."

"Send him out to help North."

"He's already on his way." She dug her feet in. "I don't need your help. I've been doing this for thousands of years."

"You intended to gather an angry mob?"

She ripped her arm from his grip. "If my other half hadn't done her mission of mercy routine, I wouldn't be in this mess."

"She wanted to be gone before word spread. If you hadn't wanted to stay, you wouldn't be in this mess either."

Her hand shot up as if to strike him. It halted inches from his face, then returned to her side as a clenched fist. "Damn her and her promises."

He put some space between them, taking halting steps toward the inn and praying she would follow. East shot passed both of them, racing to help North.

"I need to go back," Anika said.

He spun around. "Look, you said you wanted to stay in case Matouk sent more ships. They haven't. We need to get back to the Maxim. They may need you and Rice to take on the other ship."

Anika shook her head. "The other ship left shortly after we decided to remain here. I wouldn't allow the Maxim to be harmed."

"Then why the hell are we here? You said it was to protect the colony from another attack."

Anika grabbed him as if he were no more than a small child, hauling him into the shadow cast from the inn and the next building. She thrust him against the wall and backed up several steps, taking the pleasing hum of her presence away.

"My other half is weak," she hissed. "She didn't use to be, but something in her is broken. Maybe it was killing our father, dooming our offspring to live with no Unlata Kai to guide them, or she is just tired of it all, I don't know." Anika shook her head, letting out a growl that made him cringe. "She's always been too damn retentive, caught up in her own rules, but now she's made promises but took no action to feed our well. She left us empty."

"Fixing the ship, you mean? I told her to rest more."

"Rest?" Anika laughed. "Food and sleep will only do so much. She needed to gather followers and feed. I can't defeat Matouk with an empty well, not with the massive size of his following."

Dread flooded through Logan. "That's what you're doing here. Jane said-"

"My other half said too much."

She closed her eyes for a long moment and then opened them again, exhaling deeply. "What is it about you? We took you into our confidence, our bed, kept you close."

Anika licked her lips. "We've never done that before. I need to know, to feel..."

She drew closer, enveloping him with her smell and the hum that sent his senses reeling. Her hands trailed down his cheeks, his neck, resting on his chest. He wanted nothing more than to melt into her. And then her lips pressed against his. Jane's lips, moving hungrily, pleading and demanding, both powerful and sweet.

The most intense climax he'd ever felt rushed through his body, paralyzing every muscle with pleasure. Lost in the sensation, he barely noticed the blackness rushing in around the edges. The connection holding him to his body grew thin. He fought, twisting and shoving, but even as he desperately tried to pry himself away, the tenuous link to his flesh snapped. It was too late to fight her. He was already dead.

CHAPTER THIRTEEN

Jane shrieked deep inside Anika, beating with her fists, her teeth and nails tearing at the veil. The rush of incoming power from Logan overwhelmed Anika, giving Jane her chance to break free of the bindings she'd donned to protect Ivium.

While Anika was stunned, Jane shoved her back into the veil, imprisoning her as she'd been bound only moments before. Already the wrath of the elders weighed heavy upon her. If she couldn't repair the damage Anika had wrought when she'd broken her vow, their power would be revoked forever. Without her power, she'd never defeat Matouk. Even Anika had been on board with that plan.

What had she been thinking, draining Logan dry? Whether she was still dazed or ashamed of what she'd done, Anika remained silent on the matter.

Jane came into her body like a sleeper waking from a long night of tossing and turning on a bed of nails. Logan lay at her feet, his face serene, eyes vacant.

She dropped down beside him, her insides quaking. She didn't break vows, especially not this one. With him.

Bringing a person back from the dead wasn't as simple as healing. Though Anika had begun to fill their well, this would require everything she had and more.

Everything they'd gained for nothing.

The elders were normally so distant they required intense meditation to reach. Not that she'd bothered in centuries. They'd been silent to her since she'd damned herself in her father's name. Now they flooded into her mind against her will, chanting, building up the incantation that would strip the Unlata Kai essence from her being.

"Leave me alone."

She tried to shove them back into the beyond. They bore down harder, their words louder, slamming into her mind from all angles, making it near impossible to think. There was only one way to stop them.

Jane reached out to her points, drawing them to her. In the meantime, she gently took Logan's head into her lap and with her forehead resting on his cooling skin, she cast a net to capture his essence.

It hadn't gone far and it wasn't happy. The ball of hostility burned red. Orange and blue sparks fell on her as she took hold of it. The scent of burning flesh filled her nose. She tried to tell herself that the pain wasn't real, that it only existed outside her physical form, but in truth, she wasn't sure. The tears flowing down her cheeks felt real enough.

Already the energy Anika had gained from the colonists and Logan ebbed with the effort to reunite his inner being with his physical form. The two parts fought her efforts, their separation so abrupt that they didn't acknowledge the other as a separate piece of the whole. Her flesh sizzled, the stench making her gag.

East arrived first with North close behind. She drew from them as much energy as she dared, leaving them only conscious enough to return to their room. With the added strength from the two points, she painstakingly wove Logan back together.

"It's not enough." A voice she recognized with a sob as Antoni's informed her.

"I know." But knowing didn't make the process easier. If anything, the dread rose higher in her throat.

Her father's impatient voice bore down on her. "Then do what must be done."

They were all there, her family, waiting for her to fail so they could enact their revenge. Looking at the still man on her lap, his pulse faint, she considered that their revenge might be right here. Her hands were indeed blackened and her tears real. So had been his anger.

With a sigh that encompassed all the air in her lungs fleeing her doomed body, she released her hold on communications with the Maxim and silently conveyed her orders to North and West who were closing in. Rice was with them. Her points, she could face, but not him. He would accuse her of harming Logan. And she had.

She pulled up the hood of her coat and hid her hands in her sleeves. With no other recourse, Jane pumped everything Anika had taken, every reserve she herself had, into Logan to reignite the spark in his body and return him to the full state he'd been in when Anika had drained him.

Taking energy was far easier than returning it, like paying interest a hundredfold. Second by second, her power ebbed. As if all fluids were being drained from her body, she became brittle, ready to shatter with even the whisper of contact.

"Anika, get away from him," yelled Rice, bearing down on her.

Her voice was as raw as the rest of her, "Jane."

Logan's eyes fluttered, then opened. He sat up. "What happened?"

Within the deep shadows of her hood, Jane felt her lips crack as she smiled. He was again whole and well, the damage undone. The pressure in her head eased as the elders took their leave.

North and West took her arms, pulling her to her feet. Rice helped Logan up.

"I'm fine." He waved Rice off.

"She zapped you, didn't she? I told you she would. I put you on that work detail for a reason."

"She didn't zap me."

Jane, somewhat outside herself, let North and West do the job of transporting her into the inn. She was heartened to hear that he was defending her rather than hating her as he should. Maybe the transfer had knocked enough of what had really happened from his memory. Maybe there was a chance she could fix this.

While the elders had faded once she'd completed the drain, her father's laughter echoed in her mind. Logan might not remember now, but he would.

There couldn't be any future for them anyway. She'd had her fun with him, more than she'd allowed herself with any other. Now it was time to let the General get to work. After Matouk was defeated, she would go to her own beyond. Alone.

In order to do anything, she'd need to recharge. If she wasn't willing to feed from anyone other than her points, it was going to take a good long while. A long while that she'd be trapped on the Maxim with Logan and Rice.

Jane did the only thing she could think of to make that time more tolerable, after making sure Anika was contained, she stepped outside her body. Entrusting care of her physical form to her points, Jane let her body fall comatose. She hoped the Maxim kept them all safe until she was fit to live again.

CHAPTER FOURTEEN

Logan stood outside the door of the room Anika had claimed in the inn. He faced South with Rice at his back. "I need to see her."

"She said no one gets in." South stared him down, or up, more accurately as he stood several inches shorter. "Please summon the shuttle. We must return to the Maxim."

"But what about protecting the colony?" Rice asked.

Logan rubbed the sore spot on his forehead. It sure felt like he'd been burned, but Rice was adamant there was nothing there. He'd been talking to Anika. She'd kissed him. Or had that been Jane? Their conversation suddenly clarified in his mind.

"The other ship left days ago. She lied."

"What?"

"She was feeding from the colony. That's why she wanted to stay."

South pressed his back against the door, his face resolute. "She had to. She was near empty."

Rice shook his head. "What the hell are you two talking about?"

"That spectacle when Jane killed the king, shielding us on Kaldara, healing the ship, they all drained her." Logan held South in his gaze, daring him to disagree.

South gave him a single nod.

"Jane wouldn't feed from us, but Anika would, especially here, away from the Maxim."

Again, a nod.

The rest of what had transpired flooded back to him. "She killed me."

The hallway was too narrow. Rice too close. South in his way. She'd kissed him and took everything. And god or not, she was going to answer for it. Logan shoved South aside and pounded on the door, the wood reverberating under his fist.

"Anika, get out here."

"Wait," said Rice. "She killed you?"

South held up a hand. "She can't hear you. Please, just get the shuttle."

"She's not getting on the Maxim." Logan jabbed his finger into South's chest. "Neither are you. You're all a part of her, aren't you? Contaminated."

"You don't look dead."

Logan spun to face Rice. "I can't explain what happened. One minute I was dead, and then I was back, but I know what she did, what she can do to any of us."

"She promised not to harm me," said Rice uncertainly.

"Yeah, I got the same promise. Maybe she doesn't see murder as harming anyone. Maybe her promises don't mean a damned thing. Do you really want to put her back on the Maxim and find out?"

South inserted himself between them. "Please, she needs to be back aboard the ship. She wishes to remain in orbit until she recovers so that you may protect the colony."

"You said Matouk's men left," said Rice.

South nodded. "When he learns this colony was

able to destroy his ships, he will send more to learn how and to take whatever that might be for his own. You do not wish to have Jane in the hands of Matouk to be used against you."

"While that's true," said Rice, "I agree with Logan. We can't allow her aboard the Maxim. At least not until she explains herself."

South bowed his head. "It will be some time before she is able to do so. If she stays, they will take her. She is not in a state to defend herself."

"She looked just fine to me. She can start explaining right now." With South confronting Rice, Logan barreled his way through to the door and opened it. Two steps inside, he stopped dead.

Three still forms lay face up on the bed with not an inch to spare. North and East shored up the edges with Anika between them. The chests of the two men barely moved. Pale and worn, they had nothing on what was wedged between them. The glorious glowing woman he'd confronted outside had vanished. Wearing the same clothes was a sunken thing with near translucent skin. What he could see of her face and neck was skeletal, as if she'd been starved. The lips he'd so recently enjoyed were flaking, cracked and bleeding. The hands crossed upon her chest were charred black, marring the white coat with blood and seeping fluids. Someone, likely South, had taken care to pull the sleeves and hood up as far as they would go, but too much still showed.

Behind him, Rice gasped. "What the hell?"

"I don't know. She was fine."

"That's not fine. Are you poisonous?" asked Rice.

South beckoned them back out into the hallway. Logan couldn't get out of the room fast enough.

"Explain."

The young man shook his head. "I don't know. I was with him when she called." He nodded toward Rice. "She was terribly out of sorts, not making much sense. The one thing I know for certain is this is Jane and she needs to be on the-"

"Maxim. Yes, I got that," said Rice. "She wasn't in that bad of shape when she took out the King, but she healed in a matter of days. How long do you think this will take?"

South's fingers twisted together. "To be honest, I don't know. She's not responding. It's like she shut herself off."

Rice's brows rose. "I wasn't aware gods came with an off switch."

"I'm glad she does." Logan crossed his arms over his chest. At least she'd taken him out blissfully, but that didn't erase the fact that she'd done it.

Whatever had happened to her looked like payback just short of finishing her off. Doing so might be a favor.

He left Rice talking to South and headed down to the dining room. The cook was busy preparing the midday meal, the air thick with the smell of rising bread and baking fruit. He sat in one of the wooden chairs, trying to erase the stench of the room upstairs and what he'd seen inside it.

Rice came down a short time later and sat next to him. He picked at dirt under his fingernails. "South thinks it's safe to move her."

"Safe for us or moving won't harm her further?"

"Both. If she's shut down, she can't feed, or whatever it was Anika did to you, can she?"

"I'm no expert on how she works." He stood and walked to the door.

Had she been Jane or Anika when she'd done him

in? Did it matter? They were the same person. She'd sure felt like the same person.

"Can we keep whatever happened between the two of you quiet? If Tate finds out, we'll never get her back on board."

"So let's not take her back." Logan reached for the door.

"You want her on Matouk's side? We know what she's capable of. We need her."

"I don't want her near my side. Do what you want." He walked out into the afternoon sun. Children played in the square, their shouts and laughter easing the tension in his neck a fraction. He made his way through them, heading toward the job he'd deserted.

"Excuse me," said a young voice.

He turned to see Caroline, the girl Jane had healed. She sat on a bench near where the others were playing.

"You're with her, Anika?"

Logan shrugged.

"Will she come back? The others said they'd angered her, that she would leave us."

"You're better. What does it matter?"

"She's helped us. Protected us. Did you see it? When she made the ships crash with words?"

"I did."

Her eyes grew wide. "You won't let her leave us, will you? We need her."

The colony had been thriving before they'd arrived. Sure they'd helped. She'd helped. He couldn't argue that point, but they'd get by just like they had before.

"You don't need her. You'll be fine." Logan continued on his way.

Maybe he could stay. If Rice took Jane back aboard, he'd be bound to run into her. While he didn't hold his chances against her very high, it would still get ugly and that was something he strove to avoid.

He could stay at the inn until he could build his own house, maybe get to know the young woman who'd brought him lunch the day before. She'd certainly appeared interested. Of course, she didn't know him. Brin had looked the same way, as had others before he'd left Hijn. Yet, he was still wandering on his own. The only one who admitted to finding him charming was a god who had killed him.

Being on his own wasn't so bad.

Rice owed him a healthy salary. He could make a good living here doing...something. Logan surveyed the colony with its array of shops, homes, the inn, and farms. It wasn't that different than what he'd come from, just smaller. Much smaller.

While farming wasn't his thing, and he couldn't see himself holding down a shop, he didn't mind digging, chopping or building. They would have need of a strong back. He could do that at least.

Logan kicked at a rock as he walked. There wasn't anyone like Rice here, no one that would understand what he'd come from and why he needed his space. They'd either be scared of him or annoyed with him in no time flat.

Hours slipped by as he traversed the trail around the colony, venturing out along the way to see if anything here called to him. The trees rustled with a sudden wind.

A shuttle flew overhead. One of theirs.

Deciding he'd better go see Rice one way or the other, Logan headed back to the inn. By the time he arrived, Brin and Nana had gathered in the main room. Rice was filling them in on Jane's situation when he caught sight of Logan. A frown settled on his face.

"The answer is no."

"You didn't even hear the question."

"I didn't need to. Sit."

Logan dropped into the chair with such force that he was belatedly grateful that it didn't bust into bits. He didn't normally let his temper get the best of him, but Rice cutting him off was the last straw. He glared at the colonel during the remainder of the short briefing, but the man had the audacity to ignore him until the very end.

"Logan, please take Rhodes up to see Jane so she can assess the best way to transport her."

"No."

Seeing Jane again, especially like that, wasn't something he wanted to do. It was right up there on his list with visiting his ruined homeworld or walking the battlefields on which he'd fought and lost friends. Things he wanted firmly in his past so he could face another day without being the person he was just then. Some people might like losing control, giving themselves over to instinct or emotion to do what they would, but he wasn't one of them. He remained firmly in his chair.

Rice scowled. "Then find South or West and have them do it."

That, he could do. One of them had to be standing guard at the door. Logan motioned for Brin to follow him up the stairs. With her case in her hands, Brin walked up the steps behind him.

"What's up with you and Colonel Rice?"

"Nothing."

In his mind he could see her purse her lips, raising an arched brow, staring at his back as the smirk formed. He'd seen it enough times to know what her short pause looked like without turning around.

"Jane then."

The note of victory in her voice inched him closer to losing control.

"What did you do?"

"It wasn't me."

She snickered. "Men always think it isn't them, but honey, it usually is."

His fingers itched to wrap around her throat, anyone's throat for that matter, to make them pay for what Jane had done to him. To make them understand how it felt to be helpless and shown no mercy from someone they thought cared about them.

West was suddenly at his side, laying a firm hand on Logan's shoulder. "I'll take her in."

"You do that." He shook off the man's hand and headed for the room where he'd been staying.

Brin's cry of alarm halted his escape. A loud thud followed. He dashed into Jane's room expecting to see Jane attacking Brin.

Instead, Brin stood at the foot of the bed with her hands over her mouth. The case lay at her feet, open where she'd dropped it. Supplies spilled onto the floor.

Brin shook her head. "She can't still be alive."

"You tell *her* that."

After a gulp and a deep breath, Brin seemed to recover her training. "What happened?"

"She killed me. That's what happened. But I can see how that was my fault."

Brin tore her gaze from her patient, her eyes going even wider. She backed up two steps until she found herself against West. That didn't seem to calm her any. She inched away from him and gauged the distance to the door, but then glanced back at Jane. Brin returned her focus to Logan as if seeing him for the first time.

Her voice shook. "What did you do to her?"

He willed his feet to remain in place, though his fists begged to lash out at the injustice of it all. "Why do you think it was me? I was dead."

"You made an amazing recovery."

"I don't know how it happened. She looked like this when I came back to." He did his best to not see Jane, but the stench of burned flesh grabbed him and walked him right into memories of the battlefield, of Matouk's army taking down men all around him with fire from above. Smoke rose from their scorched bodies. The wet grass tickled his cheek where he lay staring up at the sky, realizing he was alive. Then his injuries registered. Pain rushed up his legs and his left side.

Logan stumbled against the wall as he fought to escape his mind. The wall was solid, the metal door handle cold in his grasp. With each blink, the past faded.

"I have to go." He didn't know where, but he couldn't stay in this room.

He made his way back down the stairs, past Rice and Nana who gave him odd looks as he passed, and out the door. His rubbery legs, still half-convinced they bore bullets, brought him as far as the edge of the garden that supplied the inn's kitchen. Logan lowered himself onto the ground and rubbed his hands over his face. The scent of familiar herbs beside him helped clear his head. He hadn't had a flashback like that since he'd met Jane. The sudden onset now made him feel ill all over again.

Rice found him there before he managed to get his feet back under him. "You all right?"

"What do you think?" Logan snapped.

The Colonel held out a hand to help him up. "I think you'd be miserable here. From the looks of Jane, you'll have a long time to cool down before deciding whether things can be worked out between you." He held up his hand. "Or not. But she's our only hope of defense against Matouk. The commander said the other ship left. The Maxim never fired a shot. You know as well as I do that more ships will be coming, if not Matouk himself. We can't leave Ivium defenseless."

"I'll be on the damned shuttle."

Rice nodded and headed back to the inn.

CHAPTER FIFTEEN

The voices tormented Jane endlessly. Some of them she recognized, her father, her mother's mocking laughter, Antoni, her brothers. Others she did not, but they threw the same words at her, telling her she'd broken her promise, that she didn't deserve to remain one of them. Farther away, on a more distant layer were softer voices, but no less cruel, seeking only to use her, saying that she was too dangerous to remain with them. Perhaps not cruel, she admitted, but boldly speaking the truth.

She'd always kept her two halves divided, under strict control. This was exactly why. If she gave herself over to Anika, she'd be no better than the others that she'd destroyed. It was only now, with Anika utterly silent that she realized how much of her attention had been devoted to maintaining that separation. Thankful for relief on that front, she let her mind wander.

Even though she felt her points near now and then, she had no desire to utilize them. If she remained in this state, she couldn't harm anyone save herself. She drifted in and out of deep sleep, the only thing that dulled the voices to a more tolerable level.

A jolt of energy pulsed through her arm, racing through her organs. Startled, Jane couldn't maintain her neutral state. Bright lights burned her eyes as they shot open. She tried to cover them, but her hands were heavy and immobile.

Doctor Adams loomed over her with a smile. "There you are."

"What..." her dry throat refused to cooperate.

"A little something to jumpstart your system. Not something I'd try with just anyone, but I figured you could handle it."

Adams puttered with the pad in his hand, holding it over her chest then slowly going over the rest of her body. He nodded to himself and made notes.

"Slow but steady progress. You need to get some food in you and some real sleep. Best medicine there is."

She became aware enough of her surroundings to realize she wasn't in the clinic. The lightest touch of her slowly returning senses informed her she was in her room.

Adams offered her a sip from a cup. Water trickled down her parched throat, making her cough. She tried to push him away but again realized her hands wouldn't move.

He stepped back, putting the cup on the table beside the bed. "You did a real number on your hands. Going to be a while before you have use of them again. Unless you can kick your healing powers into gear?"

They'd bound her bandaged hands to the bed. On a distant level that amused her. She could have gotten free in an instant. But right now the effort was too much and she didn't blame them for trying to restrain her, even if they knew it was futile.

"Not today," she said.

"We'll keep at it then." Adams patted her shoulder. "You want those boys of yours? They've been to see you every day."

"Not yet. How many days?"

"Four."

It had seemed like so many more. She sunk into the pillow and closed her eyes.

"Oh no, not yet. You need to eat something first."

The door opened and footsteps came closer. Brin, the medical assistant Logan had brought to observe her, approached with interest.

"Ah, you're awake. I guess that's a good sign."

Adams gave Jane a conspiratorial wink.

"Not really," Jane muttered.

"I see our patient is in fine spirits." Brin rolled her eyes.

The doctor turned to Brin. "Could you help her eat something? Just a little to get her system going?"

Brin nodded, surveying the contents of the container Adams offered her. The doctor headed for the door.

"I'll be back to check on you later. See if you can stay awake until then."

The moment the door closed and they were alone, Brin set the container down. She stepped away from the bed.

"Did you kill Logan?"

Jane stared at the white gauze lumps at the end of her arms. She nodded.

"Why?"

"My other half..." Any excuse she tried fell flat. "Is he all right?"

"For a dead man? Yes." Brin came closer, motioning to Jane's hands. "What happened to you?"

The angry ball of Logan's essence floated in front of her, pulsing and burning. She blinked it away. "I brought him back."

"Well thanks for that, I suppose."

Brin sat on a stool that someone must have brought

in. "They tell me you caused quite a stir planetside."

"I never should have gone there."

Brin held up the cup. Jane nodded. She took a long drink.

"Why did you?"

"Logan's idea."

She snickered. "He's terrible, but with good intentions."

"Not his fault."

"The attack? No, I suppose not." She fed Jane a bland wafer. "Colonel Rice said he had a hard time getting you out of there. The colonists rioted when they learned he was taking you away."

Jane shut her eyes, suddenly too exhausted to finish the second wafer. "Go."

"Sorry, I can't do that. Gotta change your dressings. But before that, we're going to get you cleaned up."

"Leave me alone." Why wouldn't she just go?

"Honey, you've been in bed for four days, not to mention the lack of proper facilities on Ivium. You smell." She stood and pulled the blanket back. "Now we can do this two ways. You and me right here, or I can get one of your men in here to help me get you into the bathroom."

Brin appeared determined to complete her task. The sooner she did, the sooner she'd leave. "Fine. You."

"Feeling antisocial today? Logan rub off on you?"

Jane gave her a glare.

"Alrighty, getting on with it then." Brin went into the bathroom and returned a short time later with everything she needed. She got Jane undressed.

To Jane's dismay, she realized she'd been put back into one of the thin robes from the medical facility, and they hadn't even fastened it, just tucked it in over her. Her arms remained in their restraints.

Brin frowned as she finished washing her. "You're really wasting away. I've seen plague victims who look healthier than you."

"I haven't been feeding."

"I heard about that too."

Brin dried her off, tucked a new robe around her, and covered her with the blanket before starting on Jane's hair.

"How does it work?" asked Brin.

"What?"

"The feeding."

"Can we do this without talking?"

Brin washed and rinsed Jane's hair. "Colonel Rice said it was by touch. He warned me, I should say. I'm not supposed to let you touch me." She snorted. "As if I could keep you from touching me if that's what you wanted to do."

A tiny smile snuck onto Jane's lips.

Brin smiled back. "Do you need to? Feed I mean? I'd love to see how it works."

"You're offering?"

She shrugged. "As long as it's only a light snack. Doctor Adams said you should eat, didn't he?"

"I'm sure that's not what he meant."

"I won't tell if you won't." She towel-dried Jane's hair and then combed it out.

Jane found herself relaxing, the haunting voices of elders faded away. "I can see why he likes you."

"Me?" Brin shook her head. "We had fun flirting for a couple months. However, when we finally connected for a real date, it was all downhill the very next day. It wasn't even just because of the slugs."

Brin toyed with the curls alongside Jane's face, wrapping them around her finger one by one before gently setting them aside. "Trying to have a real conversation... have you tried to talk to him? Of course you have." She laughed lightly. "Maybe he's better at it with you."

"You didn't kill him," Jane said. "I'm sure you could give it another chance."

Brin laughed. "While that's true, I think I'll just stick with trying to be friends. Besides, I'm pretty sure he's sworn us all off now. Colonel Rice said he hasn't left his room since they got back."

"You asked?"

"Well, yes. Just because we didn't hit it off, doesn't mean I hate the guy." She sat back and gave Jane a nod of approval. "Much better."

"He needs friends."

Brin nodded. "He's not very good at making them. Let's get those bandages changed."

Jane did her best to drift into the state of nothingness, but the pain kept bringing her back. Maybe Brin was right. If she did feed, she could begin to heal. But could she trust herself to do it?

"Were you serious about your offer?"

Brin put her supplies away, tucking them neatly into her bag. "Wouldn't have made it if I wasn't."

"I don't want to harm you."

"I'm sure you've done this a million times."

Jane nodded slowly.

"Did something go wrong? With Logan? Is that why you've been starving yourself?"

She couldn't meet Brin's gaze. Wrong didn't cover half of it. While everyone else in her head had spent four days berating her, it was nothing compared to the hollow disdain she had for herself.

"That is it. Isn't it?" Brin chewed her bottom lip. "What if I got one of your men for you to try it with first?"

"It works differently with them."

"But you're not feeding from them either." Her accusing tone was impossible to miss. "If it was an accident, you can't keep punishing yourself."

It wasn't an accident though. She'd lost control. Control over Anika, of her natural urges, of...everything.

"The Maxim needs you. Colonel Rice seems pretty adamant about needing you too."

Not needing. Using. That's what it was. But she *would* need to feed to have a chance against Matouk.

If only she could trust herself.

With Anika still silent and Brin willing, maybe now was the right time to try.

"Just a little then," Jane said, glancing at her bandaged hands.

"Can I touch you? Will that work?"

"Yes, but if you feel at all uncomfortable, let go and get out of here."

"Will I be able to? If Logan couldn't get away..."

"I wasn't myself then."

The lie tasted bitter on her tongue. She took a deep breath, confirming for the umpteenth time that her other half was still under strict quarantine.

Brin settled onto the stool. "Will it hurt?"

"No."

Now that she'd set her mind to feeding, the vacuum of the empty well was immensely painful. She'd shut so many things out, but now they all came careening back full force.

A soft hand rested on her neck, creating a solid place to focus, to get her bearings and rise above the swirling emotions threatening to swallow her. Energy waited right there, calling out.

This felt far too much like Anika. She didn't take

from people. It was a temptation she'd avoided to keep herself isolated from her other half. Others fully embraced their powers. Those callous Unlata Kai drained their followers without a thought, played their games with them, with their worlds. She would never be one of them.

The armies she'd led, the people who had worshiped her, she'd only ever fed from them when necessary, when her points weren't enough. Today, they wouldn't be enough. Her raging conscience eased.

Jane slowly let Brin's energy flow into her, keeping a close watch on their connection in case Anika roared to life. A peaceful smile settled on Brin's lips. Her eyes slipped shut.

"Enough," said Jane.

It wasn't. The small taste had opened up a craving that she hated. Hunger gnawed at her as Brin took her hand away, begging Jane to break free and drain the woman as dry as she still was.

"That's really quite beautiful. It feels so warm and peaceful." Brin yawned. "And apparently it also makes me tired."

"Yes."

"Better?" Brin pushed the stool aside and started to gather up her things.

"It's a small start toward better."

"I probably should have asked before, but are there any lasting repercussions beyond needing rest?"

"You'll likely be back to do it again."

Brin nodded. "I can see how that could be addictive. Is that bad though? Seems sort of symbiotic, we feed you, you help and protect us."

Her innocent words repeated what Anika had been screaming at her for most of her life. Could she never escape them? Were they the truth and her way the lie?

"That's not why I'm here."

Brin picked up her bag. "But that's exactly what's going on, so you might as well accept it and get better."

Just as the door closed behind Brin, alarms went off. The ship shuddered.

Needing to know what was going on, she reached out to her points. East was on his way to the bridge. North entered the room a minute later. The others had been sleeping and were now awaiting orders. She sent West to assist Rice. South made his way to the second level where the weapons were powered.

Before she could convey her need to be free or waste energy doing it herself, North released her from the restraints. He also handed her a stack of clothing.

"Thought you might be needing these."

Her legs shook under her, but she managed to stand while he dressed her. North did his best to not appear ready to catch her should she fall.

"Will it be easier to interface through me or to take from me what you need and do it yourself?"

The ship shook again. She didn't have time to siphon energy. "Take hold of the ship."

With North in reach, her connection with the ship was straightforward but dulled. The information flowing to her revealed a well-armed ship of equal size. The crew of the Maxim was doing what it could to defend against the heavy blows, but the shields were weak. She hadn't gotten to those yet. More importantly, she hadn't repaired any of the damaged weapons.

Knowing she only had the energy of her points to operate with, she didn't waste time. "South and East, find all operational weapons. We need to boost them. West, get me access to the shield."

Through North, she could see her target and

monitor the Maxim. The colonel's men were doing an adequate job of defense with the tools available to them. She worked through her points to give them more.

East conveyed Tate's panic at being attacked. The woman did her best to keep herself together, but she wasn't Rice and the colonel was who was needed right then. However, the woman seemed reluctant to hand over control to him. Even as she was fired upon repeatedly, she continued to try to communicate with the other ship. Their answer came via another volley.

Jane sent her demand for Rice to take control through West, then devoted herself to repairing and boosting weapons and shields as fast as she and the ship could manage. It didn't take long before black spots floated in front of her eyes. Her hold on the connection with the ship and her points slipped through her fingers. Someone took hold of her.

As her awareness came back to herself, Jane found she was sitting on the floor against the wall with North on his knees beside her.

"You need to rest now," he said.

"Have we done enough?"

"Matouk's men are determined to destroy us."

"So, your answer is no." She pressed her bare arms to the wall.

He grabbed them, pulling her away from the smooth surface. "You can give no more and we have no more to give you, not if you wish us to remain aware."

Jane nodded, exhausted. "Our fate is in the hands of Colonel Rice then."

North's body went stiff. "We've been boarded."

"Help me into a chair. I'd rather not meet my end on the floor."

He whisked her up into his arms as if she weighed

nothing. That was likely too accurate for comfort, she considered, looking at her thin arm around his shoulder.

There was only one last line of defense. Anika. Though her well was dry, her other half might be able to eke out enough to drive the intruders from the ship. But to turn Anika loose here, on the Maxim, she shook her head. Logan would be right back at her side whether he wanted it or not. Anika had tasted him and even silent within the veil, her hunger for more was palpable.

She could activate her armor, make them work to get at her, but that wouldn't protect her points or the crew. Sitting by idly while her charges died and losing were not things the General was familiar with. Being on this side of a battle made her vastly uncomfortable.

West entered her room, white-faced and weapon drawn. He closed the door behind him. "They're coming this way. Colonel Rice is doing what he can, but there are too many and he's lost four men."

"East and South?" she asked.

"Still in position as far as I know," said West. "Rice sends his thanks for all you did."

"Not that it helped." She cursed her empty well and Anika.

Footsteps pounded down the hallway outside. They stopped in front of her door. North and East stood valiantly in front of her, armed and waiting.

The door slid open. Brin and seven others piled in. She grinned. "Thought you could use a snack about now."

"What is this?" asked North.

"Some of Hanson's team. They'd be better off asleep anyway. Their big brains aren't much use once the weapons come out." She shoved the men at Jane. "You can control it, right? Like you did with me?"

On empty, Jane wasn't going to make promises.

She settled for a non-committal nod. Accidentally killing one or two to help the rest of the crew might be acceptable losses.

Weapons fired in the hallway. Brin grabbed two hands and thrust them onto Jane's bare arms. With energy right there, Jane didn't hesitate. She siphoned faster than she ever had before. Just as their hands began to lose their grip, she cut the connection. Brin urged two more to step up.

Someone shouted outside. Another blast. Another pair of volunteers stepped in front of her. The beginnings of power allowed her the strength to stand. The spots cleared from her vision. She touched her amulet, encasing herself in golden armor. The panels flowed over her wounded hands, squeezing them tight in their gauze wrappings. Intense pain raced up her arms, enraging her further.

The door opened. Four armed men entered, their foreheads marked with a thick blue line that started just below their hairline and ended between their brows. Just like the men Anika had slaughtered on Ivium after their ships had gone down. Matouk's followers.

"Down, now," Jane commanded in the reverberating voice that emanated from her helmet. Dimly aware of Brin and the others scattering behind her, Jane activated her staff, letting the butt hit the floor with a heavy thud. She hoped it had its usual effect because she couldn't do much more than throw it at someone. She was going to have to be frugal with her actions.

The men faltered, weapons in hand but not firing.

"Men of Matouk?"

One of the intruders nodded.

"You have but one choice. Leave or die."

"We have been charged with acquiring you and this

ship for our god."

Jane settled into the General with ease.
Confrontation was familiar, welcome. As long as she had
a modicum of energy, this she could do. "If he wanted
those things, he should have come himself. Now, mercy
or no?"

"Matouk does not accept failure," said one of them,
looking to the others. "We will fight. This ship will be ours
and our god will be pleased."

"This ship is mine." Jane disengaged the armor to
bare one arm. Her hand throbbed beneath its gauze. She
pressed her arm to the wall and was momentarily stunned
to find Brin's hand overtop it, followed by one from North.

"Whatever you're going to do. Make it good," said
Brin.

Jane left her body in its armor and sped through
the ship, altering and activating security features that her
mother had shown her as a child. Pouring every ounce of
energy the generous volunteers donated into her task, she
created elimination parameters, excluding anyone not
carrying the blue dye marking Matouk's followers.

As she worked, she became dimly aware of weapons
being fired into her armor. Someone screamed. Hoping
the wounded ship properly interpreted her program,
Jane returned to her body to push Brin and the others
fully behind her.

North lay at her feet, blood soaking into his shirt.
In the middle of taking a breath while deciding whether
to expend what little she had left to send a blast at the
intruders or heal North, Logan and two of Rice's men
burst in. They opened fire on Matouk's men.

One of them tried to run, but the floor surged
upward, sealing his feet in place. An oily fluid seeped up
from the floor, melding with his clothing and skin. His

screams were near deafening as the ship dissolved his body before their eyes.

Two of the others were wounded, scrambling away from what remained of their comrade. Logan killed the one remaining with a single blast to the head. Rice's men hauled the wounded to their feet and manhandled them out of the room.

She checked Brin and the others she'd brought. None appeared wounded but all were groggy despite the attack or unconscious. She turned to West.

"Go see to the rest of them. Assist Colonel Rice as needed."

He darted around Logan and left.

Her armor weighed heavy on her frail frame. With Logan nearby and armed, she deactivated it so she could turn her attention to North.

She had just sealed the wound when strong hands shoved her aside. Her face hit the wall.

"How many of them did you kill to power up? You never should have been allowed back on board."

The spots were back, dancing before her eyes. The metallic taste of blood filled her mouth. She licked her split lip and wiped at the warm wetness seeping from her nose.

"We should have let you die."

Jane got to her feet, anger lending her power she didn't otherwise have. "You'd all be dead by now if you had. But in this particular moment, and bearing that in mind, I'm inclined to agree with you."

Heat welled in her hands despite their grievous injuries. Her soul focus on the man who dared strike her.

She'd given everything to bring him back. Anger she could understand. However, despite her promises, she could not abide him striking her. She was damned already. If Matouk wanted these creatures for his own, he could have them. All of them.

Projecting a blast would cost her too much, but she could manually transfer one by touch. She stalked toward him. Logan edged away, matching her steps.

The colonel, with men behind him, ran past the open door. His body filled the doorway a moment later.

"Their ship left. We couldn't stop them," he said. "We're finding men asphyxiated, melded with walls and floors, and a few disgusting piles of slime covered clothes. What the hell is going on?"

Brin, sitting on the floor with her head in her hands and elbows propped on her knees said, "She showed the ship how to fight back."

"None of yours?" asked Jane, undecided if she hoped the answer was yes or no.

"No. All the tattooed sort."

She considered saying *good*, but couldn't quite force it out.

Rice seemed to then notice Logan with his gun still drawn, and the glow emanating from Jane's bandages. "Am I interrupting something?"

"Yes," she said.

Just as Logan said, "No."

He waved his men onward and stepped inside alone. "Brin?"

"Definitely yes. I would recommend removing-"

"I told you not to bring her back here. This," Logan pointed at the men and women scattered on the floor. "is on your head."

Brin stood, holding onto the wall. "She didn't harm anyone. We volunteered."

Several of the others also began to move, calling out to indicate they were tired but fine. Rice looked them over from where he stood.

"Like charging a battery? You use people?"

Jane shrugged.

Rice gave her a once over. "You don't look any better."

She shot him a glare. "I'm not. See them to their rooms."

The volunteers slowly made their way to their feet, some with help from Rice and Logan. One by one they filed out the door like sleepwalkers. Brin lingered, though, after offering her energy twice in such a short time, she appeared as worn as Jane felt.

Rice started to leave but turned back around. "I'd appreciate it if you kept your glow hands to yourself, Jane. With the losses we suffered today, I need Logan more than ever."

The heat had seeped from her hands as her rage faded. The moment was gone, her well again depleted. Empty and cold, she just wanted all of them gone.

"See North to the clinic. I've healed the worst of it, but I can do no more today."

Rice summoned help to transport North, but made no move to leave. "What you did with the Maxim, it won't harm any of us?"

"Not unless you have Matouk's mark."

"I'll make sure everyone avoids tattoos in the immediate future." He nodded toward the door. "Logan?"

Brin planted herself in Logan's way. "She didn't mean to kill you. Look at what bringing you back did to her. Look." She pointed at Jane. "A freaking god brought you back from the dead. And she likes you, though I can't imagine why when you're threatening to shoot her or smashing her face in. You're lucky she was on empty from saving us or you'd be dead again, you simple-minded oversized-ape." She slapped him in the chest. "We both know talking isn't your strong suit, but maybe give it a try before you end up dead for good."

"And you," she whirled around to face Jane. "You're really freaking complicated. Cut the man some slack."

Only after the three of them left did Jane summon the wherewithal to close her gaping mouth.

CHAPTER SIXTEEN

Logan spent the next several days doing Rice's bidding as long as it didn't involve Jane. Her, he avoided completely. Though, he found himself grinning whenever he recalled her stunned face after Brin's little tirade.

He was avoiding her too. In fact, he avoided everyone as much as possible because they all seemed infatuated with Jane after she'd altered the ship, and boosted the weapons and shields, and whatever else they were all buzzing about. He was living in a damned cult of Jane. Even Tate was in on it.

He was doing just fine on his own until Rice roped him into a meeting to discuss the army of Matouk. With a disgusted sigh, he settled into the chair. Tate gave him her usual pinched look, which eased when she again focused on her pet, Hanson. Rather than sit, Rice left the room.

The silence had stretched out to the point where he also considered leaving when Rice suddenly returned. Jane entered behind him, wearing her coat with the cowl hood covering her head. Once inside, she pushed it back, likely so she had a clear view of everyone in such close quarters. From what he'd heard, she hadn't been seen without it since their return from Ivium, which only added to her mystery with the crew.

Jane appeared just as excited to see Logan as he was

her. Her skeletal face offering little in the way of softening her blatant annoyance. Though she took the only empty seat across from him, she managed to continue to avoid him by keeping her gaze locked on Tate and Rice, who sat beside the Commander.

Tate cleared her throat. "You're probably wondering why I asked both of you to be here today."

Neither of them broke from their forward stares.

"While this ship seems large in comparison to our present crew, it's not large enough to encompass the tension that follows the two of you around. One of you," she gave Logan a pointed look, "at a time we can deal with. But with two of you, well, you're causing undue stress."

"What we propose," Hanson started to say.

Tate gave him a glare so harsh that, without further thought, Logan glanced at Rice and Jane to see if they'd picked up on the same thing. Jane met him with a raised brow, while Rice ran a hand over his face and took a deep breath.

"Maybe this would be better if you left the room?" Rice suggested, giving Hanson a pointed look.

"He will not," said Tate. She smoothed her shirt until her nostrils ceased to flare. "What I mean to say is, we need both of you. Logan, the colonel finds your services necessary."

"I said *invaluable*, especially now, in light of our losses."

"Right, yes." She looked to Jane. "And your knowledge of the Maxim has been quite beneficial."

"Beneficial," Jane said flatly.

"Yes, quite." Tate nodded.

Jane placed her bandaged hands on the table. "What you mean to say is that you can't currently afford to drop either of us on Ivium or elsewhere."

The commander tried not to pay attention to the bright white bandages, but couldn't seem to help herself. Hanson stared at Jane, fascination plain on his face.

Jane said, "And so you also can't seem to allow two adults their prerogative to ignore one another for the benefit of their wellbeing."

"It's not that. Exactly," said Rice.

Logan sighed. "Then what is it?"

"Brin has enlisted the majority of the crew to feed Jane. That's all well and good-"

"It isn't well or good," muttered Logan. How could the colonel even consider that it might be?

Hanson leaned back in his chair, looking pleased with himself. "And there's our problem."

"What the hell does that mean?" Not for the first time, Logan considered wiping Hanson's smug smile off with a fist.

Hanson held out an empty hand toward Jane. "We need Jane fed so she can continue to repair and work with the Maxim. The agreement is that any crewmember, at the end of their shift, may seek her out, offer what they have left, and then happily go off to bed. No one is suffering. In fact, most everyone is reporting they've never slept better."

Logan's gut clenched. The sensation of losing touch with his body overcame him.

Tate quelled Hanson's enthusiasm with another glare. "The issue is that we need everyone on board with this plan. The better off Jane is, the more work she can accomplish and the more prepared she will be when Matouk's men show up again."

He gripped the edge of the table. "What does this have to do with me?"

"It seems there is talk of Jane harming you when feeding. It's making some of the crew nervous."

"Harming? She killed me!"

Tate looked dubious. "You don't look dead."

Jane slammed a fist onto the table, startling everyone, including herself according to her pained gasp. She cradled her hand against her amulet.

For all the talk of her feeding, she was as gaunt as when she'd brought him back. She may have been healing the ship, but she wasn't sparing any energy for herself. In fact, as he stole another glance at her while she was focused on Tate, she may have been offering the crew a pleasant night's rest, but hadn't been doing much of that either. Had she always had such little regard for herself or was this something new since leaving Kaldara? She'd certainly seemed in top form there.

"That's because I brought him back," said Jane. "That doesn't erase what happened, and it could happen again if I'm not myself."

She stood and shoved her chair at the table. He braced for action, wondering if she was considering throwing it. She'd gone after Tate before.

Rice spoke calmly. "How do we help you to remain yourself?"

"Don't put me in a position that requires me to channel more energy than I currently am, like forming a shield big enough to protect a colony or destroying ships."

The twisting in his gut grew worse. He'd done that. Not on purpose, but if he hadn't taken her there...

Tate swallowed loudly. "But what about when we're attacked again? You didn't change the last time."

"I didn't have enough energy then. Thanks to your crew, I could pull it off if I had to now, but as you can see," she gestured at her still emaciated figure, "I'm still quite low. If you can get the rest of your crew involved, it would help me do more, faster. It would also mean I'd have more of a chance of slipping into my other self if necessity arises." She gave Rice a calculating look. "It's what I believe you would call a crap shoot."

"I see," Rice said.

"So," said Hanson, "as long as you're as you are now, yourself, I mean, you can't harm anyone while feeding?"

Jane gave him a withering glare. "I can harm you regardless. The difference is I have more control over whether I want to or not."

Hanson dropped back into silence, gaze glued to the tabletop.

Rice turned to Logan. "She's our best weapon against Matouk. If you could assist in keeping her armed and ready, it would greatly benefit us all."

Logan hated when Rice took on that calm, logical tone. Any attempt to argue with it made him look like an ass. And he had to admit, Jane had been integral in ending the last attack. He conceded with an almost imperceptible nod.

That was enough for Rice. "Good. Then you two are dismissed. The rest of us have other matters to discuss."

He didn't sound too thrilled about whatever else was on the agenda, but Logan gratefully took his leave of the room. Jane remained several steps behind him.

He turned to walk backward. "So..."

Deep within her hood, she answered, "Let's just go somewhere and be seen together and get this over with. I have work to do."

"Hungry?"

She shrugged but followed. They made their way to the dining room and filled their plates.

"So, Hanson and Tate?"

Jane snorted. "It would seem so."

"He's half her age."

"Really?" She pushed the hood back enough that her face was at the forefront. "That's your issue? How vast do you think our age gap is?"

"I...anyway, how about here?" Logan took a spot at an open table.

Rather than sit across from him, Jane placed herself next to him. He was about to tell her to move when he realized that they looked more intimate this way and yet didn't have to actually look at one another. He ate slowly, his stomach still in knots. She picked at her fruit.

"Do you even need to eat that?"

"It helps. I can live off energy alone if I have plenty of it, but it takes more than you'd think to keep a body functioning properly. Maintaining myself the natural way is simpler."

The memory of her blackened hands haunted him. The skin above the bandages was still pink and raw. The bandages were more compact than they'd been the last time he'd seen her, allowing her some mobility with her fingers, but her movements were stiff and awkward.

"What did happen to your hands?"

She went still. The sounds of the other crewmembers eating nearby were too loud, utensils scraping at plates, chairs creaking. Why wasn't anyone else talking all of a sudden? They were watching him. He could feel it, the skin between his shoulder blades crawling.

He shouldn't have asked. He tried to think of a way to take the words back, to cover them up somehow, to make everyone go back to whatever the hell it was they were doing and avoid him like normal.

She must have felt it too. "Not here."

He nodded. She rested the object of his awkward question on his arm and launched into a stilted report of what repairs she'd been working on. He hoped it sounded more natural to anyone else listening.

Logan tried not to think about the fact she was touching him, just like he'd seen her do when she worked the room at the inn, feeding. She'd been feeding. Like she'd been doing with half the crew here. Was she doing it now? To him?

Jane's report came to an abrupt end. Her hand slid off his arm and into her lap. She stared at her mostly untouched dinner. "Sorry. I thought it would look... I shouldn't have touched..."

She got up, taking her plate with her, and dumped the contents in the garbage. The distinct absence of other conversation and the shifting of chairs told him they were still under observation. Was it is imagination or could he really hear their heads swiveling?

He took a deep breath and disposed of his plate. It didn't take more than a few steps to catch up to her.

"What are you doing?" she asked. "Haven't we given them enough?"

"You still owe me answers."

"I suppose that's true. Where would you like to hear them?"

If the crew needed reassurance, he supposed he might as well go all in so they could both get this over with and go their separate ways with Rice's blessing. Curious stares accompanied their walk as he led her to his room.

Logan went inside. She stopped in the doorway. "Are you sure you want to do this here?"

"You wanted privacy. I want everyone off my ass. This seems like the best solution."

She walked in slowly, looking around. There wasn't much to see. The furnishings were the same as her room, his belongings few. Other than the shirt he'd worn yesterday, tossed over one of the chairs, the rumpled mess of blankets on the bed, and the absence of a layer of dust, it could have been one of the deserted rooms.

Tossing the shirt toward the bed, he waved her to the other chair.

"You haven't exactly settled in here, have you?"

She pushed the hood off her head, settling the folds on her shoulders as best as she could with her bandaged fingers. He wasn't sure if he should be relieved she still felt at ease enough with him to reveal herself when she remained covered to everyone else, or if she was readying herself to launch into a tirade that would end with a bolt of light to his chest.

"Just helping out for now. Saving up."

Her hands crossed over one another on her lap, not touching the ship or him. Could she work with the ship through the bandages? He tried to recall what exactly she'd been doing when he'd burst into her room to find Brin and the others on the floor around her.

"Saving for what?" she asked.

"That's not important. What happened-"

Her forehead wrinkled. "How can your future not be important? You must have plans for your life."

"Says the one who had plans to end hers."

She smiled softly. "You rather disrupted that plan."

"And I find myself regretting it."

Her smile faded and her gaze dropped to her lap. "You had questions?"

"What the hell happened? One minute we were kissing and then..."

"Not *we*. Anika." Jane sighed and seemed to shrink into the chair. "She's never done that before, only experienced it through me. Relationships never interested her. We're more the blow-them-up and destroy-them-all kind of god, you know?"

"So why now?"

"She wanted to see why you were different, why I hadn't moved on like usual."

Still angry but also curious, he let her continue to evade the actual question. "And?"

"And she wanted all of you so she took it."

"And you don't?"

Jane rubbed her hands over her face, dragging her thick bandaged fingers through her hair and making an utter mess of it. "Certainly not like that."

"But you're the same person. Two halves, right?"

Her gaze darted around the room. At first he thought she was calculating the fastest route to the door, or maybe searching for something to use as a weapon. Then he realized it was more of a cornered animal behavior. Deciding his own nerves could use a little fortifying, he got up and went to the cabinet in the small kitchen space. It held exactly one half-full bottle of liquor and two glasses from one of Rice's visits.

"Drink?"

Relief washed over her face. "Yes."

He poured a bit in each glass and brought the bottle back with him. Logan allowed her a sip before giving her an expectant glare.

"You ever know anyone who turns violent after drinking too much?"

"Sure."

"It's like that. The outside half, me, talking to you now, is that person sober. When I let Anika take control, the inside half that resides closest to the power well, it's like that drunk with a freshly consumed bottle of potent liquor. Still me, but with caution and any hint of compassion stripped away."

She took a cautious sip. "We share the same body

and mind. We're the same but different."

Logan nodded. "That's a bit of an understatement."

Jane set the glass down and resumed staring at her hands in her lap. "When I saw what was happening, I tried to stop it, but it's difficult to wrestle control from my other half."

"I would imagine so. Did you also see the fights she incited by getting the colonists to follow her? How she fed from us all?" He set his own glass down, perhaps more forcibly than intended as it slammed loudly onto the tabletop, slopping amber liquid onto the surface and him.

She nodded slowly. The liquor had dried to a sticky sheen on Logan's hand before she answered.

The steely tone of the General resurfaced. "Would it have been better to let them all die in the attack?"

"Of course not." For the life of him, he hadn't been able to come up with another course of action that would have saved them all, but it sure seemed like there should have been some way to prevent it. Something he should have done differently.

"When you told me to get you back to the ship, what the hell did you think would happen? How was that supposed to switch you back? Was there something I could have done?"

"No." She sounded deflated again. "I thought I was stronger, that I could have forced her back behind the veil once the need had passed, but we were both so hungry. Our well was nearly dry. The allure of followers, of feeding, it was too much."

"Why didn't you feed here?"

Before he realized her glass was airborne, it shattered against the wall. Liquid ran down the wall and pooled on the floor. Jane leapt from the chair. She started for the door, but then spun around.

"Because that's not why I'm here. That's not what I do. I'm not like them, the other Unlata Kai. I only feed from my points, not from followers. That's why my father trusted me to hold Kaldara for him. I posed no threat to his number of worshipers. When Anika needed to feed, she had my army. We didn't play games like the others, didn't take over colonies, and we didn't drain anyone to the point of death. Ever."

Jane slammed her hand on the panel to open the door and grimaced again, clutching it to her chest.

"So you lost control."

"I was starving!"

By the time the door opened, she'd stormed back over to him. Logan shifted to the edge of his seat, ready for defense.

"You know why I was starving? Healing myself from my father's death blow and this poor ship so it would have a chance to take on Matouk."

"Then maybe you should have done a little more feeding than your points could offer."

"I don't do that," she hissed.

"You *are* doing that."

She let out a fierce growl that made him wince inside. "Not by choice, I assure you. That was all Brin's doing."

He held his ground. "She told me. After the attack."

"Then you know I didn't ask for them to show up and offer themselves."

"But if they hadn't, you wouldn't have been able to alter the ship's defenses?"

She was still nearly spitting answers at him. "Correct."

He began to wonder what one might do to effectively defend one's self against a pissed off god.

The noose of logic had limited her choice in the matter, and even he could understand how frustrating that was. "Let's get back to what happened to your hands."

"You weren't happy about being parted from your physical form."

The smell of her burned flesh rushed back at him. "You're saying I did that?"

"Your essence was angry and fighting back, not understanding I was trying to return you to your body."

"But you did it, returned me?"

"I made you a promise, didn't I?"

"You did, but doesn't that also apply to Anika? I did tell her about your promise, and she still killed me."

"She disregarded it in light of your intoxicating energy. And that nearly doomed all of me." She looked ready to throw something else.

Logan grabbed the bottle and his glass. There was already one mess too many to deal with.

"So it hurt? Returning me?"

"Did it look like it hurt? Like it drained everything I had and then some?"

"Yes."

"Then why are you asking what you already know?"

Because he'd wanted to throw that back in her face, to tell her she deserved it. But now, seeing how livid she was yet still managing to restrain herself, he began to see how that loss of control ate at her.

"What do you mean, doomed both of you?"

"When we make a promise, it's binding. Anika abhors them for obvious reasons. Breaking a promise costs everything. If I wasn't able to bring you back, I would have lost what makes me Unlata Kai."

"And knowing this, your other half still killed me?"

"We haven't been able to discuss it. She's avoided

me since."

Logan drained his glass. "Just my luck to be stuck with a dually suicidal god."

Anger melted from her face, leaving her gaunt and weary. "You are not stuck with me, Logan. You are free to go where you will. Rice does need you, but he would understand if you wish to leave. Your future is wide open."

"He wasn't about to let me stay on Ivium. I doubt he'd be more favorable to the idea the next time I ask."

"Then I will make him let you go."

"Don't."

"You don't wish to go?"

"Like you said, I'm useful here. Anywhere else?" He shrugged.

She took in the mess she'd made on the wall. "I don't suppose you have another glass?"

"Just the two."

Jane went to the other side of the room, bared her arm, and pressed it to the wall. The surface blurred, seeming to spiral and waver. When he could focus on it again, it was clean. So was the floor. The remnants of glass were gone.

"Where does it all go when you do that? Those men, the glass?"

She pulled her arm away and tugged her sleeves down to their full length, allowing only the tips of her bandages to remain visible. "The ship can convert other objects into new ones it needs. Sort of like feeding. It's not a necessary function, but it takes less energy to create something from something than from nothing, if that makes more sense."

"One last question."

She sighed but nodded.

"With the crew feeding you, and I know you've been

well enough to resume repairing the ship, why haven't you healed yourself?"

She walked back to the door and opened it.

"Jane, your father isn't here. You didn't fail. Anika did."

"We're the same person."

Jane bore the scars of her past. She had a terrible temper, but she could also be kind. She wasn't at all perfect and she didn't pretend to be. Anika might appear beautiful but she loved power and being in control of others, reveled in it. She used people for food.

"No, I don't think you are. Heal yourself. We need you."

She pulled the hood back over her head. She gave no indication that she'd heard him. The door closed behind her, leaving him alone.

CHAPTER SEVENTEEN

Jane stood outside her room, as she'd done every shift change since meeting with Tate and Rice. One of Hanson's men sat in the chair she'd pulled out into the hallway. It was more relaxing for the crew to sit while she siphoned their energy. If she was going to make concessions with her own rules, at least she could be considerate about it.

The man she'd come to know as Simon had been one of the volunteers Brin had brought her during the attack. He'd been coming every day since, offering what he had left.

Today she had a line, but she still kept to her routine, asking them about their day while she fed. She touched the back of his neck, his warm skin a comfort beneath her rough hand. Feeding openly, she didn't have to restrain herself to quick touches like Anika had used on Ivium.

Simon's words slowed and his eyes drooped.

"Enough. Thank you, Simon."

He nodded and heaved himself out of the chair, making his way down the hall with a slightly dazed smile on his face. She did what she could to eliminate the addictive rush of the experience, instead giving them the impression of relaxation and letting go. It made the process slower, but she got just as much energy from it and a fraction less guilt.

For the second time, Tate took her place in the chair.

"It wasn't so traumatic as you thought then?" Jane asked under her breath.

"Just get on with it," she said with a smile plastered on her face.

Jane much preferred when Rice came to her chair. His conversation was enjoyable and his energy pleasant to channel. Yet, she saw the logic in only having one of them drained per day, leaving the other alert in case of attack.

"What would you like to talk about?" Not that she wanted to talk to Tate, but it made things appear less like feeding and more like a conversation, especially to those still waiting their turns.

"How about you tell me when the ship will be done so you can stop feeding off my crew?"

Jane slipped her hand under the collar of Tate's uniform and began to draw out the white hot light only she could see. It traveled through her palm, into the veins of her arm, infiltrating her tissues as it flowed upward. The stream gathered in her chest, settling there, funneling into the well that lay deep within the veil in the place where only she and Anika could go. A place not quite within her body, yet part of her.

"The ship has nearly finished re-growing all the missing structures. The weapons and shield are fully operational."

"And how will one ship fair when Matouk himself comes to see why his men failed to capture us or you?"

"Not well. We need an army."

Tate reached into her pocket and came out with an empty hand that she shoved upward toward Jane's face. "Oh look, I'm all out of armies. You got us into this. You damned well better get us out."

The woman had more energy to offer, but Jane had lost what little appetite she had. "We're done here."

Tate craned her head around to glare up at Jane. "I don't feel done."

The next person in line gave her and Tate a curious glance before going back to her conversation with one of Brin's co-workers.

"Then let's skip the talking." She'd rather skip the feeding, but getting Tate in the chair had been a big boost for participation. Causing a scene would only invite trouble for both of them.

"Fine."

Jane pulled enough energy to get Tate to yawn and her eyes to droop. "Feel done now?"

Tate yawned again. She got up and was quickly replaced by a more eager participant.

By the time she'd worked through the last of the volunteers, her well was full. It had taken a week of draining most of the crew daily to get her back to where she'd been before her peaceful end on Kaldara had gone wrong. And she'd hated every minute of it. Despised herself for every drain, felt Anika stirring, laughing at her, calling her weak. Anika assured her that feeding was natural, part of who she was. If she could accept that, the oppressive weight that had settled on her shoulders after her first full-fledged feeding would vanish. All her kind did this. She'd watched them all her life, basking in the energy their followers freely offered, surrounded by blissful faces.

She could barely face the crew anymore. She worked through her points, staying in her room except when it was time to feed.

Even her points knew she wasn't herself. They

constantly asked after her, offering her food, drink, and rest. Neither sustenance, nor their concern, or even the knowledge that she was doing what she had to, erased the filthy feeling that clung to every fiber of her body.

Just as she was about to return to her room, a familiar set of footsteps made her freeze. The smell of alcohol on him reached her before he did.

"Got time for one more?"

"Go away, Logan."

He dropped into her chair, words slurring. "Oh come on now, we've all got to do our part."

"Not you. Go."

"What? I'm not good enough now?"

"I will *not* feed from you."

She tried to pry him out of the chair without hurting him, but he was substantial in size, and quite belligerent in his drunken sense of duty. Giving up in removal as she didn't want to cause him physical harm, she crouched down in front of him.

"You healed yourself." He reached out to stroke her cheek.

"Only because you asked me to." He might have inebriated himself to be in her presence, but he was here, and touching her of his own accord. Hope blossomed deep inside. Could she recover what Anika had ruined?

She considered asking if he had forgiven her, but he was drunk and that brought out brutal honesty in even the best of people. She wasn't ready to have her hope crushed so quickly. And yet, every question that came to mind held the risk of just that.

"Why are you here?"

He laughed. "That's the question we all ask, isn't it?" Then he turned suddenly serious. "I don't suppose, being what you are, you have the answer?"

"I know why I'm here, the Unlata Kai, I mean, but the rest of you? Sorry, no." She risked resting her hand on his where it sat on his knee. "I mean in this chair, with me. Did Rice tell you to come?"

He stared at her hand, blinking slowly, then lifted his gaze to her face. "No."

Hope flared, but she had to be sure. "Someone else then?"

"I don't take orders from anyone else."

"You didn't really want me to feed from you, did you?"

Logan lifted one finger then another under her own, tickling her palm. When he finally stilled, his words came out clearly, each a deliberate effort. "I wanted to see if you would."

"I won't. I prom-"

He put his other hand over her mouth. "You did that before, and I still ended up becoming a tasty snack. Maybe your other half is on to something with her no promise rule."

A heavy lump formed in her throat. He hadn't forgiven her. Tears welled in her eyes, and though she fought to blink them away, several escaped. She took his hand from her mouth, kissing his palm as she did so. "I'm sorry."

Returning his hand to his lap, she stood.

He said, "I'm pretty sure the god of war isn't supposed to cry."

"I'm pretty sure she wasn't supposed to love anyone either." Jane went to the door, needing to get away before more tears escaped. "But maybe that's not who I am anymore."

The moment the door opened, she slipped inside her sanctuary and locked it behind her. Jane slumped down onto the floor, the door pressed against her back, head in her hands. Why had she let him get so close? This pain, the one he inflicted with a word, with a look, was so much worse than what she'd endured before. There was no bandage, no healing chant that could erase the ache.

Maybe she'd been foolish to break her routine for companionship. The General had never wanted for more. Even when days stretched to years and years to centuries on Kaldara, when she'd been bored out of her mind, her parents deep into the oblivion and the city running itself in utter efficiency, she'd not considered taking a man of her own. Here, away from other Unlata Kai, from the life she'd known, with no one to judge her weakness, she'd let him in. Now, even knowing she'd been selfish to want such a thing, she didn't want to let him go.

CHAPTER EIGHTEEN

The loud thump on the other side of the door startled Logan. It hadn't been his imagination or a trick of the lighting. She really had been crying.

He'd made a god cry. That had to be bad luck. It certainly couldn't be good.

"Jane?"

Her muffled voice came directly from the other side of the door. "Go away."

That would be the easiest thing to do, going back to his room. His empty quiet room with the one dirty glass and empty bottle on the table. Since he'd joined the crew, he'd memorized the walls and the shadows the lights made at the edges of the room. He'd stared at the same point on the inside of the door, waiting for some sort of sign of what he was supposed to do with the rest of his life. The only answer he ever got was Rice interrupting his silent prayer with offers to play guard.

He didn't mind the fresh air, the sun on his face, or lugging the heavy crates of equipment for Hanson's team. But for the most part, it was just another form of monotony, and none of it made the memories swirling in his head go quiet.

Only Jane did that.

He tried the panel. It didn't respond. Upon further

inspection, he saw it wasn't lit. "Jane, open the door."

Though he could hear her shifting around inside, the door didn't open.

"Please."

The operation light resumed its steady green glow. He could still walk away. Logan glanced down the hallway, but no one was there to offer an excuse to vacate the area. Heart pounding and throat dry, he opened the door.

Jane stood on the far side of the room, her back to him. She didn't turn around to vent her fury, she didn't move. She didn't say a word. Just what he wanted, to have to talk his way over this chasm gaping between them. He licked his lips waiting for a burst of inspiration, for someone to insert the right thing to say into his head. All he got was a tumble of words and none of them were the ones he wanted. He didn't even know what he wanted to say.

He could hear her breathing, the ventilation system pumping air into the room, the rustle of the legs of his pants as he took a hesitant step forward and then another. Why did everything have to be so damned loud, adding giant flashing lights to the fact he had no idea what to do. He'd hoped the alcohol would inspire him, loosen his tongue. Maybe that had worked a little too well.

Was he supposed to apologize? She had. Several times. But she'd killed him. Was he supposed to just get over that?

"Jane?"

"Would you rather I return to being the General? Maybe Anika?"

The General would have killed Tate after meeting her and would have taken the Maxim on a one way joyride to obliterate Matouk. Anika would have also gone for Matouk. However, she would have stopped to secure the crew to use as her private food stash, and then if she managed to take Matouk down, commandeered his army and set off to claim the universe as her own. He knew where he stood with both of those options. Dead.

"I'd rather you didn't."

"Then you should go before I do it anyway. I find my enjoyment of your company has come to an end."

The brief flash of hope in her eyes when they'd been in the hallway said otherwise. He was sure he hadn't imagined it. Logan stood his ground. "Returning to either Anika or the General would violate your promise."

She spun around, eyes narrowed, amulet slinging over her chest with the momentum. "I could easily set you and Rice Ivium or elsewhere and do as I wish without violating promises."

The numb encouragement he'd gained from drinking fled. He wouldn't put it past her to do just that without any notice or concern for comfort in her method of travel either. "You could, but I'd rather you didn't."

"So you've decided your future?"

Had he? He took a long look at the woman in front of him. Alone, with nothing but the clothes he'd given her, surrounded by people who weren't her kind. This crew wasn't his kind either, but maybe, in some ways, she was. Maybe they could find their way together.

His gut had told him to trust Rice and that had brought him this far. If he wanted more, he was going to have to take a chance and listen to it again.

He hadn't decided anything other than his choice to enter had been a bad one. Going along with her suggestion seemed the wisest choice for his physical safety at the moment.

"Yes," he said, feeling more solid than he had in a long time. "I have."

"I see." One hand settled on her amulet, a finger stroking the edge. "Logan, why are you here in my room?"

"To talk to you."

Jane pointed to the door. "I think you said enough out there."

"I don't think I said the right things out there."

She crossed her arms over her chest and waited, lips drawn into a tight line. "Well then?"

His palms began to sweat and the swirl of words he'd hoped would form into something coherent to convey what he felt vanished into dead air. "I'm not very good at saying the right things."

Her stance loosened and the very corner of her lips quirked. "I see."

"I tried to hate you, but I guess I'm not good at that either."

"Oh, you're plenty good at it."

Now that he wasn't in immediate fear for his safety, he took a moment to notice that her room was amazingly devoid of broken objects, dents, or other telltale signs of her temper. He scrambled for something else to say. "You like the clothes then?"

She ran her hand down the sleeve of the white shirt, her scowl entirely dissolving. "I do."

He'd never been good at this part of a relationship, not with friends and certainly not with women. Not wanting to screw things up by saying the wrong thing, he made a snap decision. "Can we just skip to the part where we're past this?"

Apprehension clear on her face, she stiffened again. "Which part would that be?"

Taking a deep gulping breath, he strode forward, took her in his arms and kissed her. The moment their lips met, his mind screamed in protest, the sensation of leaving his body, of feeling heavy, slipping through her arms to fall limp and lifeless onto the floor hit him hard.

Jane wrapped her arms around him, one hand slipping into his hair. Her body molded to his, holding him up, steadying him until the sensation passed. She wasn't the one who had done that to him. He had to find a way to separate the halves of her in his head.

She pulled back but didn't let go. "Are you all right?"

He nodded. "I will be."

"Then I might be too." She nuzzled his neck. "Does this part involve a bed?"

"It could."

"Then I like this part very much."

Logan laughed, and let his focus slip to activities his mouth was much better suited for.

CHAPTER NINETEEN

"Ined an army." Jane stood at the head of the table, her gaze steady on Tate, Rice, and the three members of the colony from Ivium who had been chosen as a delegation. The three had yet to stop staring at her like they were silently begging for forgiveness.

"I don't see how we can give you one," said Rice. "Management isn't on board with that, not to mention, they don't have resources to provide it even if they were."

Carol, the head of the delegation, shrugged apologetically. "I'm sorry, we have no ships and very few people. Is there anything else we can do? Please tell us. Come back to us."

The man beside her nodded enthusiastically. "Please, we need you. We didn't mean to anger you. Tell us what we can do."

"I'm not angry with you, but I can't stay on Ivium."

The third woman bowed her head. "We have been forsaken."

She fought to keep her temper under control. Managing an army was one thing, but consoling simpering citizens had never been her responsibility. "You were doing just fine before I came, and you'll continue to do so. You don't need me."

"We would be dead if not for you," said Carol.

"Some of you. The rest would be slaves." Having allowed herself a brief moment of honesty, she took a deep breath through her nose and focused on Logan, standing at the rear of the room.

Though he hadn't wanted to be there, he'd come when she'd asked. She needed him. He helped keep her steady, keep her mind clear.

Anika remained still behind the veil. Guilt was something she'd not considered her other half would understand. Perhaps they were both learning. Maybe, she smiled inwardly at the thought, there was hope for her after all. Inspiration hit.

"If I could provide ships, would you be willing to stand up to Matouk's army?"

Tate sniffed. "I highly doubt we have time for that. There have been rumors that a large force is amassing and moving this way. When you let the ship that attacked us escape-"

"I didn't *let* them," Jane hissed. "We knew Matouk would come. It was just a matter of time."

"They'll destroy us all," said the man beside Carol. "Everything we've worked for."

She took another deep breath and let it out. Why did helping people have to be so difficult? "I can't promise that your destruction won't happen, but I can provide you with a chance to prevent it."

That chance made her sick through and through, and even with Logan nearby, Anika let her hesitance be known in waves. That did nothing to subdue the nausea that threatened to embarrass her in front of this wary and fearful council. The General didn't embarrass easily, but vomiting at the mention of planning for war would do it. Though, it wasn't the planning that bothered her so badly.

Rice cleared his throat. "And what does this chance

entail?"

"Matouk has had centuries or possibly longer to build his army. We have a day or two at best, this ship, and scant manpower."

Tate frowned. "Forgive me for saying, but you're not inspiring much faith here."

"I agree, the facts paint a rather dim outlook." Jane sat down, admitting to herself that she couldn't voice her plan on her feet. The General was really gone. "I have fought countless wars. However, I'm usually in Matouk's position."

Jane took a deep breath and tuned out everyone but Logan. The concern and confusion on his face made the churning in her stomach even worse. So much for comfort. Comfort could come later, if they survived.

"The Unlata Kai were far-flung, living in smaller family groups rather than colonies like yourselves, meaning most didn't openly pursue war against one another. Thanks to my ambitious father, we weren't typical. I've had a fair deal of experience in defeating other Unlata Kai. Matouk likely does not."

"What if he does?" asked Rice.

"Then we'll do the best we can." She shrugged, having no better answer. "I will create ships. None like this one, it will have to serve as our main defense, but the frameworks of them, enough to hold the illusion of a sizeable force."

"How can you do that in such a short time?" asked Carol.

"I will need to return to your colony, to use resources from your planet."

She glanced at Logan. He'd gone from concerned to ashen. Rice didn't appear much better.

"And I will need to employ Anika's skills. I will also

need to feed. A great deal of feeding, in fact. To make this more efficient and for the plan to work, I will need to convert you. All of you, but Logan, actually."

Tate twisted in her seat to glare at Logan. "Why not him?"

"Because he's going to switch Anika off should we be alive when this is over."

"That didn't go so well last time," Rice stated flatly.

"I'm well aware of that." Jane's nerves were zinging, teeth nearly vibrating. "He and I will work out something more reliable this time around."

"What happens to us, if we're converted, and we live?" asked the man beside Carol.

"We will be connected to a degree, but it will not harm you."

"And who will man these other ships?" asked Rice.

"All of you. Matouk's men will need to see life signs on the vessels. I can amplify your signatures to make you appear more numerous."

"Can't he do that too?" asked Tate.

"He could if he knows how, but it takes energy and he has plenty of men. He doesn't need to."

"This energy, the feeding," asked Carol, her fingers twisting together on the table. "How will we do that if we're on the ships away from you? And it makes us tired. We can't help if we're all sleeping. How will you have enough energy to make the ships? There aren't that many of us to provide for you."

Memories of the white expanses of dead soil on Kaldara haunted Jane. She forced herself to face what must be done. "For the most part, I will take from your planet what I require."

"Will that harm Ivium?" asked the man beside Carol.

She had to tell them the truth. "Yes. But if Matouk

kills you all, it won't really matter, will it? And make no mistake, he will. You've shown resistance. He won't stand for that."

Carol chewed her lip. "So we will be connected to you and our planet will sustain damage."

"There is a cost to everything."

"Do what must be done," said Tate, surprising everyone.

Jane nodded. "Your medical team will facilitate the conversion. Afterward, you will all sleep while your bodies accept the changes. Meanwhile, Logan and I will travel to the colony, proceed with the conversion there, and create ships. When you wake, all should be ready."

She stood. "Let's just hope that your estimates on Matouk's arrival are correct or none of this will matter."

Unable to face them any longer in light of what must be done, Jane walked out. Logan followed, his footsteps falling in time with her own. They headed for the clinic.

"They agreed, but you don't seem very happy about it," he said.

"I didn't want this, but it will get the job done. Or not. We will have to wait and see."

"Can you really do that? Create ships from nothing?"

She forced a smile, hoping to gain his confidence, but she knew it was weak and tremulous. "Not from nothing, but from something. That is the way our ships are made. Like this one. I watched my mother do it once."

He came to a halt. "But you've never done it?"

"Nor have I converted so many at once, or managed them all, but it's the only chance we have."

"You sounded a lot more confident in there."

"Good."

She wasn't sure how things actually were between them, but she needed him now. Even if he didn't believe in her, he was still by her side and that counted for something. Unless, she considered, he was only there out of duty, manipulating her promise to protect him to save the whole crew. But his actions in her bed made her think otherwise. He'd come to her of his own accord, even if he hadn't been very eloquent about it.

Could it be that his lack of words had been because he was conflicted about what he had to do, just as she was now? Deep inside, where no one could see, she trembled. If she learned he was only going through the motions for the sake of the crew, she'd kill them all.

No. She quashed the flare of her temper. She would do what must be done, as she always did, and when it was over, she would complete her task—eliminating the last of the Unlata Kai.

For now, she'd enjoy his motions no matter the motive. For committing to such a momentous task, she deserved a bit of indulgence. Jane drew a deep breath and took his hand. They entered the clinic together.

CHAPTER TWENTY

U pon their arrival, the clinic erupted into a frenzy of activity. Jane lay on a bed with two tubes flowing from her body. Her blood filling bags at a rapid pace. Brin was already at work with the first bag, dividing the contents into small cups for consumption by the crew.

The thought of having to drink her blood made Logan's stomach churn. Though he wasn't excited to be the only one responsible for returning Jane to her less godly state, at least he didn't have to partake in the gruesome round of shots. On the other hand, that might make him the only sane one left once they'd all converted.

Her points seemed normal enough, until the moments when they didn't. Like when they showed up by her side without a word or allowed her to flow energy through them to expand her work. And they were utterly devoted to her. Not mindless, exactly, but close enough. The entire crew, the colony, would all be just like them. And he alone would be on the outside.

Assistants, under Adam's direction, took the trays of cups to the crew while the contents were still warm. When he disconnected the third bag and handed it off to be decanted, Jane remained on the bed, pale and sweating.

"What do you require?" asked Adams.

"My blood back, but as it is needed elsewhere, I'd

like my points."

"Can't you contact them yourself?" asked Logan. He'd seen her do it many times.

"They're not responding."

"I'll go hunt them down," he offered.

"Hurry, we need to get down to the surface."

Logan dashed out of the clinic. He'd just reached the lift when the doors opened and the four points spilled out.

"Where have you been? She needs you."

South wore a deep scowl. The rest didn't look much happier. "We heard."

They strode past him, West bumping into his shoulder with far more than accidental force. Logan followed along at a distance, wondering what had them in such a mood when Jane clearly needed them. Since the four of them had been converted, they had been right by her side unless she assigned them elsewhere.

Upon catching sight of them, Jane sat up slowly. "Where have you been?"

"Talking," said North.

The four of them surrounded her. They made no effort to hide their displeasure. Logan moved closer in case Jane needed him. She didn't appear in any shape to force them back.

"We do not approve of this plan," said West. "You're putting yourself at too much risk, stretching yourself too thin."

Jane caught Logan's gaze and shook her head. "Points have a natural sense of self-preservation."

"It sounds like this is about your preservation, not theirs." And on some level, he didn't disagree with them. However, Matouk was coming. If Jane was willing to do all she said she could and would, he wasn't going to stand in her way.

"They're connected to me, Logan. What do you think that means if I am killed?"

Logan listened to the clinic staff hurrying about their tasks, smelling the cups of blood being poured only a few feet away. Soon, everyone would be drinking them. They would be connected to Jane.

"Don't tell me they go with you," he said, "because you didn't mention that. It sure sounds like something you would have brought up in the meeting where this crazy plan was approved."

"You didn't tell them?" asked North. "He's right, you know."

"If there is no saving us, a sudden and clean death is the last mercy I can offer. Matouk will not grant such a thing. In his place, I wouldn't."

Memories of waking alone in the charred ruins, surrounded by the bodies of everyone he'd known flooded back. Alone and wounded he'd dragged himself out of the city, his uniform in tatters, scavenging for food in the few homes that hadn't been completely leveled when the bombs hit. He'd been wandering for weeks when Rice came across him, wild and considering walking right back into the ruins to sit down and starve until he'd joined his family and friends.

"So everyone drops dead but me? I get to face Matouk all on my own?

"One man can hide, disappear, start again elsewhere."

"Maybe one man doesn't want to." He couldn't go through that again, seeing their bodies, knowing there were too many to take care of and racked with guilt for not being one of them. Would someone like Rice find him again? He didn't even entertain the notion that fate would be so kind a second time.

"Then let's hope it doesn't come to that." She reached out for his hand and pulled herself up.

She was shaking.

"You need to feed. That was way too much blood to lose."

Jane nodded and let go of him. She reached out to East and South. When Anika fed, wandering through the crowd in the inn like a graceful socialite, she'd radiated beauty. Jane's lips became pinched, and he had the distinct impression she'd rather be anywhere else. She didn't glow, and by the time she'd finished with North and West, the only change in her appearance was that she wasn't pale or shaking anymore. The four men, on the other hand, were yawning and their eyes were drooping.

"You will remain here with the crew. Rest and watch over them until my return. You will not be able to reach me while I'm below. What I must do will take my full attention."

North shook his head. "We should be with you."

"Logan will be with me. He is all I need."

While those words wrapped him in warmth, the glares of the four points seared into him. He hoped they weren't able to channel her energy to the degree they could form their own light bombs. They were doing a good enough job without that.

"Maybe we should take-"

"You are all I need." She again took his hand and pulled him away. "Can you pilot the shuttle?"

He waited to answer until they were out of earshot from her points. "No."

"All right then. I will."

"Jane, two of your points have training. They can do it. You should be resting."

"They are tired and I need them here. I will manage."

She raised her chin and strode onward at a determined pace.

When they boarded one of the three shuttles, he was relieved to see that she sat right down and handled the controls as if she'd been doing this all her life. Maybe she had. Did gods of war pilot shuttles to the surface of the world they were about to destroy? He imagined her arriving in something more like a ball of fire, her armor gleaming in the dancing flames, striking terror into the hearts of the people below. Instead, she guided the shuttle downward, landed quietly, and exited the door like anyone else.

She carried the container Adams had prepared and went into the town. Carol met them, her steps halting, a hopeful smile upon her face.

"You returned to us."

"Only for a short while."

"We are grateful for whatever time you have. What must we do?"

"Drink and then you will sleep. When you wake, we will be connected. I will not need to touch you to feed. You will hear me in your mind if I wish it."

Carol's hands shook as she took the container. Thick red fluid sloshed in the clear cups inside. "Even the children?"

"Everyone."

"We will be one with you," she said with a hushed voice. "Thank you." Carol headed for the colony at a brisk step.

Logan kept his mouth clamped shut. He'd seen firsthand what Matouk's men would do to a colony who had resisted. He didn't wish to see it again, to hear the screams. And yet, to imagine all these people, even the children she'd healed, falling over dead, no matter how quick and peacefully, gave him chills.

"Come. We should hurry." Jane set a swift pace out of the colony.

When they finally stopped, he could see the colony in the distance, buildings rising over the fields, the trees far off. They'd set down in the rocky area where Hanson's men had been working.

"Why here?"

"There's plenty to work with in the soil and the damage will be less visible. I will try to expunge the mineral that the children are sensitive to while I'm pulling from the ground anyway." Jane sat, pressing her palms to the smooth grey rock.

"Wait, how am I supposed to switch Anika off?"

"There will be no need."

"What do you mean? If there's no need, why am I here and not with the rest of the crew?"

She regarded him from beneath long lashes. "Because I'm selfish. I wanted you by my side."

She had that look about her again, the same one she'd had when she'd provided the shield that had taken them out of the palace on Kaldara, committed to ending herself.

He reached for his gun. "You can't do this. I won't let you take them all with you."

Her hand slipped over his before he had a chance to draw it. "If I am given the choice, I will sever the connections before I go."

"If you destroy Matouk first?"

She nodded. "Now, let me work."

He settled onto a boulder nearby, not knowing how much space she would need. For several minutes she just sat on the ground, her hands held out before her, palms down on the surface. Then there came a subtle shift in the air, a charge. A stillness settled over the field.

Particles rose from the rock, spiraling upward to hover before her face. Her hands remained locked to the ground, eyes closed, face pinched with concentration. The particles wrapped around one another, almost slithering. A rasping sound reached him on his perch as more and more grains flowed from the ground, reds, greys, and browns, sliding over one another.

An oval formed, elongating, flat for a moment and then expanding as if inflated. Inside he caught a glimpse of pulsing veins of activity and sparks.

Her lips parted. A small bubble of light crept out, hovering before her. She blew, slowly, propelling the light into the opening at the narrow end of the spinning mass of color. Logan realized he was holding his breath. He gasped as the light flared inside. The exterior solidified, forming a shining grey surface just like the Maxim. A soft glow emanated from the opening until it sealed shut with a pop that hurt his ears.

He could have wrapped his arms around the seed of the ship. How was that supposed to carry men, to fool Matouk? And how many more could she create before she ran dry?

The seed, or maybe heart, he wasn't sure, drifted upward. He watched it go until it disappeared into the clouds. By the time he returned his attention to Jane, she'd already begun gathering another swirling mass of particles. The air had lost its sweet smell, now it reminded him of the factory where his father had worked, metals and oil. There were no lines of stern-faced men in stained heavy aprons here, only one woman in white. She breathed life into the second ship and sent it aloft.

Sweat dripped from her face. She had taken on a hollow look, though not as severe as when she'd brought him back from the dead. She sat, holding the ground, her body gently swaying.

"You need to feed."

Jane nodded. "I need you to go up there." She pointed to a rocky outcropping above the plain.

He went, glancing back over his shoulder when the footing was even. Her eyes were closed, head bowed. Once he caught her watching him. She looked entirely miserable. He wanted to run back so she wouldn't be alone. But then her head was down again and he knew sending him away hadn't been out of want, but need.

Logan chose a perch on a pile of rocks where he could see the grey plain from above. The stone beneath her had paled. He thought it might be an illusion, but the longer he watched without blinking, he knew it was real. Color leeched from the surface in a widening circle around her. When the stone had turned a sickly mix of yellow, white and pale grey, Jane stood. She took six large steps outside the circle and sat down again, palms flat on the ground. Within moments, grains began to flow upward and twist around one another.

She completed a fifth ship before standing again. Three white circles tainted the otherwise dark rocky expanse. Jane held out her hand to him, beckoning. Logan climbed off his boulder and went down to join her.

He stared upward, though he'd lost sight of the ship seeds. "Will five be enough?"

"There isn't time for more, and I must conserve my energy to make them grow."

"Can you feel them? The crew and the colony? Did the conversion work?"

"Not yet. They're still sleeping."

He noticed that for her not having time to make more ships and the fact that Matouk would be on them in less than a day, she was standing there staring at the ground, nibbling on her bottom lip. "What next?"

"I have a favor to ask of you."

"What?"

"What I must do next, when we return to the shuttle and fly with the new ships while I expand them..."

Did gods fidget? He took the hands that had pulled energy from the ground, that had created living ships from tiny particles, into his own. "Jane, what do you need me to do?"

"I will need to release Anika, to be at full strength for what lies ahead." Her fingers intertwined with his. "As there is only me, and if I fail..."

"Yes?"

She sighed. "To give us the best shot, I will need to fully merge with my other half, become complete. Do you understand?"

Not at all, but from the hesitation, he gathered there were dire implications. "You can't separate again when this is over?"

Jane shook her head. "No going back. The veil will be broken."

"You will be both halves? Not just all her?"

"Both, yes." She leaned in to rest her head on his shoulder. "Not all me either."

The thought of Anika having a say in Jane's actions, when the lives of so many were in the balance, made him cringe.

"It was Anika's kiss that killed you, and I know it would be impossible to ask you to consider sharing my bed once the merge is complete...but might we enjoy one last kiss before I go?"

"I do have other uses beyond sharing your bed, you know."

Jane stepped back and smiled. "I am aware that you are adequate with your weapons and your body is well fit for combat."

"Adequate? Really?"

She laughed, a magical sound that calmed his nerves and mind. "Perhaps more than adequate."

"You sure I'm not already talking to Anika?"

She punched his arm and started back toward the shuttle. He caught up to her just as she stepped inside, wrapping his arms around her from behind and kissing his way up her neck. She melted against him, expelling a breathy sigh that set him on fire. He made his way up her chin.

She twisted her head back to meet him. It may have been his heart or hers, but the beat throbbed through his body. "How much time do we have?"

Her hands were already undoing his pants. "Enough if we hurry."

Logan nodded and resumed his assault on her lips while she shed her clothes. With a very distracted glance, he noted that the walls of the shuttle were lined with equipment and handles of storage bins. The benches were narrow along the walls and the seats up front certainly not suited for recreational use. That left the floor. He guided her down on the discarded clothing.

Warmth surrounded him. They may be rushed, but he would enjoy every last second he had Jane to himself. She grasped him firmly, taking his breath away.

Everything would be all right.

That was the last thing he remembered thinking when he woke. He found himself sitting in the seat in the front of the shuttle next to Jane. At least he had his pants on, but the rest of his clothing was missing.

Fully dressed, Jane had her eyes closed, her face

pinched with concentration. Outside, in the surrounding blackness, floated five ships, each twice the size of the shuttle. Miniatures of the Maxim. She'd done it.

But why the hell had he blacked out?

Interrupting her to ask seemed like a bad idea. Instead, he quietly got up and went in search of his weapons and clothes. They were all on the floor where he dimly recalled shedding them. He put himself back in order and returned to his seat.

Was she Anika now? What would she be like, this mix of two halves? He really wished he could remember what had happened after they'd hit the floor.

Jane remained silent, her skin paling in degrees as time they didn't have ticked by. The ships grew, doubling again in size while he watched. The Maxim floated in the distance. From here, a trick of perspective, the new ships appeared the same size.

Her voice made him jump. "I must recharge."

"Anika or Jane?"

She cocked her head, observing him in a manner that was far more Anika than Jane. Like he was dinner. "Both."

He swallowed hard. He nodded toward the back of the shuttle. "What happened?"

"I had heard whispers, but I thought they were lies, excuses for my kind to lay with their followers. But they were true."

"What was true?" An uncomfortable shiver ran up his spine.

"Sex can recharge us. Like feeding, but more invigorating." She pointed at the ships outside. "See how much I've been able to do? And so quickly. I had not thought this possible."

"We've done this before and you never mentioned

it."

"All those self-imposed rules and iron-fisted control." She shook her head. "A foolish waste of resources. Now that we see the truth, there will be no more wasting you."

"I..." How did one politely decline sex with a fully functioning and hungry god? While he tried to work that out, he focused on the immediate issue. "Why can't I remember what happened?"

She didn't seem inclined to answer, focusing again on the ships.

Panic hit him. He was alone, on a ship he couldn't fly, with a god who had already killed him once. Jane was no longer. Everyone he knew was now connected to her.

His arms and legs felt wooden as he got out of the seat to put distance between him and Anika. "What did you do to me?"

"Nothing you didn't fully enjoy. Sit." She gestured to the seat. "We have to return to the Maxim. The ships are big enough now that I can continue working on them from there."

"Why can't I remember? Did you kill me again?"

Pain flashed over her face and she looked away. "No. It was only..."

For a moment her voice and her expression were all Jane, but it was so brief that he wasn't sure. "Which one are you?'

"Both." Jane sighed. "The transition, the merge, wasn't exactly..." She seemed to be warring with herself, fighting for ownership of her tongue.

"Smooth?"

She nodded, watching the ships rather than him. "I did not expect to merge until after we had...finished. But I lost control and Anika slipped in and, well, I thought it best to remove that memory from you."

"Why? Jane, what happened?" He held onto the headrest as if it was the only thing holding him up.

"I don't remember. Not exactly. Only that I was with you, but then I wasn't. The veil was broken, likely weakened when I'd made the choice to merge. It took me a few minutes to find my way back and when I did...I was getting dressed and you were on the floor looking angry."

"Why was I angry? What the hell did Anika do to me?"

"I don't know. My memory of the merge is hazy. So is hers. All I know is she had full control of my body. Maybe you were aware it was Anika. Maybe that's why you were angry."

That made sense. His grip on the headrest lessened. "Why erase that? You knew I'd realize there was a gap right away."

She stared at him, her voice losing its compassion. "I had work to do, and I'm far from finished. Sit."

Logan took his seat. If Matouk didn't kill him, her rapidly flipping personality would finish the job. Though they needed the General, he sorely missed Jane. Even though she sat right there, the uncertainty of what was going on inside that mind and body made if feel like that woman he'd known, albeit briefly, was gone forever.

CHAPTER TWENTY-ONE

Stepping aboard the Maxim, Jane felt the flow of energy shift toward her. The crew was awake. Logan lagged behind. Her points arrived in short order, taking up their places as she made her way to the control room.

She glanced over her shoulder to address Logan. "Wait for me in my room. I may require a recharge before Matouk arrives."

"If you think I'm going to-"

"You will do your part to protect this crew or you will find yourself no longer a part of it."

"Jane, you know-"

She scowled. "I hate that name."

"You chose it."

He was right, but that only made her more aggravated. The headache she'd developed since she'd returned to her body with Anika worsened. The merge was more complicated than she'd imagined. And now Logan was being difficult. Or maybe she was. It was hard to decipher all the conflicting emotions in her mind.

They entered the control room. Tate got up from her chair and offered it to her. The crew watched with interest.

Though it grated, Jane kept her voice calm. She forced out the word Anika despised. "Logan, *please* go. I must concentrate on preparing for Matouk."

He leaned in close, ignoring the stares of Tate and the others. "I realize that, but if you think I'm going to wait in bed for you-"

Why couldn't he just go? Was sex too much to ask for? The surge of energy that had blossomed after their last encounter taunted her. Little wonder other Unlata Kai slept with their points even though they were already connected.

He'll never accept us. Not like this. Jane cursed Matouk for forcing her into this and ruining the happiness she'd only begun to enjoy.

Give him time.

You killed him.

You brought him back. We're in the same body, the one he enjoys. Give him time.

"Fine. Then give me some room to work."

Logan held up his hands and backed away. At the edge of her vision, she could see him leaning against the wall beside the door. One finger betraying his aggravation, tapping rhythmically on the wall.

North glanced to Logan and then to her.

"Leave him. We need to focus on the ships I have created. All of you, turn to face me."

With their full attention, the lines connecting them to her drew taut. The rush wasn't as fulfilling as it had been after sex, but it was familiar, though more than she was comfortable with at one time.

We're fine. You've held us to your strict standards for too long. This is what we're meant for. It's natural.

It's not natural. Logan doesn't like it.

Anika laughed. *And he's now our gauge for all things natural?*

Yes.

Frustration flooded through her with such force that it took her breath away. This was never going to work. How could she face Matouk when she couldn't even keep her own mind and body under control?

A touch on her arm snapped her attention outward. For a second she hoped it was Logan. But it was North.

"Are you unwell?"

Yes. Very much so. She leaned back in the large chair. Built for expandable bodies like hers, it had plenty of room. Yet, not enough space to allow her to escape the room full of staring points. They would feel her unease, of course. The only one she might be fooling was Logan and knowing her as he did, she rather doubted she was successful there either.

What was she supposed to call herself now? Every Unlata Kai she'd known had adopted the name of their other half when they came fully into their powers. To call herself Anika felt wrong and she wouldn't ask that of Logan. When given the choice, she'd always preferred to use General, a name that fit both of her halves.

But she'd come here with the intention of leaving the General behind.

That is who we need. Is it not? Only the General can defeat Matouk.

Yes, that is true. But I liked Jane.

It is a weak name.

Jane bristled, her head throbbing despite the influx of energy and efforts to heal herself.

There is nothing to heal. It's only ourselves coming together. It will take time.

"I don't have time," Jane snapped.

North regarded her with clear concern. "General?"

At least he'd picked up on her silent cue. "Quiet. Let me work."

The General relaxed into the chair as much as her taut muscles allowed. She reached out with her mind, connecting to the ships she'd created. The hold was far more tenuous than she'd expected. They were her own creations, a part of her. She should have been able to speak to them as long as they were within sight. However, the ships were so young. She'd not allowed for that. It hadn't been an issue for her mother. They'd not been in a hurry like she was now. These ships had understood her touch well enough, but her thoughts and words confused them.

"I require that one man board each ship so that I may work through them."

"Men?" asked Tate.

"Any point, a matter of speech."

"We are all points now?" asked the woman at the communications controls.

Why were they so slow? She didn't have time for this. "Yes. Now, go."

Tate spoke into her com device. "They're being deployed now."

"Where is Rice?" she asked before realizing she could summon him on her own. She swore under her breath. Organizing so many points was a nightmare. Four was second nature, but the whole crew and the citizens of the colony?

The connections she shared with the crew slipped through her grasp. She held tight to her original four and the arms of the chair. Even Anika faltered, scrambling to regain control to no avail.

Organizing an attack with her own forces, with her fellow Unlata Kai at her back, that was no matter for concern. Newly merged, with so many points, with new ships under her control, with no army save a few of Rice's men, she was sure to fail.

"Jane?"

She discovered she had her eyes squeezed shut. Rice stood before her, sharing a look with North.

"General," she stated.

He nodded. "Back to that again, are we?"

North scowled.

The Colonel cleared his throat. "Right then. You asked for me?"

"Your men, arm them. They will need to be fully prepared when Matouk arrives. He will test us."

"Like before?"

"Knowing what we did before, yes."

"We shouldn't have let them escape," he said quietly

How dare he criticize her actions? She'd done all she could. Saved them, even. "It wasn't exactly a matter of choice."

"Very true." He took a step back. "So ready the men. Anything else?"

"Logan stays with me."

Rice nodded.

Logan stepped forward. "I would be of more use with him."

Why couldn't the damned man keep his mouth shut and quit distracting her? Just hearing him speak made her want to haul him off to a private space for a full recharge. If he was out of sight, maybe her attention wouldn't keep wandering to him. But then, she considered, she'd be concerned for his safety, and that was just as bad.

"You're of use to me here."

"It doesn't feel like it."

Jane shoved Anika aside. A blinding pain shot through her head. "You will be. I need you here."

"On the way here, you wanted me gone."

"Not gone." She massaged the bridge of her nose. It didn't help. "These people need someone to protect them should Matouk's men manage to board us again."

"But you're here," said Tate.

"I will be far too occupied to worry for your personal safety."

Rice took stock of the occupants of the room, who crept closer, concern clear on their faces. "What about your points?"

"They will be dispersed and also occupied. I am far more comfortable working through them than the rest of you."

"We would prefer not to leave you," said East.

Anika recovered. "No one asked for your preferences."

Jane absorbed the burst of pain Anika had intended for East.

Don't harm them. They are needed.

They lack training and proper respect.

Do you forget how well our previous points carried out their last orders?

Yes, and we killed that North for it, said Anika.

That's not what I mean. They're men, with their own minds, even that North who had been with us for so long.

With correct training, they should be of our mind. You made them weak.

Jane clutched at the amulet on her chest with one hand and sought relief at her temples with the other. "Continue with your work. We will resume when the points on the new ships are in place."

Feet shuffled back to their workstations and muffled conversations resumed. Air and power flowed through the fully healed ship. The steady pulse of it all settled in her mind. Slowly, she let go of the amulet and her head. Her breathing, the beat within her body matching that of the ship. One by one, connections with the crew fell back into place. Her vision and Anika's became one again. The sensation of being two people at once eased. The pain in her head did not.

"We will require the colonists to populate the ships. Leave the young and enough adults to guard them on the surface. I will multiply their numbers."

While Tate relayed her orders to the other two shuttles, the General ran through the chants in her head, reacquainting herself with those she would need to supplement their numbers. It would take more energy. She stole a glance at Logan, again against the wall.

She'd mostly regained her precarious hold on sanity by the time the shuttle had deposited points on each of the five ships. After some adjustments, she managed to sync communications with the fledgling ships so that she could conserve herself for growing the ships.

The faces of the five points appeared on the wall to her left. Tate stood to her right, looking uncomfortable and out of place.

The commander stared raptly at the points. "What is that? Why is everything so small?"

The points, each crouched low, with their shoulders rubbing the ceiling, stood over consoles that barely came to their knees. Their hands dwarfed the controls.

"The air is very thin here," one reported.

"Sit. You will be more comfortable while we work. I need you to all press your hands to any part of the ship, the more contact area the better." She waited until they'd dropped from view, the display still showing the control rooms of the miniature ships. The very top of one tall point's head, a few sprigs of auburn hair, served as the only visual reminder that they were still there.

She turned to Tate, then to North and past him to Logan. "Notify me if anything or anyone requires my attention."

Satisfied that the situation was under as much control as could be, she sent her awareness into the five points. The ships were undeveloped for the most part. The elements were all there, as much as she could remember how they should be from her time working with the Maxim and at her mother's side as a child. They would have to do for now. Her mother had always worked with one ship at a time, but she didn't have that luxury. This fleet would be stunted, but good enough to serve a single purpose. They merely had to be.

Her focus was life support and structure. Losing her body back on the Maxim, she spread herself throughout the ships, flowing from the hands of five points she barely knew. Their discomfort with the process was palpable. When she'd shared the sensation of working with the ship with Hanson, he'd been curious. He'd wanted the experience. These people were frightened, doing what they must to survive. Willing, but only just. If she could have spared them the duty, she would have, but that wasn't an option.

The ships had doubled again, the points now able to stand by the time her energy stores guttered. Two of them had fully developed control rooms, the furniture and consoles ready and waiting for a crew. Those two points were less resistive to her flow of energy than the others. The life support in all but one was complete. She had tried for a clear path, a developed entry bay, the main corridor, an operational lift, the control room. Everything else would come later or not at all.

When the General returned to her body, Tate and

the others were still staring at her handiwork.

"Do they have weapons?" Tate asked.

"Not yet."

"They need to have weapons." She held her arms across her chest, her hands tightly clutching her elbows. "We can't be the sole defense. We'll never survive."

"I need you all to face me. I will finish what I can and then I must rest and feed again before Matouk arrives."

With the points facing her, their energy flowed more naturally, requiring less work on her part. Worn from the merge and her work with the new ships, easier was a very welcome thing. The one drawback was that she needed the crew to remain awake, to be fully operational. She could only take so much from them. Once the colonists were aboard the new ships, she could take from them too.

Her well filled to a degree that she could continue, the General signaled the crew to return to work. She sent her four points to eat, knowing she'd need them as reserves later. She sunk back into her connections with the young ships. The colonists arrived, dispersing through the fleet. Each ship contained eight to eleven bodies. She turned inward to the chants she'd set aside, initiating the sequences that would multiply her points. Once she was finished, each body would appear as ten.

Jane checked with Anika to verify the process was going properly, only to realize they were working together without conscious thought. They were truly becoming one. The throbbing in her head had eased.

The General pulled back from the host of points, admiring the bulk of the new ships. Almost at full size, they appeared fully operational to the initial touch. Their crews working hard. If anyone boarded, they'd see the empty spaces and the mirrored bodies surrounding those of flesh and bone. All she had to do was keep them from being boarded.

"General?" Tate's voice held a tremor. "They're here."

All faces turned toward the approaching danger. The control room went silent.

CHAPTER TWENTY-TWO

What had been peaceful black space permeated with stars only moments before, was now filled with nine vessels of various designs and sizes, denoting some of the worlds Matouk had taken. All of them were bristling with weapons and boldly baring scars of previous conquests. One of them was just like the Maxim, however, Matouk's ship appeared to be in full repair. Logan's stomach dropped to the floor.

Jane's five ships were impressive. What had been mere grains, had now grown to full ships. However, seeing the odds against them, he wondered which death would be more preferable, the explosion of the Maxim or the cold of space.

He'd never seen how many ships Matouk had with him when he laid waste to Hijn, but he imagined the destruction from above had looked much like this. Ivium would suffer the same fate.

Jane had been working up until they arrived, not taking the time to rest and feed as she'd wanted. Now she wouldn't get the chance.

She shot to her feet, startling Tate and two of the crew who sat nearby. Activating her amulet, golden armor flowed over her body, leaving only her head bare. Her four points rushed in, racing to her side. They were also suddenly encased in armor, covered from head to toe in gleaming gold.

An unpleasant tingle overcame Logan. The air against his skin grew cold like he'd fallen into ice water. Golden plates rushed over his arms and legs, flooding up his chest and neck and then over his head and face. He swore as he reached for his gun, only to discover it was on the outside of his armor, rather than trapped on his belt inside where it had been. How the hell had she done that?

The display lit and then filled with the face of a man. A man with grey eyes so cold that Logan shivered within his armored shell. He bore no scars, nothing at all detracted from the image that could have been carved by the finest artist from the purest stone. The very same image he'd seen in projections on Hijn a year before. Had Jane appeared the same way to the worlds she'd taken for her father? He tore his gaze from the angelic face, seeing only the destruction of his home.

Silver scales shimmered over Matouk's chest, light dancing on tiny blue crystals inset into the center of each one. Upon taking in Jane, he flared, white light seemed to emanate from his very pores, making it difficult to stare at him too long.

Though he couldn't see Jane's face, the golden glow dancing around her confirmed his suspicion that she'd also cranked her powers to full. Her four armored points beside her made for an imposing statement even from behind.

Matouk might have the eyes to compete with Jane, but the rest of him was delicate, handsome but like a fine piece of art. It had been his appearance that had initially gained him open access to Hijn, something beautiful for the people to behold. The leaders had clamored over one another to speak to him. It wasn't until he began making threats that they realized the danger he posed. By then it was too late.

Jane, no, the General, he reminded himself, especially now, was cold all over. Her glow lent her the beauty of her kind, masking her scars, but that would not disguise who she was and what she did best. She was the sharpened axe to his elegantly sculpted figurine.

Logan hoped she was up to laying waste to her enemies this one last time. With all he'd seen her do today, he was torn between believing she could do anything and worrying that she was only a few steps away from the frail husk she'd been after his miraculous revival.

"General." Matouk's smooth voice oozed through the room. "I did not expect to see you here."

"I've been waiting for you." The General was just as brusque and toneless as Logan remembered.

"Your father, is he well?"

"I killed him. What do you want here?"

The muscle under Matouk's left eye twitched. The crew behind him did their best to not look alarmed, but their bravado faltered.

From what Logan could see, their ship was a mirror of the Maxim. That might have made them evenly matched, if not for the fact that Matouk also had eight other ships with him. Though none were of the class of the Unlata Kai vessels, they all appeared armed. Of course, Jane's new ships appeared armed too. It just happened to be a lie. He didn't doubt Matouk's were very real.

"Your army follows you?" he asked.

"Does yours?"

He scowled. "It has been a long while since I've crossed paths with another of our kind."

"I've reason to believe that's because we are all that remains of the pure."

"Then perhaps we should meet in person before we become extinct."

The General laughed. "I have no need of your services."

"Come now, we have so much to offer these lower beings. Extinction would be a travesty. Surely you miss your own tongue as much as I?"

Her chin lifted as though she was giving thought to his proposition. "I might."

She couldn't really intend to meet with him. Certainly not to sleep with him. Could she? She'd definitely had sex on the mind when they'd arrived on the Maxim, and he'd made it quite clear he wasn't volunteering for that duty.

Did she feed from her own kind in that way? If she was going to sex him to death, he might be slightly less annoyed. Maybe. No, he was rather past annoyed and getting angrier by the second.

Sure Matouk was Unlata Kai, could speak her incomprehensible language, seemed to already know her or at least of her, and had the very face he'd imagined when his mother had described angels to him as a child. As a nightmare-plagued recluse employable only as muscle and with only a modest savings to his name, he should be in the running for her attention, right? She should take his feelings into account while openly discussing the possibility of a sexual rendezvous with the enemy in front of everyone in the room after he'd told her he wasn't interested now that she'd become whole.

Definitely.

Or not at all. For all he knew, Anika was the one calling the shots now, and she'd do whatever the hell she damn well pleased.

Anika had been the one to make sure she was saved

when Kaldara was ready to implode, but Jane had wanted off the ride for good. Matouk was supposed to be the last thing on her to-do list. Now that they were one, would Anika accept walking into the sunset? He rather doubted it. Anika would want the Unlata Kai to continue.

Glad that the helmet masked his grimace, Logan focused on keeping his fists out of sight. If she met with him, if she decided the best way to keep them all alive and preserve her kind was to join up with Matouk... The frustration became almost too much to bear. He would never serve under the man responsible for destroying everyone he'd loved and known.

He got his storming pulse stifled enough that he could hear the two of them finalizing a meeting place near the colony below. How could she do that? He would see that the numbers there were drastically off from the reports of the prior attack she'd averted. Would they stroll through the town, deciding which people would serve them and which didn't deserve to live? Matouk had done much worse with newly subdued conquests. In traveling with the Maxim, he'd seen that first hand. The only difference between worlds he'd destroyed and those he'd taken under his care, were the number of survivors. The quality of life on either was too similar to call either way a win. At least Jane's people had appeared happy. She'd cared enough about them to send them off to a new world.

Tate and the rest of the crew seemed mesmerized by Matouk and the discussion of their fate, much like Hijn's leaders had been. Their fate was now entirely in the General's hands. They barely moved when the display went dark and the General left the room. Her points followed behind. The last one, he couldn't tell which when their helmets all matched, elbowed him and told him to get going.

He wasn't a point. He wasn't connected. Why did she want him near her?

The armor flowed with him as he walked, bringing up the rear. It wasn't heavy or awkward and even the helmet didn't restrict his view, almost like it was more projection than solid. Yet, when he reached up to touch it, his fingers met with cold, unyielding metal. She'd left his hands bare, as were those of her points. He spent the walk down to the shuttle trying to decide which was which by the skin tone of their hands. Not that it mattered, but it helped keep his mind off of Matouk for a few minutes.

They entered the shuttle. The one he'd decided was West took the controls. The General sat in the back, making it clear she didn't want company. Unfortunately, her points had claimed the front area. As unfriendly as they'd been with him recently, he decided to endure the flight with the General.

There were so many questions he wanted to ask, but every time he opened his mouth to say something, he thought better of it. She might as well have had a helmet on herself, as unapproachable as she appeared.

Eventually, he occupied himself with trying to figure out how to deactivate his own helmet, hoping that if they were face to face, conversation might be more likely. But as with her helmet before, there seemed to be no way to remove it.

"Stop," she growled. "He can't see you and if you blend with my points, you'll be safer. If he knows I favor you, you'll be a target."

"So you favor me."

She shot him a look. "We're not having this conversation right now. You know I do."

"So, does the General favor me or only Jane? Because it sure seems like the General is favoring Matouk at the moment."

"Logan."

The actual emotion in her voice took him by surprise. He stopped messing with the helmet.

She massaged her temples. "We can't take him by force. Surprise, maybe."

"Plan on surprising him in bed?"

Even inside the armor, he shrank back from the pure aggravation beaming from her eyes.

"Your performance will be far more sincere if you don't know about any surprises, in bed or otherwise."

"Is that what I'm doing? Performing?"

Her lips went white and her jaw stiff. She stared him down as though she could see right through his helmet. Maybe she could.

He finally caved and looked away. "You think we have a chance?"

"If you quit talking, maybe."

He couldn't win. Talking or otherwise. Logan sat back on the narrow seat, wishing that he could be anywhere else. Except on the Maxim. He'd be helpless there, his fate in her hands, and hell, anywhere else, he'd just be waiting for Matouk to eventually bring death down on him or become a slave. Maybe shadowing a short-tempered, pensive god wasn't so bad.

The faint glow of the General kept grabbing his attention no matter how much he tried to avoid looking at her.

She'd kept her scars and her curls were in disarray. Maybe Anika hadn't gained full control after all. That made the fact that they were still going to meet with Matouk rather than blasting him out of existence even more aggravating.

It got worse when they landed and exited into the

swarm of Matouk's men. Logan went along with the four points, forming a circle around the General. She had expanded to her full height upon leaving the confines of the shuttle, towering over them. She even had several inches on Matouk.

A sickeningly sycophantic smile flitted across Matouk's lips. His smooth and flawless skin barely creasing with the speed of its departure. He executed a faint bob at the waist that might have been the ghost of a bow. "General."

She examined the twenty-three men around Matouk with a flat stare. "Feeling endangered?"

"You do have a reputation."

"As do you." She looked him up and down, scowling. "Do you take these worlds of your own accord or have you let yourself become a slave to your people?"

He sniffed. "They are *my* slaves. Only a fool would make promises to such as them."

She nodded. "Indeed."

Watching the two of them, Logan felt small, insignificant. Did she think herself a fool to have made a promise to him? If she hadn't, would she have let Matouk's men take Ivium rather than protecting them because he happened to be there? Though the question swirled in his head, he saw her healing the children. She'd done that on her own. She would have saved the colony too. Jane was good.

Matouk switched to their own language, the almost musical cadence was beautiful, soothing. Logan's muscles relaxed as they talked. From the dazed expressions on Matouk's men, he wasn't the only one affected. In the back of his mind, he knew they were trading insults and sizing each other up and that he should be on alert, but the lilting sounds unlocked something inside, something he'd been seeking for as long as he could remember.

Despite two magnificent beings butting heads in front of him, it was as though everything was right in the universe and he could be at peace. Time slowed as his very soul felt at ease.

The General approached Matouk, his men parting the way before her without hesitation or show of fear. She kissed him, long and deep. Matouk's arms wrapped around her, one lodging in her hair, pulling her even closer.

None of Matouk's men seemed alarmed. The General's points stood silently. He didn't know about any of the rest of them, but the sight of Jane wrapped in Matouk's embrace erased the ease that had enveloped him and replaced it with a boiling rage. Was he supposed to just stand there and watch them?

The General tugged at Matouk's armor with an urgency Logan knew too well. His entire body vibrated with the need to do something.

Matouk glanced around the General, taking stock of the sedate force. He pulled away and spoke again. His words danced in Logan's mind. His thoughts slowed, the words lulling him back toward peace.

The General never faltered, never looked at him, offered no hints of her plan or the surprise she'd alluded to. She touched the amulet set into her armor, retracting the plates until she only wore the white shirt with silver threads and white leggings with gold-plated boots up to her thighs. The sparkling amulet rested between her breasts. She reached for Matouk.

He placed his palm upon his chest. The silver armor began to retract, slower than hers, but in much the same manner, sliding down his neck, up his arms and shoulders and then down his chest. It stopped at his waist. He spoke again, holding out his hand. The General lifted hers and stepped forward.

Matouk pointed to Logan and the four men beside him with his other hand. The General turned then, enough that he caught the glowing light in her eyes. She looked just as she had when she'd blasted her father with the first beam of light.

The light built again, around her, inside her. She met Logan's gaze for a split second and nodded at her points. Were they supposed to do something? Had she sent them some message through their connection that he wasn't privy to?

She switched back to his language. "You hesitate. Why?"

Matouk jerked his outstretched hand, "If you wish to join me as you say, give me this one small token."

Her hand hovered over his, not quite touching. "You must give me one as well."

"What would please you?"

"You ask for the lives of my five. They are worth ten of yours."

Lives? She was going to blast them, blast him, to join with Matouk? Damn her surprises, he had one of his own. Logan drew his gun and fired at Matouk's unarmored chest. And kept firing. It wasn't until he'd run out of charge that he realized Matouk was still standing and the last of the searing holes in his chest had already sealed shut. Light flared in Matouk's eyes. He caught Logan in his gaze.

Run. That's what he had to do, what he tried to do, but his body didn't respond. Instead, screaming inside himself, inside the armor, he watched in horror as light built inside Matouk and shot from his chest.

In that same instant, the serpent staff appeared

in the General's hands, landing with a loud crack on Matouk's head. The god went to his knees. Blood dripped down his forehead, staining his hair, dripping down his nose and cheek.

The edge of the blast of burning light hit Logan, dropping him to the ground. He curled onto this side, trying to find any ease from the heat and pain fast overtaking his senses.

Light flared again. This time from the General directly at Matouk as he struggled to his feet. Silver flooded up his body, but the light hit before it reached the upper half of his chest and arms. For an instant, his skin blackened, eyes and exposed teeth stark white against the charred flesh. His hair turned to ash.

Then he was back to his former beauty. Matouk growled, baring his teeth, now again behind full pink lips. "Kill them all."

His men, as if awoken from a trance, sprang into action. A golden form hovered over Logan, sinking down beside him. He tried to make sense of the barrage of gunfire and the golden figure before him, trading blasts of light with the silver one. One of her points, that's who was with him. North, by the color of his hand. The hand that rested on his head. Where had his helmet gone?

Logan blinked several times, trying to clear his vision. It didn't help. Then he figured out it was a shield around the five of them that was causing the blur. Soothing warmth flowed from North's hand into Logan's skin, slipping through his body.

"Why aren't you out there helping her?"

"We're feeding her. She'll draw from the ground and the colonists if she needs more than we can give."

Men threw themselves at the General, at Jane. They were swarming her. He needed to help her.

North held him down. "Let her heal you."

"Let me go." What the hell was she doing, healing him in the middle of being attacked anyway? "Stop. She needs to focus on Matouk, not me."

"I agree, but she demanded that you be saved." He lifted his hand seemingly grateful for the excuse to stop the healing.

Logan got to this feet, shaking, but with a tolerable level of pain. The shield she'd placed around them kept him contained. "How do we get out of this? We have to help her."

Matouk sent a blast of light at her back while she was busy flinging men off her body as if they weighed nothing. Yet they kept getting back up, kept coming. Like they were possessed. The blast hit her armor, knocking her forward. She staggered but remained standing.

East went to his knees, wavered left and right and then collapsed onto the trampled grass. South followed suit seconds later.

"Get us out of here," he shouted at North.

The man regarded his fallen comrades. "She's protecting her food source."

"I'm not food," he growled. "Remember how to be a soldier? You aren't only food either. Now, get us out of here."

The General flung another man off. His body hit the shield with a muffled thump before bouncing off and landing with his head at an unnatural angle. His arms and legs shuddered and then he went still. One down, but there were still far too many of them distracting her. She shot a blast in Matouk's direction, incinerating two more men who had been racing toward her.

West's legs went out from under him.

Matouk sent a blast directly at the shield. The

blinding light turned everything white, then black. Echoes of the bomb thundered through Logan's head. His vision cleared enough that he could make out the growing gaps in the blurred shimmer that had surrounded him with safety. He'd wanted out. This was his chance.

North ran beside him as they raced toward the General. She flung two more bodies away. One of his own men struck Matouk in the chest. The two armor-clad, towering Unlata Kai traded intense blasts of energy, buffeting him with gusts of heated air that penetrated his armor. How did they stand it?

This was far different than any combat situation he'd been in before. He spared a second to check the charge on his gun. It had only recharged enough for two shots.

Twelve of Matouk's men were still on their feet. He took aim at one of their heads and made it eleven.

Just as he'd chosen his next target, a dark splotch in the sky caught his attention. And then was another. The blackened shapes falling toward them, getting larger by the second as they sped closer. Not full ships, but bits of debris.

North gasped. "One of the ships."

"Ours or his?"

His words came slow and halting. "I don't know." North's eyes rolled back into his head. He collapsed.

"We have to go," Logan yelled. If the ships overhead had engaged, they needed to protect the Maxim. There were too many people onboard.

Matouk waved a silver plated hand. Logan found himself propelled through the air. He landed on his back, his breath knocked from him.

"The only way you will leave is in chains." Matouk sent another blast at the General, driving her back. "Your points are drained. Save the lives of your army and end this now."

The General snapped the neck of the next of Matouk's men to accost her. She dropped the body to the ground as if it were merely a mild annoyance. She grabbed for another one.

A glimmering shield expanded directly overhead, protecting their corner of the battlefield. The burning debris rained onto it.

Now that there were fewer men to swarm her, she swung her staff with an ease and effectiveness that made Logan envious. Color leeched from the ground below her. With each obstacle removed, light gathered within her.

Matouk sent blast after blast, but it did not halt her progress toward him other than to cause her to stagger for a step or two. Three of his men dropped to the ground in the same manner North had.

Logan rolled to his side and got to his knees. The General was so bright now he couldn't look at her. The pale grey circle of dead soil beneath her grew, creeping toward him. He got to his feet, still hunched over, but moving away from the circle.

Matouk continued to fire until one of his men encountered the circle. The moment his feet encountered the sickly ground, he froze, his body going rigid. The man shriveled, his body caving in upon itself, crumpling into a blackened mass of boneless flesh and cloth.

The voice within the silver helmet shook. "Those powers are forbidden, ruled anathema by the elders. You will never join them in the beyond."

Logan hazarded a glance at the General. Her golden armor seemed to melt away, its departure from her body back into the amulet so smooth.

"You will join them now." She bolted straight for

Matouk.

A massive charge filled the air, raising the hairs all over his body. Everything seemed to vibrate.

CHAPTER TWENTY-THREE

Matouk stood before her. His armor would mean nothing once she unleashed her overflowing well upon him. Whether she found herself amongst the elders or not meant nothing compared to completing her mission. In seconds, the Unlata Kai would exist only in the beyond.

Anika screamed in her head. *You cannot do this. We must live.*

We can't hold this charge much longer. Already, boiling energy bled from the well, burning her from within. She had to remain in control long enough to propel the energy forward when she let it consume her. If it burned through before that, Matouk would survive. He had to be eliminated.

One hand went to her amulet, fighting to release her armor. The other grabbed it, holding it back. She spoke the beginning of the command to sever the ties with all those connected to her. Her tongue refused to complete it.

We must let it go now. The General threw her head back, trying instead the chant to open her chest and channel the swell of energy straight at Matouk. The vibrations from the chaos writhing within threatened to tear the flesh from her bones.

You will destroy our child.

The memories of what had transpired during their merge clarified in her mind. Anika had taken complete control of her body and in doing so, taken the one step she felt would guarantee their continued existence.

Shaken beyond even the near critical well tremors, Jane sunk into herself to seek out the truth for herself. The fast multiplying mass of cells within her confirmed Anika's gamble.

He will not be pure, but he will be ours.

He will not be. The General again picked up her chant.

Anika's voice rose. *Please. I will remain silent in the veil forever if you will vow to allow us and our child to live.*

Do not think to trick me. Our joined power will be needed if you wish to take Matouk another way.

My power is your power. We have always been one.

Could that be true? She again focused on the beginnings of a child growing in her womb.

The excess energy she'd built up inside her well sizzled and snapped. She spared a split second to fortify the shield above Logan and wrapped it around him for what was to come either way she chose. And she had to do it now or forfeit the ability to do so at all.

The walls of the well shook. Matouk stood right before her. All she had to do was finish the last line of the chant and let go.

Please. There is no beyond for us. Let us enjoy this new life a little longer.

All her life her other half had made her feel weak. She'd hated having to turn control of her body and mind to another to accomplish what must be done in her father's name. But now, to hear that half pleading with her, the gratification she'd expected wasn't there, only sadness. Her mind had held itself in two halves for too long to unify her thoughts and goals. She couldn't even agree on the very act of living itself.

Anika flooded their mind with memories of waking up beside Logan, of his hands on her body, of the heated way he looked at her just before they hit the mattress or floor. She rushed through flashes of an imagined future where they raised this child together in his way rather than hers.

Silence behind the veil for the rest of our days.

Hope swelled within her, rising up from her womb to wrap strong warm hands around her heart, steadying the vastly unstable well.

I do so vow.

If I strike him now and do not follow, our pain will be immense.

I will protect our child as long as he is with us.

A thick lump formed in her throat. *Then it shall be so. Go.*

For the briefest moment, another woman's lips pressed against her own. And then the sensation passed, leaving an emptiness behind. Her mind grew quiet.

Shocks rocketed through her body. A scream leaked from her lips as she fought to harness the energy. With every ounce of control she possessed, Jane calculated how much energy it would take to obliterate Matouk and how much she could expel without killing herself. Shielding Matouk's continuous attacks during the calculations meant she had to continue to draw from the ground to maintain her current level. The numbers did not allow for error and she did not have time to recalculate to take her own armor into account. With a silent apology to Logan if she had it wrong, she released the iron grip on her well.

Bolts of blinding light tore from her chest, hands, and out of her mouth. They shot into Matouk. His well violently exploded with a force that knocked Jane backward. With her feet off the ground and the sun arcing overhead, she distantly wondered if Logan's shield and armor would be enough. She hoped so.

Her back hit the ground, driving the breath from her body. Her head hit next. Blackness swam before her eyes, turning the blue sky grey and the clouds a sickly yellow. Pain erupted throughout her body, pulsing through shattered bones. A light breeze fluttered over her burned skin, setting it afire.

She couldn't see if Matouk was dead, or if Logan was safe. She had to heal before she could move. Swallowing the mewling cries that her raw throat insisted on producing, Jane let go of everything on the surface. She sunk her awareness deep into the ground, drawing out Ivium's raw energy to begin healing.

CHAPTER TWENTY-FOUR

She hadn't acknowledged his pounding fists on the new shield that had suddenly enveloped him, swallowing his pleas for her to find another way. She hadn't looked back at him at all.

Jane had stood there, within yards of Matouk, unarmored, trading bolts of light, her face knitted in sheer determination to destroy him. And then she'd stopped firing.

At first he, and likely Matouk too, had thought she'd run dry. Matouk had continued to fire, his own points dropping around him as he used them up.

And then the silver armor had shattered, the body inside blown apart by the beam erupting from Jane. What remained of Matouk, was spread over the area where he'd been standing. The blackened armor-encased smoking remnants. Jane had vanished in the blast of light.

The shield surrounding Logan crackled and dissipated with a loud snap. He finished off the staggering remainders of Matouk's men with weapons he pulled from the dead.

Nightmare inducing smells of blood, seared hair and flesh, permeated the air. The field became the tumbled ruins of a city. Blackened bodies lay everywhere, some recognizable as soldiers by the singed remains of their green uniforms. Most weren't. He dropped to his knees at the sight of a woman curled around her child, another only feet away, her little hand outstretched, forever reaching for her mother.

His heart swelled at the sound of faint cries. The city vanished, returning him to the pale grey field littered with bodies. He followed the sound to a blackened figure. The chain around her neck bearing an amulet that lay over her shoulder on the ground confirmed his worst fears. Jane. And then she fell silent.

His throat closed off and tears streamed down his face. He reached down to touch her, but there seemed to be nowhere untouched by the blast.

An odd distant feeling came over him, one he recognized a second later. Feeding.

She wasn't dead.

Logan jumped back and ran for the edge of the ruined soil. He kept going until he'd put enough space between him and the expanding circle that he could keep an eye on her in case he'd missed any of Matouk's men.

The edges of the plain of grey grew, absorbing tall grass, trees and the bodies of several of Matouk's men. The area where her own points had fallen remained untouched. As he watched her body heal, he wondered about what Matouk had said. Had Jane truly damned herself by drawing energy from the ground instead of people? And if she'd said that her father and the others were in the beyond, that could only mean one thing. She'd been the one to destroy Kaldara.

Jane sat up slowly, straightening her whole and clean clothes and pulling the amulet from over her shoulder back to its rightful place on her chest. She shoved her curls back from her face and rubbed her eyes several times.

Dressed in white, the woman before Logan seemed to rise from the pale ground itself. Her movements were slow, like the ground didn't want to give her up.

Logan rushed to the edge of the circle. It had stopped growing.

"Jane?"

She held up a hand. "Stay back."

"We have to get back to the Maxim. His army is still up there."

She spotted her fallen points and nodded. The voice that had traded deadly calm barbs with Matouk now wavered. "We'll come back for them."

"Can you manage the shuttle?"

"Yes."

Though she was clearly shaken, he didn't question her. If she couldn't fly them, they would have to wait because he certainly wasn't getting them anywhere.

The grass beneath her feet remained green once she'd breeched the circle. Before he could say anything his armor clicked away into nothingness. Jane's hands ran over his body.

"You are unharmed? The armor should have kept you safe."

He caught her arms. "I'm fine. You, on the other hand..."

"Good." She landed a quick kiss on his cheek. "I am well enough. I took what I required."

They jogged to the shuttle, got inside, and slid into their seats. He waited until they were racing upward before he dared ask.

"What happened back there?"

"Self-preservation." Moisture glistened in her eyes, reflecting the lights of the control panel.

She'd removed her armor during the battle. "You

looked damn well ready to go with him."

"I was."

"That was your big surprise?" He sprang up from his seat and inserted himself between her and the controls she seemed to be so focused on. "You were going to go up in a big ball of light without so much as a goodbye?"

Her brows rose. "That was the agreement, wasn't it? I take out Matouk, and your people get a fully operational ship?"

He'd forgotten her cold logic. Was he imagining that she cared about him?

She gave up on the controls with a heavy sigh and finally met his gaze. "You were my surprise. I gave you armor so he wouldn't see you, see the hate burning in your eyes."

Jane rubbed her hands over her face, shoving her hair back. "You distracted him, as I knew you would. He thought you weak, your mind sedated by our speech, but I've seen you resist it before. You're stronger than most. Your anger makes you even stronger."

For now, she seemed wholly Jane. His muscles eased a fraction. "You could have just asked me to shoot him."

"I did put your gun within reach for a reason." Her lips parted into a half-smile. "I know it wasn't ideal, but you were my only hope of catching him off guard. He was in full power, not like my father. I needed every advantage I could get."

The realization that she'd depended on him, that she considered him strong, filled him with satisfaction.

"Without Matouk's connection, his points will falter. They've been under his influence too long to act on their own. Your people haven't. They should be able to take on Matouk's ships before they recover."

"And we would know that how? Did you think to discuss this plan with the colonel?"

"He's a smart man." She reached around him to the panel of buttons.

He grabbed her hands. She didn't resist.

"You changed your mind. You healed yourself. Why?"

She was doing that thing again where she could see into him. He could feel it now that he knew what she was doing, a momentary discomforting intrusion in his mind. Tears escaped down her cheeks. With her hands in his, she couldn't wipe them away. It struck him odd but touching, that a god would cry. That someone like her could cry, now that she was one with Anika.

"You wish me to say that you are the reason I am still here."

Did he? Is that what she saw in his mind or was she merely guessing based on what she knew of relationships? Maybe it was his own misconceptions of romantic gestures that she'd happened upon.

"You have seen much loss, but you would have survived mine too."

"Maybe I'm sick of *surviving*. Is wanting something beyond that too much to ask?"

"No."

She stood, pulling her hands from his to wrap her arms around him. Her moist cheek pressed against his. "If we get through this, I would like to do more than survive with you. If you are agreeable?"

Logan chuckled. Finally, he'd met someone as inept at romantic conversation as he was. "I am, but what about Anika?"

Something struck the shuttle. They sprang apart to maintain their balance. Jane grabbed the control panel.

"Debris," she said in the distracted voice that let him

know she was half within the shuttle itself.

"Theirs or ours?"

"Not ours."

In the distance, he spotted the Maxim. The five new ships hovered behind it, though they all showed signs of battle. Two of Matouk's ships were actively firing upon them. A number of smaller vessels, likely deployed from the largest of the enemy fleet, darted between their ships, delivering beams of white light that left gaping holes in the hulls of the newly created ships. They'd been at this for a while if the shields were down. The Maxim's seemed to be holding.

"Sit." She waved him to his seat.

Not taking any chances, Logan strapped himself in. They sped toward the Maxim faster than the shuttle should carry them. Three of the small fighters peeled away from the others, now heading straight for them.

"This thing doesn't have enough firepower to take them out."

Jane gave the three incoming ships a calculating glance before returning her attention to the controls. "Good thing my well is again full then, isn't it?"

She got down on the floor and wedged herself under the control panel, hands pressed against the metal to either side. Her eyes slipped closed just before her head lolled forward onto her knees that were drawn up against her chest.

"Jane?" He craned his neck as far as he could manage within the confines of the straps, but couldn't see or hear any response.

The shuttle shuddered then rolled. Logan's eyes squeezed shut. Flying under normal orientation was one thing, but this was about to make him sick. He much preferred solid ground under his feet.

A high-pitched whine rose in volume until he clapped his hands over his ears. Even muffled, the whine set his teeth on edge. He pried one eye open long enough to see the stars blur as they shot past. The ship rolled again, darting to and fro. A swath of white light lit the front display. The shuttle shifted again, knocking him around in his seat despite the straps. He didn't look forward to the bruises the forced motion would cause if he lived through this.

Explosions sounded all around the shuttle. Everything shook like it was ready to fall apart and expose them to a quick death. His ears popped and then there was silence.

Logan pried his eyes open to see they were safely inside the Maxim's bay. The shuttle shuddered as the doors sealed behind them.

Quickly, he freed himself of the straps and slid from the seat to help Jane out from under the controls. She appeared tired and pale, but otherwise no worse than when she'd been when trading blasts with Matouk at close range.

The shuttle hadn't fared as well, but it was still whole for whatever that was worth. He didn't look forward to stepping inside it again anytime soon.

"I need to be in the control room."

She knew her way, but she had one hand out, reaching for him. As soon as he got close, she took his arm and walked beside him, her gaze unfocused.

"They're all points," she said, her voice distant. "But it was so much easier with my four."

"Any chance you can give the new ships weapons?"

She smiled. "Only enough to be an annoyance to Matouk's fighters, but yes, I'm on it."

"And repairs?"

"Just the critical ones."

"Good plan." He patted her hand. "Your food supply is limited here."

Jane walked alongside as though she were blind. She nearly missed the door to the control room. He pulled her inside before she walked into the wall. "I'll need them. Can you have Tate gather everyone together?"

"Yes. Where do you want to be?"

"The chair."

He helped her settle into the large chair, the high back creating a welcome rest for her head while her attention was stretched far beyond her body. Now off her feet, she didn't need him. He got the Commander's attention and relayed Jane's instructions.

"Do you think we can do this?" Tate asked quietly.

"She destroyed Matouk. Now it's only his army."

"His very large army. You do realize this is only a small portion of it?"

As much as he hated her for pointing that out, she was right. "Where's Colonel Rice?"

"Overseeing our defenses with his team."

"I should go help him."

"You'll stay right here. You're the only one who has any control over her."

Logan laughed. "You really believe that?"

She shrugged. "I've seen the way she looks at you, and I can tell you, as a fellow woman in charge, we don't do that in public unless we're serious."

"So you're saying I'm not her Hanson?"

Tate scowled, making the lines around her mouth even more severe. "Yes, and I'm also saying you're a tactless ass." She spun around and returned to the panel where she'd been working since surrendering her chair to Jane.

Sirens sounded throughout the Maxim. Logan planted himself next to Jane's chair while the rest of Tate's people shouted frantic reports at one another. The full host of fighters sped past the display, firing at the Maxim's shields.

Soft grunts grabbed his attention. For each shot the Maxim absorbed, Jane winced. Three of the largest ships closed in.

Still, the Maxim didn't return fire beyond what the young ships were capable of. Surely she'd repaired more weaponry than that. The Maxim had to have something larger if it was able to subdue entire planets.

The shield shimmered and fizzled, allowing two blasts through. Tremors rocked the ship.

Tate yelled over her shoulder, "Make her do something."

The other crew members began to gather inside the control room. Finally, something he could do. Logan left Jane's side to direct them to stand around her, yet out of the way of those frantically working.

The rest of Matouk's ships surged forward. The display revealed the five young ships had retreated, leaving the Maxim surrounded. The shield shimmered to life again, but with gaps. If she had any sort of plan that could get them out of this, she would need access to more energy.

"Form lines," he told those that had gathered. Though she'd been able to pull energy from her points from a distance, she was highly distracted now. Physical contact would be best. "Join hands. Those closest to the chair, touch her."

The shield vanished again. The fighters had likely returned to their ship. The larger ships fired. Alarms rang through the Maxim. Her white-knuckled grip on the chair did little to assure him that she had this situation under any semblance of control.

Her lips moved though no sound came from them. Behind her eyelids, her eyeballs danced. Beams of light shot from the Maxim and into the opposing ships. Rice must have finally gained access to the larger weaponry now that the ship's energy wasn't concentrated on the shields.

Alarms rang on as the Maxim rocked again and again. Someone in line whimpered and others cried out for Jane to save them. Several people muttered prayers. Logan didn't care who they were praying to as long as something happened to turn the tide in their direction.

Tate's people continued to barrage her with reports. The phrase *venting atmosphere* grabbed his attention.

"Jane," he said, hoping she could hear him as deep within the Maxim as she was. "If you plan on doing something other than watching us all die, now would be good."

With so many people crowded into the room, the air turned hot and stagnant. Or maybe that was because there wasn't much air left. He swallowed his own panic down. If Jane's supply lines saw him begin to doubt her, they'd really lose it. The prayers grew louder and more prolific.

The alarms came to a sudden end.

Jane went stiff. She drew an impossibly long breath, her body expanding as she did so, filling the chair. Those that had been touching her gasped, whether in pain or awe, he couldn't tell. The lights went out, leaving only the soft golden glow of Jane to illuminate the room.

Her chanting became audible, the tinkling music of her own language. Silence fell over everyone connected to her. The same sensation he'd encountered when she and

Matouk had spoken, seeped into him again. He fought. If he was about to die, he wanted to see it coming.

A ripple passed through the ship, blurring his vision. He swore as the walls separated to form a horizontal slit across the room and into the next. That was impossible. Logan blinked and tried to focus on the display. People in Jane's supply lines crumpled to the floor. He could see space, but he could still breathe.

The line raced around the entire ship until the top half floated free from the bottom. Light flared around Jane. Her hand clamped down on his arm, a shield flowing from her to spread over everyone in the room. Wisps of it sped out the door.

A deafening thunderclap filled the air. Energy radiated, spinning outward in a circle all around her like a slender blade. It raced outward, flashing and expanding, until like a blast wave from a bomb, it ripped into every ship around the Maxim.

The blade tore into the enemy fleet, severing Matouk's ships and exposing his army to the cold death of space. As soon as the ring blade exited the last of the ships, it evaporated.

The two halves of the Maxim came back together. The wall sealed before his eyes as if it had never separated.

The Maxim pulled away from the wreckage. The five young ships followed, drawing closer.

Lights flickered to life overhead, revealing he alone remained standing. Jane sat slumped in the chair, her size back to normal, her skin pale and taut as though she'd drained herself again.

He moved through the fallen, making sure no one was obviously hurt. Upon spotting Brin, he pulled her out of one of the toppled lines of bodies, hoping he could wake her to take care of the others. She appeared to be in a deep sleep. He shook her, but she didn't wake.

They'd all exhausted themselves for Jane, for their survival. He might be alone for the moment, but they weren't dead. This wasn't like before, he assured himself. This time, they were victorious.

He went in search of the colonel and his men. He found one on the floor in front of one of the weapons stations. Scouting the other stations, he located the rest.

After making sure no one had sustained any injuries, he made his way back to the control room in the hopes of ascertaining if the life support systems were back online. Though he poured over the panels, most of the readings meant nothing to him. Finding no big red blinking warning lights, he could only assume they were safe enough for now.

He wandered the ship, feeling like he should be doing something, but unsure what that might be. He ended up in the dining hall. Though his mind was still reeling from Jane's destruction of Matouk and his ships, his stomach informed him in loud angry rumbles that it had been a long time since his last meal. He gathered a plate together and sat in the empty room.

Chewing without tasting, he focused processing all he'd seen and what it might mean for his future. A future with Jane...if they could get past her suicidal streak, power-craving Anika, and the apparent soul-damning ability to suck the life out of planets. Then there was the fact that she was Unlata Kai and he was very much not.

He set his fork down, no longer hungry. No longer sure of anything. Was finding an average woman who would tolerate him too much to ask for? He sighed. Like surviving, he also craved something beyond tolerating.

He craved Jane.

Logan walked the quiet ship until he found himself

again back beside Jane and the lines of sleepers. If he couldn't pilot a shuttle to retrieve her points, competently monitor the Maxim, or revive anyone who could, at least he could provide Jane with what she sorely needed.

She looked even worse than before he'd left, face gaunt, dark circles around her eyes, skin so pale it seemed almost translucent. She was small and frail in the large chair she'd filled only hours before.

Continuously draining herself couldn't be good for her. Not that he could think of a way around what she'd chosen to do since they'd met. She'd done what was necessary to protect them no matter the cost to herself. But she was also the one who had drained Kaldara and only she knew how many other worlds. Did that mean she was evil?

Was it Anika who had done those things or Jane, and did it matter if they were one and the same? They shared a body. Their faces were the same. Could he really look at one without seeing the other, knowing she was in there and how differently she saw through the same eyes?

For now, it didn't matter. The silence ate at him, making his mind spin. Just then he needed the peace and contentment of the sound of her language, but to speak she needed to be conscious.

"Jane." He shook her gently.

She didn't stir. Maybe he should carry her back to her room so she could rest properly. He tried to pick up one of her hands but encountered resistance. Both hands were splayed, palms down on the chair. Was she still connected to the ship? If she'd lost consciousness before disconnecting, she'd still be draining herself. She'd accidentally done that before.

He pried her hands off the chair and picked her up, not taking any chances that any skin to ship contact might drain her further. Jane may have been a substantial woman, but she seemed much lighter than he remembered, almost hollow. Her body filled the same space in his arms and against his chest, her hair tickling his neck as he walked, but it lacked substance. Did energy have weight?

Logan paused, panic striking hard and fast. He held his face close to hers. His heartbeat eased when he felt her breath against his cheek. Still breathing. Still alive.

When he reached her room, he took her inside and set her down on the bed. She definitely needed to feed. He tried placing her hand on his arm, like she'd fed when they were in the colony. Nothing happened. He brought her hand to his neck like she'd done when she'd fed from the crew here. But it was only her chilled hand against his skin, none of the relaxed detachment or pleasure that accompanied her feeding.

He returned her limp arm to the bed and covered her with the blanket. With nothing else he could do, he gave into his training, knowing there would be plenty to occupy him soon enough. Logan slid under the blanket, wrapped an arm around Jane, and went to sleep.

CHAPTER TWENTY-FIVE

Jane drifted up through the utter blackness of sleep and though the milky haze of waking to find herself in her bed. The warmth against her back and weight of a thick arm around her chest told her she wasn't alone. Elated, she snuggled closer. Logan's soft breath against her neck brought a smile to her lips.

And then the hunger hit her. It had been so long since she'd indulged in so much energy. Sharp pangs raked along her empty insides, driving her from the comfort of Logan's body to the chair farthest from the bed.

She would not feed from him.

Disgust flooded through her as she recalled draining the entire crew, the crews of the other ships and even those on the colony. All of them, not only her points who had agreed to give all if needed. She'd just taken. Always in her mind, it was Anika who took without asking, who did what had to be done. But they were one.

They had always been one. The words drummed in her mind, echoing, overlapping.

Had she been talking to herself for centuries, sure she was the only sane one left? Uneasy laughter tried to escape her mouth. She clenched her teeth together.

Anika had banished herself. But she was Anika. She was the General. She was Jane.

Could she bury that part of herself for good? Anika's vow rang in her ears. A vow. One she had to uphold, even to herself.

She gnawed on a fingernail, rocking back and forth in her chair, watching Logan sleep as hunger and disturbing revelations unraveled in her head.

"Jane."

When had she closed her eyes? Logan sat on his knees before her, looking so earnestly concerned that it made her heart ache. It also made her very aware that she was running on empty and he was the only source of energy on the ship. The others would be again, in time, but they would need to recover for at least a couple days from the drain. Her points were still far away and though they would rejuvenate before the crew, it would only be by hours. She reached out for him but caught herself before making contact.

"You can, you know. I can see how badly you need to feed."

She did, and not only for her. Another life depended on her now. A life she hoped she hadn't damaged with the influx of so much power.

Warm reassurance caressed her thoughts. Anika had said she would protect the child. Or had that conversation all been her imagination, high on the overflow of energy. She was Anika, and Jane. They were one.

"Am I crazy?"

Logan nodded and started to answer, but then paused. "I'm supposed to say no, aren't I?" He rocked back and stood. "You've done a lot of crazy things and I'm pretty sure you've tried to kill yourself at least twice since we've met. So to be honest, yes. If you mean insane, off your rocker crazy, then maybe no."

"Maybe."

He shrugged. "I don't pretend to be an expert on the minds of gods."

"I wish you'd stop using that word."

"You used it."

She huddled in the chair, keeping her hands and arms firmly locked around her knees. Talking with him was taking her mind off the hunger. As long as he didn't get too close.

"I have. But I don't want to be that with you."

Logan grabbed the other chair and moved it to face hers. He dropped into it with a relaxed flop that the tight muscles in his neck and shoulders belied. After an audible swallow, he asked, "What is it exactly that you do want to be with me?"

"Good. When I'm with you I want to be good, not Unlata Kai, not the General, not a god to anyone. I want to be, to see, to do the things that your kind do. Not mine. I've done that for far too long."

"But why with me?"

"You've taken care of me, even when I didn't want anyone to. You don't look at me like the rest of the crew does, like I'm a magical prize, or something to be feared and worshiped."

"I'm pretty sure I have done both."

She loved when he smiled like that, a little bashful, a little daring. He did that a lot when they were alone, like he wasn't sure if he should say something but blurted it out anyway.

"Perhaps, but not like the others." She tucked her curls behind her ears and tried to mimic his relaxed pose. If he could play casual when he knew she was starving and dangerous, she would do her best to give him no reason to doubt her. "If you're asking for a list, I also like your hands."

He raised one eyebrow.

"Particularly when they are on me, but that's not a good idea right now."

Logan laughed. The deep rumble made her insides twist and flip. Despite her discomfort, a smile broke out on her face.

He studied her thoughtfully. "I could be courting disaster here, but you did mention that there was an alternate way to recharge that didn't involve draining energy. At least not in your typical sense."

She had mentioned that, or Anika had, but that had also been her. Jane sucked on her bottom lip, trying to think his suggestion through before she got too excited. He hadn't seemed any worse for wear the last time. Conversely, she'd been elated and energized. They were creating energy together. She wasn't taking anything from him.

But was that just a rationalization to get what she wanted? She'd promised him and herself that she wouldn't feed from him ever again.

There was also that other byproduct of their last encounter.

She cleared her throat and made herself meet his intrigued gaze. "You had asked about Anika on the shuttle."

He nodded, sitting straighter and decidedly less relaxed.

How could she explain her delusions without making him run for the door? "We are the same person."

"I saw you split the ship in half and create a massive blade of energy that obliterated Matouk's army. Sure everyone is still knocked out from it, but no one else could have done what you did. Ivium now contains a rather large swath of dead land, but you also eliminated Matouk, who was a threat to a hell of a lot more than uninhabitable land. If being the same person allowed you to do that-"

"I've always been the same person."

She wanted to crawl inside the chair and hide, but he deserved to know the truth. "A long time ago, my Father wanted an edge, something that would allow him more power than other Unlata Kai. My brothers didn't dare tap the forbidden. I did. And yes, there is no beyond for me. What Matouk said was true."

Logan leaned forward, almost touching his hands to her knees but not quite. "Did you do it for him or for yourself?"

"Both. I proved that I would do anything for him and it gained me his favor."

"But you didn't suck the life from Kaldara for your own benefit. You did it for him."

"There were a lot more worlds than Kaldara, and I may have done it in his name, but that doesn't erase the fact that I did do it, does it?"

He exhaled loudly and shook his head. "Are you trying to convince me that you're evil?"

"I think I've kept myself divided in my mind so I could tolerate things I've done. Part of me is every bit as evil as Matouk." She swallowed hard. "I want you to know the truth, a truth I've only now come to accept.

"Why does it matter to you what I think?"

"Because I hope we will be together for a very long time, but that can't happen without truth between us."

Logan shrank back into his chair. "Your long time and mine are far different."

"They don't have to be."

"If you think I'm going to swallow your blood or whatever crazy-"

She held up a hand. "You may have noticed that I'm

not that enamored with living lately."

"Now you're just confusing me."

"I've realized that it's not that I don't want to live, but that I don't want to live how I have been. You've shown me another way."

"You looked plenty ready to go when you confronted Matouk."

"Part of me was." Her heart raced. A sickly tickle plagued her throat. She coughed her way past it. "The other part allowed herself to get pregnant so she'd have a reason not to."

Logan stared blankly forward. His gaze finally wavered into a blink and then another, but his lips remained firmly clamped together.

Nerves made her insides quake. If he stormed out she wasn't sure what she'd do, not with the hunger writhing inside. "I need you to show me how this is supposed to be, having a child. I will ruin him on my own."

"Him?"

He might not be jumping for joy, but at least he was still in the chair. She nodded.

"On the shuttle, when Anika took over?"

There was no easy way to explain how her split personality worked. "Yes."

"But that just happened. How would you know already? Not to mention, knowing it was a boy."

"I'm not like you, remember?"

He did jump out of his chair then, baring down on her with a stormy glare that made her wince inside. "How could I forget?"

He turned away and started for the door.

"Logan, please. I could turn this all off, grow old, die like everyone else."

"You could just turn off being Unlata Kai?" He spun

around. "Why would you do that? You can heal people, save them, protect them. You would let them suffer and die?"

"I thought you'd want that." She ran her hand through her tangled curls, fingers snagging on a knot that offered a welcome dose of pain. "Tell me what you want."

"Will he be like you?"

She stood cautiously, wanting to go to him, but also doubting her control. "He will also be like you."

"What I mean is, will he live forever, like you?"

"Unlata Kai don't live forever, Logan. You have noticed I'm the only one left?"

"Because you've killed the rest," he grumbled. "Naturally though, how long would you continue to live?"

She couldn't lie to him. Not now. "A very long time."

"And so would this child?"

"First generation hybrids do tend..."

His narrowed eyes urged her along.

"He would."

"Then he will continue to need you long after I am gone. There are no others who can help him."

Jane dared to take a few steps closer, the desire to touch him becoming almost unbearable. "You're wrong. There are thousands of others like him. Those who left Kaldara would welcome him. There are other worlds we've left that would also be a suitable home if he wants options."

"He's barely begun to form and you've already planned his life?"

Jane smiled. "Hazards of longevity. My planning thirty years ahead is like you planning your week."

Just when she'd thought she was making progress, he appeared more agitated than before. Unwilling to take the chance that he would leave, she closed the distance between them. With her arms around him, she pressed her cheek against his. He stiffened for a moment before returning her embrace.

To her surprise, even touching him now, her control held. She squeezed tighter, welcoming the comforting sensation of familiar arms around her, his solid chest against hers, the broad shoulder under her chin and the dark silken hair that tickled her nose.

"I need to breathe," he whispered.

"Sorry," she eased her grip, smiling as she nuzzled his neck. He eased against her, their bodies fitting neatly together.

"Do you really want to know what I want?" he asked.

"Yes."

"Your points not to shut me out when I want to be near you."

The rivalry between her points and Logan had not escaped her notice. "Do you wish for me to release them?"

"You need them."

Did she? Having other hands to work through did make her tasks easier, but if her task was to be a guide, perhaps reining in her powers a little wouldn't be such a bad thing now that Matouk was gone. Logan had been after her repeatedly to stop draining herself. If her well was limited to recharging naturally, it would force her to do just that. She turned her options over in her mind, contemplating the future.

Logan slipped out of her arms, standing just out of reach. "The rest of Matouk's army is out there, leaderless. I doubt they will disband nicely and go home."

She nodded. "That has not been my experience. They will either unite under one of their own or fracture into smaller groups."

"We should make sure they fracture in a more

permanent sense."

Jane regarded him thoughtfully. "I don't know that your crew would agree with that. Our deal was to destroy Matouk for one operational Maxim."

"You created five more ships, and after what you did today, I'm sure you could motivate them to finish what we started."

"I could...if that is what you want."

He nodded. "They destroyed my people, everything I knew. We can't allow them to do that to anyone else."

"Then my points will remain until we have completed this task, but then I will set them free."

The relief on his face assured her she'd made the right choice. "Would you want to go to Hijn when we have finished? Return to your home?"

"There's nothing there."

"We could build something there, if you wish."

"I'm not really the colonizing type."

She laughed in his ear. "With a body like this, any enterprising colony would want you."

"Ivium wants you."

"Not there. They want a god. I've already severed my connections with them. Ivium will find its own way again."

He stilled her wandering hands. "What about you? Now that you've been on one of your ships, wouldn't you miss it?"

"Yes, but I also miss my people. I may never see them, the ones I raised up out of my father's war, but I miss caring for them. The beautiful city we built has crumbled, but the plans are right here in my mind. It could live again."

"So these people who you would care for..." He nibbled her ear. "Would you be their god?"

"Guide." She shivered. "I'd prefer, guide."

"And what about this crew?"

"Tate has her mission. These are her people. Rice can protect them well enough under regular circumstances. The deal was for Naptcha to control the Maxim."

"And the other five?"

She bumped into one of the chairs, only then realizing he was backing her further into the room. "I might be persuaded to trade one of the stunted ships for her cooperation in hunting down the rest of Matouk's men. The others would be ours. After all," she let out a startled yelp as her knees buckled against the edge of the bed, sending her sprawling backward.

Logan laughed and landed next to her. "You were saying?"

"We'll need somewhere to live while we recruit colonists, search out a world that needs us, and then get our city underway. You will be my guide."

"How so? I don't think I'm qualified to tell a god what-"

She silenced him with a finger to his lips. "You've done just fine so far."

"And we'll raise our son in a place without war?"

"Until he is ready to go his own way." She sat up and pulled his shirt over his head, running her hands over his chest. "Until then, we will remain as we are now."

His hands faltered in the middle of tugging her pants down. "You can do that?"

"I have held your life in my hands. For you, yes, I can do that." She kissed him gently. "But only until you say we are ready. Then we will grow old together, and my well will slowly seal so that it will harm no one when the time comes."

"Even knowing you have no beyond waiting for you?"

She shrugged. "Maybe yours will take me."

"It just might." He slid on top of her, pinning her to the bed. "The first step would be getting you recharged then, wouldn't it?"

Jane grinned. "I'm quite empty. It might take a while."

"Oh, I think we have plenty of time before everyone else wakes up." With a wicked smile, he proceeded to introduce her to a future she'd never thought to have.

About the Author

Jean Davis lives in West Michigan with her musical husband, two attention-craving terriers and a small flock of chickens and ducks. When not ruining fictional lives from the comfort of her writing chair, she can be found devouring books and sushi, weeding her flower garden, or picking up hundreds of sticks while attempting to avoid the abundant snake population that also shares her yard. She writes an array of speculative fiction.

Find links to all of her books, updates on new projects, and sign up for her mailing list at www.jeandavisauthor.com. You'll also find her on Facebook and Instagram at JeanDavisAuthor, and on Goodreads and Amazon.

Made in the USA
Columbia, SC
08 June 2021